THE CLOCK IS TICKING!

Miranda Gray and the Colonel are back! They're in a race from Cairo to Crete to find an ancient treasure, but will a thief and a ghostly Minotaur beat them to it?

The Queen and courtiers of France are dying, and Adelaide's miraculous invention could save them, but will her mentor's thirst for power force her into obscurity forever?

The governor of the State of Jefferson has a full schedule of visitors this month, but it's nothing a little sasquatch charm, a pound of bacon, and a couple of chocolate shakes won't fix!

Ghost never had a problem working for Mr. Bacchus, until the prize at the deb poker game was a fifteen-year-old girl. Can Ghost beat the House and set her free?

Vivian is tired of the social whirl—nothing but teas, balls, parties and picnics. Surely there must be some adventure waiting for her somewhere. Surely!

Kenna can play in 'Raro, City of Guilty Pleasures and Never-ending Buffets, or do time to find the one person that can stop a war and break him out of prison. Choices. Choices.

Sparky McTrowell wouldn't hurt a fly, but the man that drove her father to an early grave is fair game. Will she risk her prized partnership with Erasmus Drake for vengeance?

Fifteen pairs of stories, thirty days of action, adventure, romance, and intrigue—Steam forward through time with the Treehouse Writers!

FIND OUT WHAT HAPPENS THIRTY DAYS LATER!

THIRTY DAYS LATER

STEAMING FORWARD:
30 ADVENTURES IN TIME

EDITORS

AJ SIKES

BJ SIKES

&

DOVER WHITECLIFF

Thinking Ink Press
Campbell, CA

Published by Thinking Ink Press
P.O. Box 1411, Campbell, California, 95009
First printing, 2016

ISBN 78-1-942480-07-5

Printed in the United States of America.
Library of Congress Control Number: 2016931610

Project Credits
Cover design: Keri Knutson
Cover image courtesy of Cottone Auctions, Geneseo, NY
Layout: BJ Sikes and Dover Whitecliff

This book is dedicated to the memory of
Vicki Rorke, Treehouse Writer.
On August 10, 2015, we lost Vicki to cancer.
We will miss her wit and wisdom on Authors' Row.

A Note from the Editors

Four years ago a group of steampunks from the greater San Francisco Bay Area started up a convention to celebrate all those things they loved: the styles and times that never were. They came with passion and creativity in hand and to share. They came to have fun. And they succeeded. Since that storied weekend in 2012, every Memorial Day has seen Clockwork Alchemy return to San Jose, California, with artists, artisans, musicians, performers of all stripes, and authors in tow.

It has been our pleasure to number ourselves among the talented, imaginative writers who dwell on Authors' Row at Clockwork Alchemy. A better bunch of friends and fellow storytellers would be hard to come by. For 2015, we gathered the collective wit and wisdom of the Row and produced *Twelve Hours Later*, an anthology of stories that showcases who we are and what we do as Clockwork Alchemy authors.

This year, we're thrilled to present to you stories ranging from the light-hearted and the grim to the marvelous, the fantastic, and the downright weird (and we mean that in a good way). The 2016 anthology, *Thirty Days Later*, gives readers a taste of everything that Authors' Row has to offer. We have some new names in the crowd this time around, too.

These are memorable tales and tales told in memoriam. These are stories of intrigue and deceit, stories of high adventure and low behavior. We have comeuppance, conspiracy, catharsis, and contraband. We have myths and monsters, time travel, time to waste, and time to kill. We have stories of derring-do and dastardly deeds, stories of defectors and dilettantes, and the warmth to be had from détentes.

In editing the works herein, we were in turns delighted, surprised, stunned, and always excited. We hope you'll enjoy this collection and, if you're in the area on Memorial Day weekend, consider stopping by Authors' Row while you're out and about exploring the many wonders to be found at Clockwork Alchemy. We and all the authors would love to meet you and thank you personally for reading *Thirty Days Later*.

Have we run out of time?
Time is the one thing we can't make
but we can kill.
—Unwoman

The Story Begins

Thirty Days Later

THE STORY BEGINS

A Linear Mystery

or

How All This Madness Got Started!

By T.E. MacArthur

The Nile River, South of Cairo
November 23rd, 1893

A lost codex found, a vast treasure recovered, and death by a ghostly Minotaur. What could possibly ...

The concept had been so intriguing that Miranda Gray hadn't heard him coming.

What a stupid mistake.

"Do you really want to kill me?" The knife he held at her throat warranted the urgent question. Slowly she set down the pages of her meticulous notes. Her hand shook a little as she settled it on top of the Old Explorer's journal, praying he wasn't planning to take that from her.

He gently swept his lips up her ear and kissed her temple, scratching her skin slightly with his rough facial hair. "Not if I don't have to." Such a proper English voice.

The desert wind cut across the water and sent a shiver through the sails of the *dahabeah* as she waited to see what he'd do next. The *Neshmet-Osiris* slid quietly against the river's flow, counting on the breath of the gods to get it up river. It was as cold as the time of year would permit, and in the blood-colored dusk, the river was strangely empty. No one was around to see the two foreigners seated under the boat's canopy.

"Tell me, *Nefer*, have you enjoyed my gift to you?"

The knife notwithstanding, Malcolm Drummond Davies was an appealing, wild looking rake, with a slight beard defining his jaw, a linen shirt he left partially open, and thick dark hair. Were she not aware of his history, she might have mistaken him for a local aristocrat, with his dusky appearance and flashing black eyes. But, no, Davies was very English. "Yes, as a matter of fact."

"Tell me what you've discovered from the old man's cryptic ramblings and I promise we will remain the best of friends." The knife turned slightly, pushing the blade a little more into her skin without cutting it.

"Why not," she said with remarkable calm, satisfying her self-esteem. Would he really harm her? What might Davies do for untold wealth? "Do you know what a 'Perigee-syzygy 'is?"

"The Moon at its closest to the earth. It appears enormous in the sky. Very romantic."

Smart boy.

"Do you know, then, what happens if you have a Perigee-syzygy at the Winter Solstice?"

"A very long, well-lit night," he smiled slyly.

"And a Moon that appears even larger than ever."

Davies kept nuzzling her ear. "Obviously important or you wouldn't mention it."

Taking a substantial risk, Gray cautiously pushed the knife away. Turning to him, she smiled. "It so happens that there had been such an event on the equivalent of December 23rd, 1424 BC, a year after the Mycenaean invasion of Crete. And again on the Winter Solstice in 1597—when Sir Charles disappeared, but left this journal on board his ship."

"Any chance we have such an event coming up soon?" Davies lowered his knife, but kept a tight grasp on it. "I gather strong moonlight is essential to find the location of the treasure? And we might just discover whatever happed to old Bellingsfield and his codex."

"The find of the century."

He leaned in toward her. "Then come with me to Crete, *Nefer*, and we'll find it together. I know where to look; you understand the Old Explorer's book."

"I do wish you wouldn't call me *Nefer*."

"But you are the Beauty of the Gods."

"Oh nonsense. What are we *really* looking for, Mr. Davies?"

"The Bull of Heaven and the Heart of the Sea." He leaned back on the pillows, grinning.

"What?"

"Allow me to explain ...."

Timing, as the saying goes, is everything. The Ministry Agent, whom she did not like, and two of the boat's crew mounted the stairs in three bold steps and leveled various guns at Davies. "Get away from her!"

Gray tried not to roll her eyes.

Bloody stupid ....

Davies took up the knife and placed it firmly again under Gray's chin. "Don't block my way. The lady and I are leaving."

"No, Mr. Davies, we're not." Gray slid her left hand under his and pushed it away as she turned. Regrettably, while her knee did find its way between his legs, it did not strike with enough force. It did convince him to drop his knife.

Davies shoved her backward with both hands into the on-rushing men: simple, inelegant, effective. There was no escaping down the ladder—the *dahabeah's* crew was in the way. Instead, he smiled, turned on his heel, and dove headlong into the river.

"Damn it!" she shouted, rushing to the rail and searching for Davies in the water.

"Such language, Madam. Let the crocodiles have him," the Agent snapped. "Be grateful I arrived to rescue you."

"You arrived to interrupt me. He was about to tell me what we don't know: where to be on the 23rd of December."

The Agent looked down at her. "I don't care. He would have killed you."

"No. He needs me to provide that which *he* doesn't know yet. We have the Old Explorer's book and he has the location along with additional clues."

Signaling the crew that all would be well, the Agent folded his arms tightly across his chest. "I'll have to go after him." The man was a retired Army major, too set in his ways to be of any use to Gray. She still wondered just what the Ministry was thinking when they sent him to her. "Stay put and work on that book. You'll be safer here. I'll take care of Davies." He picked up the delicate, old journal and dropped it back onto the table. "Thirty days. Can you do it?"

"Finish translating a rambling Elizabethan diary written in Latin, which may be a fake, and locate what Mr. Davies suggested is somewhere on Crete, so that we can discover the ultimate treasure? In thirty days? Perhaps we can."

"*We*, Madam Archaeologist?" he asked, pompously.

"Indeed. I'm afraid I'll need to call in specialized assistance. You do understand, don't you?" She didn't wait to hear his protest. She quickly wrote out a note on the back of one of her papers, folded it, and handed it to the Agent. "Please send that urgently to London: to the Punjabi Club."

It read very simply: *Colonel – you are needed.*

ೞೞ

The Nile River, headed north toward Alexandria

Her black hair whipped around her face and she casually pushed it away. The sun was setting in the West, casting a glow of orange out across the fields and sands. Birds cried out their last of the day and a huff of water in the distance suggested a hippo was warning off the human craft approaching too near to shore. Ethereal music sweetened the air, coming from a distant mosque, or was it only the exotic meditations of an imaginative mind glimpsing the Giza Pyramids silhouetted in the distance? Gray pulled her right knee up toward her chest and lifted her chin into the breeze. Seated on a set of ornate pillows under the canopy, she was pleasantly alone, surrounded by scattered research. She'd done an incredible amount of work.

Children called and waved at her from the shore; their robes maintaining a two-inch hem of caked mud. So many Europeans, women included, were flocking to Egypt. Most stayed on the elegant steamers or the Trans-Mediterranean Airships that offered tours up and down the Nile. Gray preferred the tried and true method of the *dahabeah*. The *Neshmet-Osiris* was a medium sized craft in that particular Egyptian style: a barge with sails, a shallow draft, and a canopied rooftop that doubled as seating for guests. Should the wind fail, oars could be reluctantly dipped into the water. The barques of the Pharaohs had been of the same design, though far more opulent. Why change what works?

Gray stared for a moment at the bottles waiting on a tray, touching each one with her fingers. Water: boiled for purity and cooled. Pomegranate juice: likely over-sweetened. Acceptable Champagne.

She did not hear the report of a gun and yet the bottle shattered. *So much for the water.* Gray grasped the Champagne with a dramatic flourish and hid it in the pillows. She was being watched.

Not even allowing a smile to form, Gray loosened the cork on the bottle of pomegranate juice and held it slightly aloft. The cork burst out of the bottle, shot away with only the whistle of a bullet.

Gray poured half a glass, set down the bottle, and reclined on the pillows, the Champagne bottle protected by her side.

One hundred yards away, waiting at the end of the dock, she could see her partner—the Colonel. A typical British male: overdressed, overheated, and over-confident. Yes, acceptably handsome, intriguing, and intelligent—she could imagine that any woman might fall in love with him, but no sane woman would ever marry him.

The Colonel lowered the barrel of his Von Herder .455 caliber air rifle and lit his cigar as the *Neshmet-Osiris* slipped into the quay.

∞∴

Aboard the Neshmet-Osiris, Alexandria

"Damn embarrassing, to say the least—it was damn stupid too, Madame."

So very proper, Gray thought, *until of course, he opens his mouth.* Quite the opposite of Davies, the Colonel's crusty military voice often amusingly contradicted his distinguished appearance. Yet, after all that they'd gone through—what *he'd* put them through—he was still the agent she preferred to work with.

The Colonel watched the river tensely. He'd finally allowed himself to be talked out of the brown twill suit he'd worn since leaving England. Reddish full beard, blue hound-dog eyes, and a keenness of bearing that reflected his military experience. Lanky and time-worn. Nothing missed his gaze. As was the custom with Agents of the Ministry, she was neither privy to his real name, nor he to hers. She was still certain they knew who the other was, but chose to play the game.

"I could kill *him*," the Colonel said coldly. "He's certainly proved to be a right pain in the ...."

"What, and rob me of the little amusements he brings?"

From the look on the Colonel's face, Gray knew he hadn't understood. She held out the journal for him to examine. "It's Sixteenth Century—not quite my usual period of interest."

"Why give it to you then?"

"It appears to be the log book of the dubious explorer, Sir Charles Bellingsfield. After pestering Cadez on behalf of Elizabeth the First, curiosity—and rumors of treasure—drove him into the Mediterranean."

"So what?" the Colonel replied, not at all disinterested.

"It seems he may have done in 1590 what Arthur Evans has only scratched at this year. He found a codex on Crete that he claims he used to translate early, pre-Mycenaean texts. Minoan, as they call it." Gray began earnestly flipping pages back and forth. "It is possible that this is a fake. There's no record of Bellingsfield being on Crete, let alone discovering anything significant. And he was known to be quite mad."

"*This* is an official Ministry assignment, Madame Archaeologist?"

"Well, not entirely. But I thought you wouldn't mind another shot at Malcolm Davies." The Colonel responded by taking her glass of pomegranate juice and drinking half. "I rather expected you might like that," she said to his slight smile.

"The book is in Latin."

"Hardly difficult to translate." It was no surprise to her that an Elizabethan gentleman wrote his formal observations in the accepted language of learned men. The drawing on the right-hand page was a copy of a circular tablet, with the letters tracing a path down toward the center.

The Colonel stared at the snail of symbols. "Davies translated this gibberish?"

Gray shook her head. "Nonsense. Arthur only just found ancient hieroglyphs like these on Crete last year. 'Linear A.' That is what Arthur and Flinders Petrie are calling it. The text is a complete mystery. No one can translate it." Gray turned the book, following the spiral of the writing. It appeared to be a labyrinth that the reader's eyes were drawn into with numerous drawings of strange shapes.

The Colonel leaned forward. "Can you translate all the rest?"

As Gray's eyebrows rose coyly, she knew that she was going to be a very determined Archaeologist. *Poor Colonel.*

"I have a proposal, which I believe you might actually like, and that could be linked to the greatest find in archaeological history. Bellingsfield disappeared in 1597 while searching for the fabled Treasure of Minos. If he had a codex to translate Linear A, he took it with him. And, per his book, he was headed to a site on Crete, on a specific date, to observe an astronomical event that happens infrequently. But, one that points to Minoa's greatest secret."

"Look at you, you're excited."

"And concerned. The Mycenaeans pillaged the whole civilization—it is ridiculous to think that one coin survived the invasion, let alone a whole treasury—we could be chasing after rumor only. This could be a gigantic failure."

"And Davies will be there?"

"Of course." Noting the Colonel's returning smile. "I'm sure you two will have plenty to chat about?"

"Isn't this where that ghost of the dead Minotaur protects the treasure, blah, blah?"

"Oh my, yes." Her hazel eyes twinkled. "Locals say they hear it howling in the mountains and by the sea."

"Wind."

"Are you absolutely certain?"

Ghost and the Birdman

By AJ Sikes

Ghost squints in the dim electric light and writes the address on a matchbook. The dark skin of his fingers stands out against his sharp white suit, and Ghost thinks about what it means to *go up in smoke*.

He's worked for Mr. Bacchus going on five years now, since Christmas 1923. This isn't the first time he's had reason to question their affairs. But it is the first time Ghost feels strongly enough about things to actually open his mouth.

Mr. Bacchus plays a mean hand, but never lets things slip too far one way or the other. Now here he comes with this address and this job, and Ghost is thinking.

He slips the matchbook into his hatband, puffs on his cigarette, and cocks an eye at the man by the window. Mr. Bacchus didn't move an inch while he spoke about the job, and he keeps his near three-hundred-pound self statued now.

Ghost takes a long drag and holds the smoke in his lungs, lets the fingers of calm trace their way through his chest and mind. He reclines against the cushions of the chaise lounge, the only seat in Mr. Bacchus' office, and one Ghost would rather not be in. But it's where he was told to sit, so he sat.

"Are you sure, Mr. Bacchus, about me bringing the girl in?"

Ghost's employer shifts his bulk and rotates where he stands until his wide back aims at the window and his wider front aims in Ghost's direction. The slanting light haloes the man's dark face, and Ghost forces his lips to stay straight. Mr. Bacchus is no angel, and everyone in New Orleans knows it.

"Am I sure, Ghost? I believe I am. Are you sure you want to remain in my employ?"

Ghost nods.

"But?" Mr. Bacchus says, arching an eyebrow.

"She's fifteen, Mr. Bacchus. I know it's only for—"

"Fifteen's as good as sixteen when it's just a month between them. She can stay here until her birthday comes. Now answer my question, Ghost. With words this time, not just a nod of your fool head."

"Yes, sir, Mr. Bacchus. I'm sure."

"Acceptable. But this is a first for us, and I'm of a mind to caution you. I don't need to caution you, do I, Ghost?"

The heavyset man holds his hands over his midsection, resting them across the roll of his stomach protruding from under his waistcoat. The gold rings on his thick fingers shine like fireflies in the dim room.

"No, sir, Mr. Bacchus."

"Then what are you waiting for?"

Ghost stubs out his cigarette in an ashtray on the round table beside him. He stands, straightens his slacks and shifts his jacket on his shoulders. With a tip of his hat, he leaves Mr. Bacchus alone in the gloomy space of his parlor.

Ghost departs his employer's house. He steps fast to his sedan and drives away with gloom and suspicion swirling in his head like whispers of crimes gone by.

∞⋈

A block from the house, Ghost cuts the engine and coasts to a stop out back of the property. The gas lamps flicker and flutter along the street. The new electric lamps are supposed to go in soon. They just have to come down the river from Chicago City. It's been a decade of dirty work since Ghost has seen his hometown. Maybe now's the time to head back north and see if his roots can hold him steady.

Maybe after this job.

The house hugs the ground, like it's afraid it'll fly off the earth otherwise. Across the alley, two old steam cars gather rust in the warm night. A horse and buggy pull away from a house a little down the way. The horse *clops* by Ghost's sedan, and the driver wisely keeps her eyes on the road.

Ghost rolls up a new smoke and has it half gone when two bicycles clatter by. Young boys out late, racing each other around the city, like Ghost and his brother used to do once upon a time. A dog howls from the next yard over. Ghost gets out of his sedan.

He's putting a family out of their home tonight, and Mr. Bacchus is set to have him do much worse. Five years of working for the man and Ghost has avoided the gala house mess. He's made sure his employer gets paid what's owed him. And he's made sure Mr. Bacchus has never had to teach a lesson more than once. More often than not, Ghost shows up and that's lesson enough. People pay their debts when they have to look down the barrel of a stare like the ones Ghost sends their way.

This family is different, though. They just have it rough, and sometimes having it rough is just a matter of how the cards come down.

Ghost stamps out his smoke and follows a stone path around the house. Along the side he spies movement through a window. He pauses to look in and sees the girl and her mother arguing.

The girl's long dark hair hangs down in strings and tatters. The mother grabs at it and the girl swats the woman's hand away. Then two little boys come in, all pasty faces and filthy cheeks. Ghost recognizes the bicycle racers.

Ghost shakes his head and wipes a hand across his brow. Five years gone and not once did he have to do a job as dirty as this.

The man who called himself your father would tell you different. If he could still speak.

Ghost sniffs at the memory trying to force its way into his conscience. He has a job to do tonight, and he'll do it. He follows the stone walk up to the front door. He lifts a hand to knock and pauses when the door flies open. The girl stands there, eyes wide and full of fire.

"Momma," she says, tears spilling down her pink cheeks, squelching the flames. Nearly sixteen she might be, but Ghost would have a hard time believing it if he didn't already know.

"I'm here to see your mother, yes," he says, hating the words as they leave his tongue.

The girl steps back, putting a hand to her heart and letting the mother come between her and the threshold where Ghost stands waiting, one hand on his lapel, the other by his side.

"Mr. Gh—Mr. Ghost," the mother says. "You here for the rent money, I expect."

"No, I'm here for the house. The empty one," Ghost says, glancing around the entry way at the ceiling, the walls, and the dirt on the stoop. He looks the mother in the eye. "Mr. Bacchus tells me it should be right here, seeing as how no rent's been paid now two months gone."

The mother nods and stammers a few sounds that don't quite make it into words. Ghost finds the girl with his eyes, but keeps talking to the mother. "I get it now. You're just here looking the place over. Mr. Bacchus is happy to let the house, but he needs two months up front."

"Mr. Ghost? I don't—"

"Go on," he says, flashing his eyes on the mother. He uses the other stare, the one that makes people run from him instead of freezing them solid with fear. "Get some things together. You can't take much. Car's in the alley. I'll tell Mr. Bacchus you snuck out on me. Saw me coming and lit out the back."

The mother stares at him, and he can see she's half ready to believe him. But she balks, stands there like a dummy in an uptown showroom window. Ghost puts both eyes into the work now, and the mother whips a hand up over her mouth as her eyes jump left to right looking for safety.

"I said get a few things together. Better do it now before I change my mind and do like Mr. Bacchus wants me to." Ghost lets his eyes slide over to the girl and he does his best to send her a look that tells the story. The mother picks up the plot.

"Go on, Namah. Take your brothers and get some things together. Just some clothes. That's all we need."

"Momma?"

"I said go, girl! Dammit, get moving and do it fast!"

Ghost nods and keeps his face stony. The mother waits until the children are out of sight before she follows them into the house. Ghost stays on the front step. Sounds inside tell him they're getting a few clothes together. Drawers slide in and out, closets and cupboards slam and clatter.

Ghost sends an eye around the street, looking for inconvenient passersby who might throw a wrench into his plans. Sure enough he spots two of Mr. Bacchus' finest specimens along the way. They stand by a street lamp, the weak gaslight glowing the night above their heads and giving them parodies of the halo Mr. Bacchus wore earlier.

The men spot Ghost, too. He knows it, even if they keep up their smoking and jawing like they haven't seen anyone or anything at all.

The back door opens and closes and Ghost reaches into his jacket for his revolver. He draws it as he runs inside, shouting and cursing. The two men came running his way as soon as he reached for his gat. He knows they'll be inside the house, and behind him, before he can set up any signs of a story about how the family got the jump on him. He'll have to hope they were too far away to overhear what he told the mother.

The boys come in as Ghost reaches the back door. He gets there in time to see his sedan go roaring off the curb. Ghost yanks the door open and jumps out like he'll chase the car, but he draws up short when he sees Mr. Bacchus step out of the shadows to his right.

"I believe my instructions were to bring the girl in. Was I not clear, Ghost?"

"Mr. Bacchus," Ghost says, lowering his gat so his boss doesn't get any more wrong ideas. It's plain enough from the look on the man's face that Ghost has overstepped his radius. Better to just take the beating, he thinks, than risk getting cut off his tether and set adrift. Or handed a pine box to occupy. But Mr. Bacchus has other plans, Ghost discovers, and too late.

A rustling like dry paper and the scraping of steel on stone comes to Ghost's ears. He turns on his heel, bringing his revolver up slow, and too slow he finds, as a dark shape covers his vision and the night goes black around him.

A stabbing pain rips into Ghost's eye. He feels and hears himself screaming. He smells the musky damp of a barnyard and then the night rushes back in, billowing out in a spray of black feathers and gaslight and a laugh he hasn't heard since he left Chicago City.

"Ghost," Mr. Bacchus says. "I apologize for your unsavory treatment. This is done out of necessity, you understand. Word on the wind is that new blood is coming down river. New names and new games, and this is my New Orleans. I'll not lose her to anyone.

"Your services are no longer required, Ghost. This, I am sad to say, is the parting of our ways."

Ghost's eye is on fire. He turns on his heel and stumbles, trying to find Mr. Bacchus in the night. He turns and turns, looking for the man, but all he hears is his employer's voice. Then he puts a hand to his face and feels the wet smear on his cheek, smells the coppery tang and knows he hasn't just lost a job.

"My eye," he says. "Why'd you take my eye?"

"Precedent," Mr. Bacchus says. "People respond to threats when there exists precedent to prove the threats are not empty. That precedent is *you*, Ghost. The threat," Mr. Bacchus says and laughs once. "I believe you already know the man."

Ghost searches the night with the eye he has left. He turns slowly, watching shadows, hunting movement in the corners. The street is empty and quiet except for the rumbling of his sedan's engine a few blocks along. He sees the family there, and the boys from the krewe gathered around them, holding the girl apart from her mother and brothers.

"Over here, pal," says a voice from Ghost's past. He spins to the right and sees the man, standing just inside the house and clutching a dark mass tucked under his arm. A rooster. The bird is big and black, and its beak is smeared with blood. The man is tall and thin, and his pale brown skin looks like cigarette papers in the weakening light of the street lamps.

"Good to see you again, brother," the man says. "Thanks for the tip 'bout finding work down this way. All but dried up in

Chicago City. Capone pullin' back. But New Orleans? Man with both eyes on the street, he find work. Ain't that what you told me? When you left me in that flophouse, alone?"

Ghost stares his one eye full of hate at his brother as the man steps out of the house and into the night. Before Ghost can offer any reply, Mr. Bacchus clears his throat and fills the last line on the balance sheet.

"She turns sixteen come next month, Ghost. That's fine by me. Thirty days is all the time I need to send word to New York. Then we'll have another of our debutante games. Now, if the man with the bird will accompany me, it is time I take my leave of this alleyway."

Mr. Bacchus steps to the curb and Ghost watches his sedan slowly roll backwards down the street and stop beside his old boss. One of the boys gets out and opens the back door for Mr. Bacchus to climb in. Ghost's brother trots by to join them, whistling a happy tune as he steps up to the car. "Be seein' ya, Ghost," he says over his shoulder and laughs at his joke.

Ghost watches them drive away. He watches the mother and her sons shuffle down the street in his direction. They shiver as the sedan roars past them.

"Be seeing you, Birdie. Someday soon," Ghost says. The mother comes closer but keeps a few feet between them. She holds her sons to either side, hands around their backs and clutching them tight.

"Mr. Ghost," she says. "What do I do? They took my Namah. What do—"

"She'll be at the debutante table next month."

"The deb— I don't know what that means."

"It means Bacchus is making her the grand prize in a game of cards. She'll be won by whoever takes the game. And that means this one-eyed sonofabitch has a fortune to earn and he's got only thirty days to do it."

Visitor from the East

By Harry Turtledove

"Oh, hell," Bill Williamson said when the alarm clock assassinated a particularly juicy dirty dream. Cussing at it didn't make it shut up. Resigned that the dream was dead—he'd never be so limber in real life—the governor of the state of Jefferson hit the top of the clock with a massive fist. He got the OFF button and didn't break the clock, though not from lack of effort.

Yawning, he sat up in bed. "So early?" his wife muttered.

"Sorry, Louise," Bill said. "But I've got to get to the coast to greet the visitor, and Yreka ain't exactly coastal."

He lumbered into the bathroom and did what needed doing in there, then pulled a pair of shorts up over the thick, reddish hair on his legs. His wallet sat in one pocket; his keys clinked in the other. Out he went, to grab some breakfast before he hit the road.

Ceilings in the Governor's Mansion were thirteen feet tall. Doorways were ten feet high. Bill, at nine-two, didn't need to worry about ducking or bashing his head every time he went through one. Charlie "Bigfoot" Lewis, the second Governor of Jefferson—and the one who built the mansion during Coolidge prosperity—had been a sasquatch himself, and ran it up on a scale that suited his own comfort. Too big for humans, he'd figured, was easier to deal with than too small for his own folk. Bill blessed him for that.

"Here you go, Governor," the steward said when he walked into the dining room. "Coffee's hot, and breakfast'll be up in a minute."

"Thanks, Ray." Bill drank coffee by the quart mug. He was halfway down his first cup when Ray brought him eight fried eggs, a pound of bacon, and a dozen slices of wheat toast. As he plowed through the food, he hoped he wouldn't get hungry while he was driving.

The Stars and Stripes and the state flag of Jefferson flew in front of the mansion. Jefferson's banner was green, with the state seal centered on the field: a gold pan with two X's that symbolized the double crosses northern California and southern Oregon had got from Sacramento and Salem till they formed their own state in 1919. After World War I, self-determination was all the rage in Europe, and they'd run with it here, too. That neither Sacramento nor Salem was exactly sorry to see the seceders go hadn't hurt.

Below the flagpole sat the Governor's car: a 1974 Cadillac Eldorado he fondly called "the Mighty Mo." The Detroit behemoth wasn't quite the size of a battleship, but it came close. It was five years old now, getting long in the tooth, but he kept it anyway. Since the Arab oil crisis, cars had shrunk like wool washed hot. For someone Bill's size, they'd gone from dubious to impossible. The Mighty Mo got next to no mileage, of course, and gas was six bits a gallon. Bill didn't care. If the state wouldn't pay, he would.

He slid into the left rear seat: the driver's seat, with a long, long shaft for the steering wheel. The ignition was on the column, not on the dash. *A good thing, too*, he thought, starting the car.

Like the Governor's mansion, the Capitol had gone up before the Depression hit. Wings and colonnades and gilded dome showed off Jefferson's wealth, or maybe delusions of grandeur. The government office building next door? A square WPA block, as ugly as it was functional. The miracle was that it had got built at all.

Barbara Rasmussen waited in front of the office building. The Governor's publicist was highly functional, too, but far from ugly: a shapely blonde with big blue eyes. To use Jimmy Carter's immortal and immoral phrase, Bill had looked on her with lust in his heart a time or two. He was married, but he wasn't blind. Sasquatches and little people had been getting it on since long before blondes came to Jefferson—not all the time, but every so often. Some stories said one of Bill's great-grandmothers was a little person. He didn't know if that was true, or care.

Barbara got into the right—and only—front seat. "Morning, Governor," she said. "Early enough for you?"

"Oh, pretty much," he answered, miming a yawn. She laughed. He sometimes wondered if she was interested in a roll in the hay with him. Some little women (not at all in the Louisa May Alcott sense of the words) hopefully looked for sasquatch men to be big all over. They were seldom disappointed in that. Other ways? Men were men and women were women, big or small. Sometimes they clicked, sometimes they didn't.

None of which mattered right now. His size thirty-two right foot swung from brake to gas. Away the Mighty Mo went. He drove south on Jefferson State Highway 3 to the 299, then west toward the coast. What Jefferson called state highways would have been narrow, twisty, no-account two-lane blacktop roads anywhere else. That was partly because the state hadn't really bounced back after Hoover's name became a swear word, partly because the terrain was so rugged.

From Yreka to Eureka was just over 200 miles: three hours on an uncrowded freeway, assuming there was any such animal. Setting out just after six, Bill pulled into Eureka just before eleven. The overturned logging truck sure didn't help. The ship he was supposed to meet was due in at eleven-thirty. That cut it closer than he liked.

His back crunched when he unfolded himself from the Eldorado. A car that big wasn't meant for those roads, but he didn't fit into anything smaller. "Hey, Gov!" somebody called. Bill waved a broad-palmed hand. Sasquatch or little person, no pol could ignore constituents.

A few reporters and a couple of camera crews waited at the base of the pier where the *Heiwa Maru* would dock. Its arrival would be news here and in Yreka and Redding and Ashland and Port Orford and the rest of Jefferson. Maybe one of these birds was an AP stringer, in which case the story might go farther. But the gentlemen of the Fourth Estate just stood idly, some smoking cigarettes. "What's happening?" Bill called.

"Not a damn thing," a Eureka newspaperman answered. "Harbormaster says the ship's running an hour late." He sounded disgusted.

Bill was delighted. "In that case, we've got time for lunch. C'mon, Barbara. Let's hit Freaky Willie's."

The diner was only a block from the harbor. BIGGEST SHAKES IN TOWN, a sign painted on the window bragged, next to a picture of a sasquatch doing a swan dive into a strawberry milkshake. Bill didn't think he'd want to try that. He'd never get the goo out of his pelt afterwards. But the food was good and abundant and cheap, all of which mattered even if he was on state business and putting it on the taxpayer's tab.

He inhaled three Ginormous Burgers and half a farm's worth of fries, along with two of those big shakes (chocolate). Barbara ate, well, rather less.

Another citizen greeted him as he came out. Bill's hand didn't quite engulf the other man's when they shook. Haystack Thornton was a little man, but a big little man, close to seven feet tall and wide in proportion. He might have been part sasquatch himself. His bushy russet beard rose high on his cheeks, while his hairline came down almost to his eyebrows. He wore bib overalls and a Pendleton underneath; Eureka had to be twenty-five degrees cooler than Yreka.

"Just wanted to tell you thanks for all you've done and for all you haven't done, Governor," he said. "Me and my friends appreciate it, believe me."

"No worries, man," Bill said. Haystack Thornton and his friends were the leading growers of some highly unofficial crops around Eureka. Jefferson looked the other way, and wouldn't help the Feds when they didn't. *Do your own thing* had been a way of life here long before the hippies found it. Besides, Bill thought smoking marijuana was more fun than drinking beer, though nothing was wrong with beer, either.

Thornton ambled into Freaky Willie's. Bill and Barbara went back to the harbor. Sure enough, the *Heiwa Maru*—Japanese for

Peace Ship—had come into Humboldt Bay. A pavilion of saffron cloth stood on the deck before the bridge. *Good thing it's August,* Bill thought. *I wouldn't want to cross the Pacific under canvas in January.*

Snorting tugs nudged the *Heiwa Maru* into place. Lines snaked out from the ship. Longshoremen secured them to bollards. Down came the gangplank. Bill, Barbara, and the reporters and cameramen strode down the pier to meet the ship and its important passenger.

"Permission to come aboard?" the governor called to the Japanese skipper at the far end of the gangplank.

"Permission granted," the man said in good English. He added, "Have no fear, sir. It will bear your weight."

"I expected it would." Onto the *Heiwa Maru* Bill went. The skipper bowed. Bill bowed back. As he straightened, a Japanese sailor snapped a photo of him.

Bill walked toward the pavilion. The saffron cloth on one side folded back and the Yeti Lama came out to greet him. "Hello, Governor Williamson," the holy man said, his English more hesitant than the skipper's. He wore a loincloth and cape of scarlet silk to show his rank. Two other yetis, both in saffron loincloths and capes, followed him. So did two saffron-robed human monks. The big folk never could have used ordinary cabins.

The Yeti Lama was someone Bill could look up to—literally. He overtopped the Governor by six inches. Anyone seeing them side by side could tell they were of the same kind but different races. In little-people terms, they might have been Mongol and Swede. The yeti's pelt was browner than the sasquatch's; he had broader cheekbones and lower brow ridges.

"Welcome, your Holiness," Bill said. "Welcome to America. Welcome to Jefferson."

"I thank you so much." The Yeti Lama bowed and held his hands in front of himself with palms pressed together. Bill imitated the gesture. The newcomer looked to be in his mid-forties, near the Governor's age. Along with many pious members of his folk, he'd fled into exile when the Chinese invaded his mountainous Tibetan homeland twenty years before.

One reason more reporters weren't here was that Washington and Beijing had been thick as thieves since Nixon went to China. To the State Department, the Yeti Lama was just another tourist. Bill had all sorts of reasons for feeling otherwise.

A newshound who worked for a paper in Redding called, "Your Holiness, can you tell us why you came to Jefferson in particular?"

"Oh, yes. It is my pleasure." The Yeti Lama's English wasn't perfect, but he used what he had. "Jefferson in all the world is where I most feel a sense of, ah, communing—"

"Of community, you mean, sir?" Bill said helpfully.

The Yeti Lama smiled. His teeth were large and broad. One bore a gold crown. "I thank you. Yes, that is the word. A sense of community. You have in Jefferson mountains, and I of course grew up in mountains. Yours are small, but that is a trifle."

"We think they're pretty good-sized." Bill waved east, toward the Klamath Mountains serrating the horizon.

"I hear many have trees all the way up to top." The Yeti Lama smiled again, mischievously now. "Next to the Himalayas, that makes them foothills. Is right word, foothills?"

"Foothills is the word, yeah. You've got me there," Bill allowed.

"But this is not important," the Yeti Lama said. "It is only land. People on land, they are what matters. You here in America, you here in Jefferson especially, you set example for the world. Here you have small folk and large, living together in happiness and harmony. Here you have one of a large race, chosen peacefully, freely, by large and small to lead all. Not like this in land I come from. Chinese call us *xueren*—snowmen." His heavy features twisted in sorrow, or perhaps anger. "They treat us abominable— ah, abominably."

"I'm not even Jefferson's first sasquatch Governor, either," Bill said. State pride counted. The less said about earlier times, when this land was squabbled over by Russia and Spain, then split between California and Oregon, the better. But little people with guns hadn't hunted sasquatches for the fun of it in more than a hundred years. That was progress, any way you looked at it. Sasquatches had guns of their own now, too.

And, when you thought about what China was doing to yetis and Tibetans alike, Jefferson had to look like heaven on earth by comparison. No wonder the Yeti Lama wanted to call here.

Barbara said, "Can we all get together for pictures to show this harmony?" She turned to the *Heiwa Maru*'s skipper. "Captain, please join us with some of your men. Everyone gets along in Jefferson."

"That's right," Bill said. "Next month I'm going up to Port Orford to visit a businessman there. He moved to Jefferson from Japan more than fifteen years ago."

The captain spoke in Japanese. He and three sailors joined the Yeti Lama, his retinue, the sasquatch Governor, and the blond publicist. Barbara was taller than any of the crewmen from the *Heiwa Maru* or the human Buddhist monks, but even she barely came up to Bill's chest.

Well, that was the point of this exercise, wasn't it? Sure it was. Big people and little people could all get along together. Different kinds of big people could, too. And so could different kinds of little people, even if their countries had fought a ferocious war only half a lifetime earlier.

The skipper's wrinkles and bald spot said he was old enough to have fought for Japan against the USA. But, again, even if he had, so what? He was here in Jefferson in charge of the *Peace Ship*. He'd brought the Yeti Lama, one of the greatest peace symbols in the whole world (except perhaps China). That was what counted.

"Smile, everybody!" a cameraman called. Everybody did.

The Compassionate Moon

By David L. Drake and Katherine L. Morse

A horse blanket. And an in-barn water pump. A sack of soap flakes. A bucket. A sleepy draft horse. And I have you, my Harvest Moon.

So tonight I will scrub my clothes and body, getting the smell of the last week off me. Your light will aid my midnight chores without risking an open flame or lantern in a dusty hay barn. And while my clothes dry, I get to sleep close to that sleepy grey mare. Oh, how ironic, you say? A grey spot on the moon is also called a mare? Yes, yes, I know. But did you know mare means "night goblins" in Old English as well? Like the ones that chase me? Of course they are not real goblins. I know that. All too well.

What's that? You want to hear my story again? Do you mind if I whisper it to you? I don't want to wake the farmers, or find out if they have a dog. Where do you want me to start? How I used to have a room at the opulent Casino di Venetia that was all silks and brocade? How about the simplistic beauty of the card game *ventuno-et-un*, or as I have learned to say in English, twenty-and-one. Well, I have these breeches to wash, and what's left of my shirt, so allow me to entertain you with my tale.

It all started in my beloved Firenza, Italia, in my print shop. Things were going well for me as a young man, until my gambling debts outpaced my income, when I decided it was better to take the last of my finances and move myself and my press to Shrewsbury Street in Worcester, Massachusetts. I remember hanging the sign over the door, "Annunziato Venator—Printer—

Architectural Drawings," the gold letters gleaming against the black background. Why take my print shop there? Simple. The nearby Tempo watch works had their own designs and they did a good business. Tempo was known for their willingness to machine specialty watches: stopwatches, scientific timepieces, mechanical fuses, and many things with gears and springs. All for a price. I provided two complementary services: redrawing components in the style required by Tempo, and making copies of those drawings for each manufacturing station.

It all went well for two years. The conservative people of Massachusetts abhorred betting on games of chance, so it was easy for me to stay away from the private gambling clubs. I had a good relationship with John, the shop master at Tempo. One day John stopped by to pick up some illustrations, and he asked me to look at some drawings for a device he wasn't sure was a good fit for a watch factory. He plopped a notebook of drawings on my counter. The man who brought them to the factory didn't have much money to finance a new timepiece, so John told me that I shouldn't spend much time on it. And then he walked out.

I flipped open the book, somewhere in the middle, I believe. The drawings were painstakingly detailed, both graphically and in description. Nine layers of gearing, two separate mainsprings, three hands, and a three-color watch face. This was no ordinary specialty watch. Ordinary specialty? Does putting those two words together only make sense to me?

I spent the night studying the manuscript. All night. Until the rooster crowed I read through those pages at least three—no—four times.

The fool didn't understand what he had designed. The simpleton had completely underestimated the value of his creativity. He would have wasted it all. It was I who saw the usefulness of it. It was I who had the vision. I alone.

To the casual observer, it appeared to be a well-made pocket watch. And it worked as such. The long black hands moving as time passed and all that. It was the four extra buttons on the left side and the one on the right that added the hidden treasure. By pressing all the buttons at once, the timepiece would reset its internal counters to the standard set of fifty-two cards of a fresh deck. By pressing the buttons in a pattern, like playing a chord on a piano, the owner could mark which card had been played in a game. Another chording of buttons revealed how many of each card-type remained in the deck.

For any game where most of the cards are revealed and decks aren't reshuffled between hands, it was an incredibly accurate memory aid. But every page of the manuscript repeated that the instrument should only be used by casino owners to verify that their dealers weren't cheating. Slipping in an extra ace or two. Or dropping cards off the bottom of the deck. Tricks like that. What utter foolishness.

This was the tool for a winner. In my hands, a card game would be mine to control. As the bottom of the deck neared, I could escalate the betting and have an edge over all other players and on the casino, creating a gambler's paradise. And the detailed drawings for this mechanism were right there in my hands.

I meticulously copied every illustration, every paragraph, one by one. It took three long days. Then I struck a devil's bargain with John. He returned the engineering notebook to the fool, and I sold my work and the new merchandising strategy to Tempo. They planned to sell each of the instruments for hundreds of dollars, clandestinely of course, since in the right hands, such a device could pay for itself in days. They gave me a small fortune and the first Gambler's Friend that they made. That's what they called it. The Gambler's Friend.

Massachusetts is a horse- and dog-racing place, certainly not a place for high stakes card playing. I longed for Italia and her palaces of gaming. That was the end of my printing business. I headed back to the island of Castello, and the glorious Casino di Venetia.

With my little helper, the mistress of fortune was my devoted courtesan. I tried to stick to playing against the other patrons; no need to upset the house. I developed a habit of toying with my new "watch." Flipping the lid. Turning it over in my hand. Opening and closing it. Checking the time. All the while, I was manipulating those little buttons. And I always got lucky near the end of the deck.

What is that? How did I get here in this barn? My lunar friend, you are too impatient. A tale must not be rushed to be properly told. And I am hardly through my laundry duties, as you can see. You have never had to pump water quietly, have you? No, you slosh the oceans around without a care in the world. I have to rinse all the soap out of this shirt and that takes a lot of water and wringing. So allow me to continue both my labors and my narrative, please.

The money came easily. I bought luxurious Italian clothes. Quite nice. Not like these filthy rags. I bought drinks and dinners for entire rooms of acquaintances. I stayed in the best rooms in the casino.

But as the years went by, I started to get sloppy. I'd make foolish bets that I assumed I'd recover from. Fortunes were gained, but then lost. Not everyone was fooled. Dealers noticed, and had to get their cut of the winnings. I had to buy my way out of a potential scandal more than once. I reluctantly made friends with very unsavory characters.

My glorious run came to an end three months ago; the mistress of fortune abandoned me. The Casino, where all the staff knew I was gaming their patrons, ejected me. I was down to the coins in my pockets and literally owed a crooked lender an arm and a leg. For my own safety, I had to leave the island of Castello. I caught a ride to the nearby town of Treviso, trying to get the means to move farther away. I started playing small card games in the taverns there, avoiding anyone that I had hoodwinked at Casino di Venetia.

While there, I saw a broadsheet announcing a Twenty-and-One card game competition in Edinburgh, Scotland. Huzzah! A new location. No one would know me. The perfect game to get my fortune back. This was it! Back to my world of silks and brocade.

It took three days of crafty card play, but I was able to afford the airship fare, two exceptional Italian suits for presenting myself properly as a gentleman of means, and a new steamer trunk. I caught the one-hop airship flight from Venice that took me straight to Scotland's capitol. When I landed ... well, that was when the tables turned.

The competition sign-up booth was at the Edinburgh airship port. While waiting for my trunk, I queued up to register for the games. A friendly gent struck up a conversation, asking if I was excited to try my hand at the international event. I, of course, answered with an excited "yes," given that I knew this would be my grandest opportunity to regain, and perhaps surpass, my previous fortunes.

He introduced himself as Angus Sutherland, and asked if I had heard of a Gambler's Friend. Without waiting for an answer, he quietly asked if I was interested in purchasing one. He surreptitiously pulled one out of an interior vest pocket, and gave me a quick peek at it. I proudly replied, perhaps bragged, that I wasn't interested because I already had one. He retorted that the quality of the instrument declined precipitously after the first nine were made; he could sell me serial number nine, the last of the well-manufactured ones. "Not interested," I responded with a smile, "I have serial number one!" With that, he grabbed me by the shoulder of my coat with one hand, and dragged me out of the line. "Unhand me this instant!" I shouted in my best English to gain favor with the crowd. Instead, three or four men stepped out of the line to help him drag me over to a constable's stall.

"We have found him! We have Venator!" Angus shouted. "Send a telegram to Drake and McTrowell! Tell them to get here as quickly as possible!"

I writhed against his grasp, slipped out of my coat, and blindly ran. Of course, I initially headed straight for a dead-end hallway. As I skidded to a halt, I heard Angus shout behind me, "Get him! That's Nunzio Venator!"

Now, I am not known as a fast runner, but on that day, my patron god Mercury couldn't have caught me. I sprinted through the terminal, knocking down a couple of people who got in my way as I made my way out of the front double doors. Once out in the evening dusk, I hopped upon the first unhitched horse I saw, kicked it into a gallop, and headed north out of town.

That mount gave me a good ten-mile run before it flagged. With the cover of darkness, I slipped into an old barn that was much smellier and unkempt than this one, and pilfered water and grain for my ill-gotten steed. I assessed my situation. I only had the clothes on my back and a few coins in my pockets. And what useless bits of metal they were! My lire weren't going to do me any good here in Scotland. I decided to sleep there despite the disgusting stench from the dairy cows crowding the place. I awoke in the middle of the night to the sound of baying hounds and a man yelling that they had picked up my scent. I remounted my nag and was out in a flash, again heading north in the moonlight. The Grain Moon, I believe. And thank goodness for its light, as I was without a torch. Or any sense of self-preservation either. Careening over hills, fields, streams, and all of it uneven and rocky. The nag must have gotten another five miles before breaking her hind leg. I pressed on by foot without looking back. That was a month ago.

And here I am today. After a month of skulking from barn to barn, moving only at night. What's that, you say? They are still following me? Is that barking I hear? My clothes are soaking wet! I am dressing anyway. Oh! Oh! These clothes are painfully cold! Wake up you stupid horse. I need a fast escape.

What's wrong with you? Oh no, you're a plow horse! You aren't going to be fast enough! That box of matches, I'll start a fire and burn this useless barn down! That will slow down those that hunt me! Burn! Burn!

Outside I shout jests at my pursuers and their band of nimrods! I call them stupid and foolish, and head north, ever north, under you, my faithful Harvest Moon.

The Fall of the Falcon

By Anthony Francis

Somewhere in Edinburgh was a rat, and Liberation Academy Cadet Jeremiah Willstone was determined to find it—even if it got her expelled. But as she flew crazily through the city, she was increasingly unsure whether she was more likely to be expelled—or killed.

The tracker swung left, and Jeremiah followed suit, banking so hard with her "borrowed" Falconer's wings that all of Edinburgh seemed to barrel-roll around her ... then, as she feared, her ever-vivacious inner ear decided to get in on the spinning, too.

Dizziness swept over her, followed by nausea. Her gorge rose, even as her body fell, and she barely avoided a church steeple. The maneuver hooked her into a narrow four-storey alley—but even as she lost her way, her tracker showed she was gaining ground.

ↂↃ

Earlier, the Lady Georgiana Westenhoq had dismissed her plan. "Its directionality won't be the best," the computer pronounced from her clockwork-and-vacuum-tube throne, inspecting the device Jeremiah had cobbled together to track the infectious Foreign gearwork which lurked in the streets of Edinburgh. "You've got the resonances right, but the antenna's too small—"

"Oi!" Jeremiah said, protectively taking the dish, no larger than a salad bowl, from her roommate. Georgiana might be the best computer at Liberation Academy, but she was no engineer. "*You* try fitting a larger detector within the weight limits of Falconer's wings—"

"I thought you grounded," Georgiana said suspiciously. "Given your inner ear—"

"The *Dean* told me 'tracking those bloody gears is of highest importance,'" Jeremiah retorted, but Georgiana raised an arch eyebrow, and Jeremiah sighed. "Navid said he had it on good authority they could replicate, infest living tissue, even meddle with *time*—"

"Navid also said 'be effective, not reckless.' You were grounded for a reason—"

"Unless you've a better idea for tracking those clockwork parasites," Jeremiah said, "this is our best option: a ranged detector, capable of scanning at Falcon-wing speed, so we can scan whole neighborhoods from the air—Georgiana? What have you thought of?"

"A better idea," Georgiana said, turning to the locator board opposite her throne. "Apply your approach to the city-wide network for tracking cadet locator brooches. Then we can scan the whole of Edinburgh at a single stroke—and find any trace of those monsters."

଼ଓଔ

There! Her quarry wasn't a rat, but a *bat,* a glittering of gears showing it had succumbed to the mechanical plague. Jeremiah grinned, even as her stomach churned. Dragonflies might be her favorite flying creatures, but she wore Falconer's wings, and falcons ate bats, didn't they?

But the tiny bat, guided by a clockwork brain, darted quick and clever through stovepipe and antenna, and the indicator beads on Jeremiah's propulsion canisters fell dangerously low. She found herself hard pressed to keep up with the creature—or to keep down her lunch.

Her wings clipped a guy-wire, and she heard a scream behind as something toppled—but she opened the throttle on her wings to full power. She only had one tracking nodule left, and the dart gun was a projectile weapon; miss your target, and who knows what you might hit?

With only a minute's flight left, she had to close the gap!

ॐ

"Hacking the locator might get me expelled," Georgiana said, slotting Jeremiah's wax cylinder into a reader slot in the opened hood of the locator array. "But if I feed the resonance profile into the locator network, switch the network to active sensing, then ... gotcha!"

The spectroscope's screen lit with the glowing green lines of the streets of Edinburgh—speckled with hundreds, perhaps *thousands* of red glowing dots, like a bird's-eye view of an enormous swarm of luminous ants, all moving slowly with purpose.

"Like a villainous Christmas," Jeremiah said, stepping closer to the huge glass disc, looking at a dense concentration of dots northeast of campus, a curdling swarm in a riverfront warehouse on the Waters of Leith. "We should start our investigation ... here—"

But as her finger neared the dial, all the red dots fled outwards at once, like cockroaches fleeing a sparked kitchen gaslight. "Did I do that?" Jeremiah asked, whirling to Georgiana, who was plugging herself back into her computer throne. "The whole city's on the move!"

"Blood of the Queen!" Georgiana said. "They've detected the active scanning!"

"Blast!" Jeremiah said. "We'll head them off. Uh ... where are they going to?"

"I—I can't tell," Georgiana said. "There's no pattern! They're fleeing at random!"

Jeremiah turned and stared at the dial. The fire ants *were* fleeing at random—that is, not just fleeing outward in an ever-expanding ring, but losing time by crossing back over themselves. But these gear-infested monsters weren't stupid—it had to be *deliberate* randomness.

"This isn't random flight," Jeremiah said. "*We* know where they're coming *from*, but *they* know they're being tracked. They'll have to flee the city entirely, get out of range—but a caravan to a safe house is as useless to them as a big red arrow pointing straight at it!"

"They can't converge on a safe location," Georgiana said, beginning to comprehend. "So they need to flee in a way that obscures their ultimate goal. But how does that help us? They've got us thoroughly baffled—"

"*Use* those vacuum tubes embedded in your head," Jeremiah said. "Run a, what was it you called it, a Pearson component analysis to see where the different masses of them are going. No—where they're mostly *not* going. *That* will show what they're trying to hide!"

Georgiana sat bolt upright in her chair. "Signal and noise," she said, and her crown of vacuum tubes crackled. "Factor apart the major movements, exclude random noise, map to the compass directions—and find the stragglers on routes deliberately *not* chosen by the mass!"

She pointed. "There!" she said, and Jeremiah gasped as the map reformed itself into rainbow brigades as regimented and orderly as military maneuvers—with one big gap in the formation, with a red dot at its center. "*That's* what they're trying to hide—"

"Like a general," Jeremiah said. "Hiding in plain sight—in Holyrood Abbey!"

೪೦೮೩

Jeremiah swooped under crumbling buttresses, weaving in and out of the girderwork slowly transforming the ruins of Holyrood Abbey into the cathedral of the Church of Scotland. But the chaos of restoration made a perfect home for her hypothesized "clockwork general."

The bat threaded in and out of scaffolding ahead, but at full power, Jeremiah flitted like a dragonfly, barely a stone's throw behind. Then the bat reached free space, devoid of cover, and Jeremiah squeezed out a bit more power, stabilizing herself just as she was ready to fire—

Her left canister sputtered out. The Falconer's wings faltered, dipped—and her wing clipped a gargoyle, decapitating it. With a nauseated groan, Jeremiah realized that destroying either her wings *or* a historic monument would wash her out of the Falconry program.

Then whirling begat vertigo, her nausea overcame her—and she vomited.

℘

"Yes, Georgiana, sound the alarm, but we can't let whatever it is they're trying to hide just slip away," Jeremiah said. "I know I'm grounded, at least until my inner ear surgery; but don't be a mother hen. They may have taken my wings, but I'll steal a pair—"

"Jeremiah!" Georgiana hissed, seizing her hand. "What if this is just a sensor artifact? What if there is no 'clockwork general' running this army? Or what if there *is*, and he's got human confederates at his disposal? Leave this to the faculty—"

"When have we ever?" Jeremiah asked. "And—honestly—have we the time?"

"At least leave your locator!" Georgiana said. "You'll be tracked—caught—*expelled!*"

Jeremiah's free hand jerked towards her locator brooch—then froze, and clenched.

"If something were to go wrong, wouldn't I *want* to be found?" she asked. "I've nothing against skulking, I'll have to do it to succeed. But I'm a grounded Falconer. Stealing wings violates the honor code. I'm not out for gallivanting. Does this need to be done or not?"

Georgiana released her hand, and Jeremiah nodded curtly.

"As I thought," she said. "Keep an eye on the tracker—I'm off to the Aviary."

℘

Grimacing, in tears, clenching her teeth, Jeremiah shot out of the buttresses in pursuit of the bat, her wings spiraling as her remaining canister rocketed her off balance. They'd grounded her for a reason; she knew that now. She couldn't take the maneuvering demanded of a proper Falconer: otoliths in the ear, *paroxysmal positional vertigo* in a textbook; *benign*, they called it, until it made a dizzy, reckless cadet upchuck her innards midflight. Jeremiah *would* crash—but as her quarry fled into a canyon of five-story slum houses, she got it dead in her sights.

"Gotcha," Jeremiah said, and fired.

Missing her target—and hitting godknowswhat.

Jeremiah whirled after the bat into the rising canyon of crumbling buildings, in a full, uncontrolled barrel roll now. Nausea surged, her stomach clenched—then she sprayed her guts out as even her namesake will was no longer able to hold back the rising pressure of bile.

As Jeremiah spiraled back to earth, vomit trailing around her in a corkscrew, she realized the only way she could make this cock-up more undignified would be to have forgotten her uniform and have crashed these wings wearing no more than a night-shirt.

Jeremiah impacted, wings breaking with a vicious crack, then disintegrating around her in a spray of brasslite, balsa, gears and wires as she rebounded into the air. Tumbling, she got one last airborne glimpse of sky—before it was snatched away, as she definitively went down.

Jeremiah slammed into the street face first, skidding to a painful almost-stop three meters later. At the last moment, a final bit of wing caught a drainage gutter and flipped her over, throwing her onto her back in a puddle of slime that was almost certainly not water.

Lying in agony, Jeremiah stared up at her lost sky. Surprisingly, she was conscious, and miraculously, her body was a sparkle of blossoming bruises, not spreading numbness from that horrible wrench to her neck. But her dreams of falcons and dragonflies were dead.

She heard a tread, swallowed thickly—and looked up.

The figure that loomed over her was no savior. Tall as a man, its body was covered in a hooded duster of mismatched scraps of ballistic cloth and Faraday mesh. The coat disguised the figure's outline—but beneath the hood was a near-featureless cylinder of steel.

"The clockwork general," Jeremiah whispered. "You're real—and, sir, under arrest."

But the figure did not hear her. Jeremiah stared up in helpless horror at the single offset eye, glowing red, shielded with wire, that stared down pitilessly from within the hood. Beside the eye, the clockwork bat nestled—then the hooded figure raised an enormous shockgun.

Jeremiah's eyes went wide as the crackling vacuum tube charged—then she kept her face carefully frozen as a clockwork rat climbed up onto the figure's shoulder, with Georgiana's tracking nodule embedded deeply in its fur. Miss one target—you might hit another.

In the instant before the figure fired, Jeremiah's final thought was: *gotcha.*

The Engraved Chest

By Kirsten Weiss

April, 1849
San Francisco

Ely:

It's the damndest story. I'm not sure what to make of it.

There's a pleasure in bringing a lady exactly the right gift, especially when the lady is a friend, like Miss Grey. She'd been holed up in her room at our boarding house for weeks. Since you and I share some responsibility for that, I decided to bring her what we'd found. Just to check on her, you understand. We're responsible for delivering her to Washington, after all, and you were in Sacramento.

I knocked on her door, parcel in hand. Another door down the hall opened. A man stuck his head out, stared at me, retreated.

A bolt drew back, and Miss Grey opened her door. "Mr. Sterling. Good afternoon." Her British accent was stiff and starched as ever. She wore her white blouse, chemical-stained at the cuffs, and that brown, leather waistcoat. Her copper watch chain dangled from one buttonhole. Strands of dark hair escaped her chignon.

In the room behind her, the blue bedspread was rumpled. The wardrobe door stood ajar. A tiny sweeper mechanical bumped, trapped, between a folded-over corner of the rag rug and the rickety wooden desk. The desk, at least, appeared normal, scattered with papers and splattered with ink.

I reached up to tip my hat and remembered I wasn't wearing one. "You shouldn't open the door to just anyone, you know."

"An angry mob wouldn't have bothered to knock. Besides, I'd have smelled the tar and feathers. Or at least the tar."

I liked that she could joke. But I didn't like to see her beaten, cynical, hiding. I was going to make it right.

"Have you any news?" she asked.

"Soon."

She walked to the window above her desk and looked out. "We're not leaving San Francisco, are we?" Her tone was flat, defeated. Her brown skirts seemed to fold into the gloom.

"Not yet," I said. "Your equipment is loaded on the Navy ship. All I need do is complete the inventory." That would be more easily accomplished with her assistance, but I didn't like her moving about the streets. A miasma hung over the boomtown, the San Francisco fog oppressive rather than cooling, and tasting of ash. There was a lot I could protect her from, but angry mobs were unpredictable and dangerous. The town still blamed her for the harbor fire.

"This must feel like prison," I said. "No mechanicals to toy with, no workshop, can't go out. But it won't last much longer."

The rattle of hammers and horse carts, invisible in the fog pressing against the thick glass, seeped beneath the windowsill. Miss Grey touched her fingers to the glass. "I need to go … somewhere."

Something in her gesture made me shift my weight, uneasy. "This may cheer you up." I laid the parcel atop an open book on her desk, and a spring of tension between my shoulders released.

Twin wrinkles appeared between her brows. With a snick, a knife popped from her sleeve. She cut the strings and returned the knife to its hidden sheath. Unwrapping the paper, she frowned at the engraved metal chest. "I don't … Where did you find this?"

"Soldiers retrieved it from what's left of your workshop." I'd polished the black from its strange symbols, but the chest smelled of soot and ruin.

"I'd forgotten about this," Miss Grey said. "Strange. It should have been in my safe, not lying in the rubble."

"What do you want to do with it? Send it to the States by steamship, or carry it with us overland?"

She frowned. "It's not mine. A traveler asked me to keep it in my safe for two weeks. But he never returned."

"How long ago?"

"It's been three months."

"The man's not coming back. Maybe whatever's inside will indicate where he is or what to do with it."

Miss Grey turned the chest over in her hands. "Perhaps you're right."

"It's locked. Can you open it?"

"Mm."

I could have picked the lock but didn't want to deprive her of the pleasure. It would keep Miss Grey ungainfully employed for at least an hour. "Is there anything else you need?"

Miss Grey traced her fingers over the lock. "To depart San Francisco as soon as possible."

I reached again for my missing hat, bowed, and left, satisfied. If that uncanny box didn't lift her spirits, nothing would.

There was the usual chaos in the streets, drunken miners and swearing cart drivers and sailors slipping in the thick mud. A madman crawled on all fours, ranting. "It's fastened on me. Hollowing me out. Make it stop!"

Watchful, wary, I walked to the blasted harbor. Burnt and sunken ships protruded from the sand. Planks had been laid over the ruins, stretching to abandoned ships farther out in the bay.

At the shore, a soldier in blue saluted and led me to a beached rowboat. Another soldier guarded the vessel. I helped shove it into the water and splashed inside. They drove the boat through the mercury waters, the swells gray and seething, to the steamship.

A rope ladder with wooden rungs hung over one side. I clambered aboard.

A man waited on deck, his face hidden beneath the hood of his slicker. He held a ledger between gloved hands. Though the captain had told me the man covered himself due to a lab accident, dislike tightened my spine. I like to look a man in the eyes when I'm talking to him.

"And where is Miss Grey?" His voice scraped, thin and squeezed.

"Safe."

"I do not require her safe. I require her assistance cataloging the items."

"I'm here to help catalog."

I felt his stare for a long moment. Pivoting, he strode down the wooden deck, his slicker flaring about his knees.

I followed him into the ship's hold. Lanterns swung from above, and weird shadows danced across the open crates. The scientist led me through rows of boxes, pointing to the contents of each crate, demanding a response. I didn't like his attitude, and what I didn't know, I invented. The man's response was the same in any case – a hiss, a flick of his pen across the page.

Finally, we finished.

"This is not everything, I think," he rasped, setting my teeth on edge.

"It's everything to be shipped. We plan to travel overland to Washington—"

"I must see it all."

"Why?"

"The US Government—"

"Has no authority over Miss Grey's personal effects."

"And are mechanicals included in her personal effects?"

"Of course, but—"

"Then I will judge whether I have authority over them."

"No, you will not." Jaw clenched, I turned and strode from the hold.

ॐ॑

Day Two

"The ship can't leave until that scientist is satisfied," the Colonel said. Lamplight glittered off the brass buttons in his blue uniform.

"He won't be satisfied until he's pried through each of Miss Grey's carpetbags."

"Most likely." Rubbing his knuckles along a blond mutton chop, he leaned back. His chair creaked. The Colonel sighed, grim. "You'll have to negotiate a truce, Agent Sterling. I haven't time. This morning a man from that very ship washed up with the tide."

"From the steamer?" I asked sharply.

He nodded. "Drowned, most likely. But his expression ...." His expression grew distant. "Such horror."

"Sir?"

He shook himself. "A sad business. Well, that's all."

"Yes, sir." Tipping my hat, I took my leave.

On horseback, I made my way from the Presidio. Night had fallen, fog twisting across a blood moon. Rectangles of light from nearby houses splintered the road. Tinny piano music floated from a distant gaming hell.

Some instinct made me veer toward the burnt wharf. New buildings were already rising, skeletal in the gloom. At the ruins of Miss Grey's warehouse, I slowed. A steady scrape and thunk floated from the burnt and broken beams—most likely a two-legged vulture scavenging for metal. I stiffened. It was still Miss Grey's property, and she had lost enough. I drew breath to urge my horse forward.

The piano music, the lap of the nearby bay, the scrape-thunk from the ruins, all stopped. A wall of silence descended. Even the jingle of my horse's harness quieted.

A shadow glided across the broken beams and mounds of ash.

And then I smelled it.

Fear.

I've smelled fear on other men, but Ely, this was the first time I smelled it on myself. And I'll be damned if I knew why.

The shadow vanished, and not knowing its location was worse. A clammy vapor brushed past me, prickling my scalp.

As if released, a wave of sound crashed down. Men shouted. A buggy jingled on a nearby street.

I slid from my horse and searched the ruins but couldn't find that damnable shadow. After twenty minutes, I gave up and rode to the boarding house.

At the door to my room, I hesitated. That shadow had got my wind up. I walked down the hall to Miss Grey's room and knocked.

No response.

I knocked again. "Miss Grey?"

She opened the door.

Haggard smudges bruised the skin beneath the inventor's unfocused eyes. A hank of brown hair fell loose across the front of her leather waistcoat. It looked like she'd slept in yesterday's gown. She seemed thinner, shrunken.

I stepped backward, shocked by her alteration. "Are you all right?"

The lady swayed. "Perfectly."

I strode inside and looked around. The gas lamp was low, and in its flickering shadows I saw the room was no more or less disordered than the day before. The mechanical bumped against the same carpet hillock. "How'd you get on with that box?"

"I opened it last night," she said in a dreamy voice.

"What was inside?"

"Nothing." Miss Grey's shoulders twitched. "And the ship? Are they prepared for departure?"

I turned my hat in my hands. "I'm afraid not. The government scientist in charge is worried he doesn't have everything."

Eyes glazed, Miss Grey said nothing.

"I explained your personal items would be traveling overland, but he needs to see them."

"He has everything he needs." She stumbled sideways and banged into her desk. The oil lamp trembled, shadows shooting about the room. Something metallic clanked to the floor, one of her aether guns.

I'd already confiscated one of these weapons. The government scientist would no doubt want this as well, but the gun would come in handy as we traveled east. Besides, I hadn't the heart.

"I'll take care of the scientist," I said. "Get some rest."

"I am rather tired. Thank you for speaking to the man. I'd prefer no more delays to our journey."

I took my leave, struck by the sensation she was already on a treacherous voyage.

ೞಣ

Day Three

The town reeked of smoke from a thousand woodstoves, cooking dinner. Angry shouts drifted up the darkened street, and I urged my horse to a trot.

My fist clenched on the reins. That damned scientist had complained to the Army commander, who'd put his booted foot down. I'd wasted another day at the Presidio, arguing and losing. The Army couldn't allow one of its ships to sit in the harbor indefinitely. Three soldiers had already deserted for the gold fields, plus the one who'd drowned.

If he had drowned.

I pulled up short in front of our boarding house. A brawl was in full swing. Men tangled, a body being flung from the knot at random moments. Our landlady, the diminutive Mrs. Watson, stood at the top of the porch steps, a sawed-off shotgun in her hand.

I waded through the combatants to her. "What happened?"

"That there man tried to push his way into Miss Grey's room." She pointed.

That-there-man was the government scientist. I rubbed my chin. Now I don't like six on one, but he was holding his own against the miners. And I didn't like that he'd tried to bully Miss Grey. "And the other boarders defended her?" That was a good sign. Not all San Franciscans wanted Miss Grey punished.

"No. That man beat on her door so long and loud, the other boarders got fed up with the racket."

"Well, I won't spoil the fun. Is Miss Grey in her room?"

Mrs. Watson frowned. "Don't rightly know. I didn't see her leave. She never does these days. But she didn't come down for meals today, and I don't know how she could have ignored all that banging."

I took the stairs two at a time and pounded on Miss Grey's door.

It swung open.

Invisible ants crawled up my spine. I edged into the room. In the dim lantern light, everything appeared as it had yesterday, with one exception: Miss Grey was absent.

The window, latched from the inside. Wardrobe, empty. I lifted the bed skirt. Miss Grey did not hide beneath it.

I raced downstairs. Men stumbled inside, lips swollen, blood streaming from noses and foreheads, clothing torn and dusty. No Miss Grey in the parlor, dining room, kitchen. I barreled through the kitchen and outside, to the yard. The privy door hung open.

Unsettled, I walked down the steps into the muddy yard, nearly decapitating myself with a clothesline. A steam-powered washing machine—another of Miss Grey's creations—sat, cold and unmoving, near the water pump.

I paused on the plank walk to the privy. Where the devil could she be? She hadn't left the boarding house in over a month. The thought that she'd strike out now, in the dark, made no sense. Unless she was on a mission of her ...

The fog parted. Moonlight edged the mist with silver and silhouetted a feminine figure on the roof.

I gasped. "Miss Grey!"

The lady stood, unmoving, at the roof's edge, her hems bleeding over the side.

"Don't move!"

A ladder leaned up against the plank wall. I scrambled up it and onto the roof. "Miss Grey, I'm ..." My voice dried in my throat.

The moonlight turned Miss Grey's face ghastly, immobile as a Greek statue and frozen in horror. She clutched the metal chest in both hands. Its lid was open.

"Miss Grey?"

"I've seen them. Unspeakable things," Miss Grey said, hoarse. "Good God, they're coming."

"Who's—"

A winged shadow swept behind the lady.

"Miss Grey!" I leapt toward her, but the thing knocked us both down. We sprawled on the rooftop.

I whipped my pistol from its holster. One shot. Two. Three. Ely, I hit it. I know I did.

Claws scrabbling, the creature landed. Its inky wings coalesced behind it. It flowed across the roof like oil, a malignance freezing the blood in my veins. The thing swooped upon the fallen box and snapped it shut. "At last," it rasped

My throat tightened. It was the government scientist. "What do you want with that chest?" I rolled, angling myself between that monstrosity and Miss Grey.

"The world, sir. The world."

Blackness flattened us. Fog and stars spun, a whirlwind, and the corruption vanished.

The Clockwork Writer, Part I

By Steve DeWinter

Had I heeded the final message from the clockwork writer, I would look like the mirror image of my twin brother pointing a loaded pistol at my head. Instead I had refused to follow a direct order, was now unarmed, and about to pay the ultimate price for my disobedience.

My brother's hand was rock steady as he squeezed the trigger without remorse. I watched in slow motion as the hammer snapped forward a heartbeat before the gun's discharge would blind me at the same moment the bullet would end my life.

ⅎℛ

Thirty Days Earlier

The attic of the palatial family estate in the country just outside London looked as if no living soul had touched it in two generations. Despite spending every summer at the massive estate in my youth, I couldn't remember ever setting foot on the stairs leading up to the attic, let alone entering the attic proper before today. Joseph, born two minutes before me to our same mother, seemed more at home in the crowded space, as if he had spent some time up here before. He pointed to a particularly suspicious looking mound under a faded dust cloth.

"That one," he said. "That looks like it might be it."

"Might be what?" I asked, unsure about touching the dust enshrouded cloth with my clean hands.

He smiled at me from across the open space. "You'll see."

I shot him a withering look. "Why don't you just tell me?"

"Grandfather made me promise to never tell. But can I help it if you discover it on your own?"

I sighed heavily. Joseph was always good at keeping secrets. Unlike me. Maybe that's why he and grandfather became so close that one summer when I lay sick in bed for two months. Joseph never did tell me what they did together while I slowly recovered from the fever. His devilish smile told me maybe now I was about to find out.

I quickly pulled back the dust cloth and sent a plume of particles erupting into the air like a miniature volcano spewing ash. I coughed harshly and blinked away the tears, unable to see more than a few feet across the attic in the sudden dust cloud.

Joseph waved his hands frantically back and forth, which only resulted in the dust swirling around the stale air with very little of it deciding to accept that gravity existed. "Easy, James. You don't want to choke us to death before we receive our fortunes."

I was about to ask him what he was talking about when the dust settled and the air cleared visibly, revealing a strange wooden boy seated at tiny student desk poised with quill in hand as if ready to write something. It drew my attention to it so rigidly that I nearly forgot the words poised along the edges of my lips and stared at it in silence. Through an open panel on the side of the tiny desk that had sprung open from disrepair I could see rusted old gears and springs.

Joseph leaned in beside me and smiled at the tiny figure. "Hello again."

The mechanical boy jerked and we both jumped back. I'm not too ashamed to admit I yelled out in surprise. The boy dipped his quill into the inkwell and then scraped the pen across the top of the desk. The inkwell had dried up long ago. And without any paper to write on he ended up giving us his message in the dust that had only recently settled on the desk. The same dust I had unceremoniously tossed into the air with the canvas dust cloth to reveal this strange contraption.

When he was done, he settled back into the position I had first seen him. Joseph, always the more brazen of the two of us, moved closer and twisted his head to read the message scrawled in the dust. Keeping my distance, I met my brother's confused expression with one of my own. "What does it say?" I asked tentatively.

His eyebrows met at the middle of his forehead. "Paper and ink."

೮Ꮔ

It didn't take us long to drag the mechanical contraption out of the attic and clean it up properly. We set it up on the dining room table and Joseph filled the inkwell while I located paper to place into the spring-loaded holders on the corners of the small desk. As soon as we were done, we stared at it in silence.

I looked at Joseph and noted the smile spreading across his face.

"Now what?" I asked.

"You ask it a question."

"And?"

"And it answers."

I frowned at the small wooden boy. "Are the answers broad or something? It can't possibly understand us."

"Watch this," he replied, a twinkle of excitement sparkling in the corner of his eye.

He cleared his throat and directed his question at the clockwork writer. "How do I get rich?"

I visibly flinched. "What kind of question is that?"

"It's a perfectly valid one. Father left us with practically nothing but debt and junk. Look at us. We are out here only a day before the bank is to reclaim our summer home, digging through the attic hoping to stumble across something of value. Now we have the chance to re-write our story." He pointed at the boy with his quill poised over the blank page. "He can rewrite it for us."

He turned back to the boy and repeated his question. "How do I get rich?"

The clockwork boy sat perfectly still.

We looked at each other and I shrugged. "Maybe your question is too open ended."

Joseph nodded and looked at the small wooden boy. "Where can I find some money?"

The clockwork writer jerked into action and I jumped even though I had been half expecting it. He wrote slowly and steadily. We watched in anticipation until he finished and resumed his waiting stance. Joseph removed the paper from the desk and read it out loud. "Visit the Old Lady today at precisely seven minutes past the hour of three. Take only one."

He stared perplexedly at the doll seated at the desk. "What is this?"

My mind raced as I worked out the solution and then my face broke out into a massive smile. "I think he means the Old Lady of Threadneedle Street."

Joseph held his hands out and shook his head, indicating he still didn't understand.

I had to use words he would know. "The Old Lady of Threadneedle Street is another name for the Bank of England."

He stared at the paper again and then at the clock on the mantle above the dining room fireplace. "Seven minutes after three? That's in an hour." He grabbed the mechanical doll and lifted it from the table.

"What are you doing?" I asked.

"Hiding this in our old room. And then we are going to see what is so special about the Bank of England at seven minutes past three."

₧℣

Imagine my surprise when we arrived at the bank a couple of minutes before three only to discover stacks of gold bars on display in an effort to prove everyone's money was safe with the Bank of England. So safe, they saw no disadvantage to leaving stacks of gold bars piled up out in the open for everyone to see.

We stood just inside the door and I struggled to keep my mouth from hanging open in shock. How had the doll known about this? Joseph nudged me in the side with an elbow and whispered. "He said to take only one. Do you think he meant only one gold bar?"

I tore my eyes away from the glittering bars stacked waist high and focused on the several armed guards standing around them. I nudged Joseph back hard with the sharp point of my elbow and whispered loudly. "He didn't say anything about guards with guns."

"Let's wait and see what happens in seven minutes." Joseph winked and strode deeper into the bank, walking around the edge of the bank interior, his gaze fixed to the bars of gold in the center.

The clock on the wall above the front door ticked away the time and, as it slowly swung past the five minute mark, my heart rate increased to match each twitch of the second hand as it juddered ever forward towards providence.

Joseph took one last look at me and then moved towards the stacked bars in the center of the room. A guard eyed him suspiciously and I glanced up at the clock. In less than thirty seconds, it would be exactly seven past three o'clock. I looked back at Joseph who was standing his ground as one of the guards broke from his post and started wandering closer to my brother.

I couldn't take my eyes off what was about to transpire between the guard and my brother when I collided with a young boy carrying a bag of coins.

The bag took that moment to split open and coins rained down noisily on the polished marble floor around my feet, echoing loudly throughout the bank lobby, and turning every head in my direction. The boy cried out as he watched his life savings spread away from him. I bent down and started helping him scoop up the coins. I glanced up to see Joseph walking past the guard, tipping his hat as he walked up and bent down to help me scoop coins into a pile.

The boy's father bent down and started sliding coins away from us. "He has been saving for five years. You better hope we recover every penny."

I smiled weakly. "I'm really sorry. I didn't see him there."

The father scowled at me. "Watch where you're going next time."

Joseph stood and pulled on my shoulder. "You've caused enough trouble. We should get going."

Before I knew what was happening, I was ushered through the bank doors and into the street. I followed as we rushed around several corners until Joseph ducked into a dark alley and paused, looking around to ensure we were alone. I stopped next to him and the smile across his face threatened to tear at his cheeks.

"Why are you smiling?"

He glanced around surreptitiously again and then lifted back the lapel of his frock coat. I caught an unmistakable glimpse of bright yellow before he slapped his hand against his chest. I stared at his chest for a moment and then looked at his eyes. "Is that ...?"

"Yes," he laughed, his hands visibly shaking from excitement. "I didn't hesitate for a moment. As soon as I saw the minute hand click to seven past I reached for a bar of gold. I heard all the commotion, but didn't look until I had tucked the bar out of sight." His eyes shifted back and forth quickly as he looked into my eyes and gripped my shoulders. "I don't know how you did it, but thanks to your distraction nobody saw me. We did it."

I shook my head, unable to fathom what had just happened. "But I—I didn't do it on purpose. I wasn't looking where I was going. I ..."

Police whistles blew out in the streets and men ran from every doorway into the view. They poured from the public houses and private residences in response to the rising alarm and headed as one towards the Bank of England, all shouting and blowing their whistles to alert other officers nearby that something was amiss. Joseph squeezed my shoulders and released me. "Looks like they finally noticed it missing. Let's get out of here and back to that doll. I have more questions."

The Light of the Moon

By Michael Tierney

The carriage finally reached the end of the hot, dusty drive up from the valley and pulled to a stop in front of the brick building. Its sole passenger, Professor Augustus Lawrence, attempted to climb out, but the bumpy trip had made his injured knee stiff, and bending it was difficult. Finally, he was rescued by a man who hurried toward him.

"Professor, let me help you down. Please. How is your leg? Is it feeling any better?"

"Thank you, Simpson. At my age, injuries heal much more slowly than they once did. The doctor says I have a few more weeks until the stiffness subsides. He quite scolded me, 'You're lucky you didn't fall from higher up on your telescope.'"

Lawrence did not own the Great Refracting Telescope *per se*, but as director of the newly built Lick Observatory, he decided who was granted time on it. While he enjoyed having less-senior astronomers have to ask him for the opportunity, Lawrence kept access to the telescope tightly controlled. All the more time for his own observations.

One day, maybe those prestigious East Coast college astronomers will stop looking down their noses at my "frontier observatory" and come begging to me for observing time.

Lawrence was an active man, not used to being limited physically, and his injury both pained and annoyed him. The pain he could control by judicious doses of an elixir he obtained from a highly recommended druggist. It was the annoyance he could not bear.

If my astronomical colleagues found out that I had tumbled off my telescope's observing platform, they'll think me a fool. It would reflect badly on both myself and the observatory.

"I plan on observing the Petavius region of the Moon this evening, Simpson. Who is on duty to assist me?"

"I'm afraid it's Miss Branham, sir."

"Afraid? Why are you afraid of her, Simpson? She has performed satisfactorily in her duties, or else I wouldn't have kept her on. Let's not assume all members of the fairer sex are less able than you or I."

"Yes, sir," said Simpson rather sheepishly. "I meant no disrespect to Miss Branham, sir. It's just that ..."

"Well?"

"It's just that ..."

Lawrence left his tongue-tied assistant, entered the spacious observatory dome, and looked up at the telescope. The observatory's 36-inch refracting telescope was the largest of its kind in the world. Perched on Mount Hamilton above the agricultural town of San Jose, it was a bequest by James Lick to the University of California—and, it must be said, a monument to himself. At the base of the brick telescope mount was a bronze plaque which read, *Here lies the body of James Lick.* Lawrence nodded towards the plaque and muttered, "I will make those Ivy League astronomers take notice, Mr. Lick. They may look down on us now, but soon they will know what discoveries we're capable of."

Coming out of his reverie, he noticed a young woman watching him. "Good afternoon, Miss Branham. Is the telescope prepared for tonight's observing?"

"Yes, director. Mr. Simpson told me you were interested in some areas on the terminator of the Moon?"

"That's correct—the southern hemisphere, right at the edge of the sunlit section where the slanting light throws the terrain into sharp relief. Petavius Crater, to be exact."

The area of the Moon he wanted to investigate had some very interesting features and was best observed only a few days after the new Moon, when the Moon was still a thin crescent and only visible just after sunset.

"I've prepared some filters to reduce the glare of the Moon's light," said Miss Branham. "Do you want to expose some photographic plates, or will you be observing directly through the eyepiece?"

"Mmm, yes, please prepare the camera, but I will let you know if I decide to use it."

Lawrence left her to finish the preparations for that evening. He limped back to the director's quarters, favoring his injured knee. In his apartment—sparsely furnished, as his wife absolutely refused to live on a mountaintop and preferred to remain at their San Francisco home—he unwrapped a bottle prepared for him by Dr. Perrin, by reputation the best pharmacist in San Jose. The embossed lettering on the bottle read, *Mor-fo-caine Elixir* and the paper label claimed, "The Cure for all types of muscular and skeletal Pains and Inflammations. Restores Vital Functions and infuses New Life and Vigor." Despite the flowery language, he questioned the pharmacist's skill. He had already emptied the first bottle with little to no reduction in his pain. "Up the dosage!" was Perrin's reply when Lawrence visited his pharmacy. "Some patients, especially professional men of determined nature, are resistant to its effects."

Lawrence did as his pharmacist recommended, and measured out twice the amount he had taken previously. The liquid burned as he swallowed, then its warmth spread throughout his body. He imagined his pain fading. He smiled and lay down on his bed, and rested until the golden sunset's light faded to blue shadows. Soon, his night's work would begin.

಄಄

"Good evening, Miss Branham! How are we this evening?" asked Lawrence jovially as he bounded into the dome. "Are we ready for tonight's session?"

The elixir had indeed worked. The pain in his knee had subsided, and even its stiffness was gone. He bounced on his injured leg to test. No pain.

"Yes, Professor. The telescope is already trained on the Moon."

"Excellent, Miss Branham. And how is tonight's seeing?"

"The air is warm and slightly hazy at the moment, Professor. The atmosphere looks to be fairly still, but not perfect."

"Let's try anyway, Miss Branham, shall we?" he laughed. "The wide-angle eyepiece, please." Lawrence looked over at his assistant. He had hired her because her teachers at San Jose Normal School had told him that she was much more interested in astronomy than in becoming a teacher. She had proved competent, he thought, maybe more than competent, as she was obviously bright enough to anticipate his requirements. He noticed the red light from the safety lamp catching the highlights in her auburn hair and thought it rather fetching.

He shook his head and brought himself back to the work at hand. He jumped up on the observing platform and sat down in the large chair. "Engage the tracking drive, Miss Branham." She tightened a knob which locked the telescope into place against a clockwork gear that slowly moved the exquisitely balanced instrument to track the Moon across the sky. Lawrence leaned forward and peered through the eyepiece. He gingerly turned two brass wheels until the image of the Moon was centered in his view.

"Higher magnification eyepiece, please," he said, continuing to look through the telescope. This eyepiece revealed only a small portion of the Moon's cratered surface. Turning the fine positioning wheels again, he found the area he was interested in: Petavius, a medium-sized crater only visible at a slanting angle as the surface of the Moon curved back toward its far side. He centered the image and asked for a yet higher magnification.

Miss Branham looked up at the slit in the dome far above. "Are you sure, Professor? The atmosphere is becoming more turbulent. The image may become blurry and shaky."

"Nonsense, my dear. I can see the Moon's features distinctly. Very interesting indeed."

She handed him the highest magnification eyepiece they had. It was almost never used in the Great Telescope, even when the atmosphere was extremely clear and still, as it magnified the smallest aberration.

Lawrence peered through the telescope for several minutes, moving the fine positioning wheels from time to time to look at different features, and adjusting the focusing knob furiously. He was silent except for humming sounds that originated from deep in his chest. Lawrence leaned back, blinked his eyes several times, and rubbed them vigorously.

What am I seeing? Could it be ...? I've always wondered about Petavius. It looks too perfectly round, and that ridge line, too uniform to be geological.

He took a deep breath and brought his eye up again. The eyepiece magnified the turbulence in the air, and the image came in and out of focus. At times the focus sharpened to crystal clarity, only to suddenly jump to a soft wavering blur. Several more minutes passed, then a smile slowly grew across Lawrence's normally sober face.

"Just what I've suspected all along! I felt that crater's features did not seem natural."

"Excuse me, Professor?"

"Petavius Crater. It ... I can barely say it ... it holds a city at its center. A city with buildings and a causeway running to the city from the crater's edge. Too straight to be made naturally. It must have been made by the hand of man, or rather, Moon-man. Here, look for yourself."

She climbed one step up on the platform and contorted her body around the control wheels.

"I can see the crater, but I'm not sure what else, Professor."

"Do you see the buildings in the center? And the causeway?"

"The image is dancing about. I see what look like central mountain peaks inside the crater, and I think I can see a line running to the edge of the crater."

"Nonsense, girl. Look again. Wait until the image momentarily clears."

Miss Branham strained to see what Lawrence had, but gave up. "I'm sorry, Professor. I can see nothing more."

"You merely do not have the experience to be able to interpret what you are observing," he said. "You are young yet. With time, it will come."

"Are you sure, Professor? You are making some fantastic claims."

"Fantastic?" he said, offended. "Do you think I'm imagining it?"

"No. Perhaps 'fantastic' was a poor choice of words. I mean only that if there were a city on the Moon, it would be an unthinkable discovery."

Lawrence stared rather blankly at her for several seconds not seeming to understand her, then regained his focus and said, "Please hand up my notebook, and I will draw the features I see. I want this discovery recorded properly."

"Wouldn't it be easier to expose a photographic plate, Professor?"

"Easier, but not as accurate. At this magnification, the image is bouncing all over. A plate is too slow; all we'd see is a blur. By drawing, I can capture details from the brief moments that the image is stable."

Miss Branham started to say something, then seemed to think the better of it. Lawrence noticed her fiddling with the plate cases, and reprimanded her again.

"All right, Miss Branham, I am finished with the sketches. The atmosphere is getting too unstable. I will retire to my quarters and clean up these drawings. Please close up the telescope."

Miss Branham approached him rather meekly and said, "Professor, I mean no disrespect, but are you sure you saw what you think you saw?"

"Miss Branham, I have been more than patient with you. Your work, I must say, has been very good, but not so good that I would not let you go if you continue to question my judgment."

"Sorry, Professor. I am merely asking if it would be worthwhile to double-check the data."

"My data needs no double-checking. Not when it's this important. Don't you understand? This discovery will change the way Mankind sees itself. It will literally change the world."

"Yes, Professor," she said, giving up. "I'm sorry to have doubted you."

Lawrence spent the night re-sketching what he had seen through the eyepiece and preparing his scientific report to be submitted to the Astronomical Society Journal. Towards morning, as he paced his room organizing his thoughts for the next day, he realized his knee was stiffening again, and he took another draught of *Mor-fo-caine.* The fragrant liquid again burned his throat as he swallowed it.

No, he decided, the news was too important to rely upon the slow deliberations of the Astronomical Society. He telephoned down to the San Jose News that an announcement of an important astronomical discovery was to be made the next morning. He did the same to the San Francisco and Oakland newspapers. He would have loved to notify the East Coast newspapers as well, but there was no time. *No matter,* he thought. *Once the news was out, newspapers world-wide will pick it up and repeat it.* In one month, Petavius Crater will again be most easily visible. Observatories around the world must be notified and be prepared to confirm his observations—and then recognize him as the most accomplished astronomer since Galileo.

ℰℭ

In the rotunda of the courthouse in San Jose, Lawrence lectured to the newspapermen that had answered his invitation. "Last night, at Lick Observatory, just outside the city of San Jose, a discovery was made that will change Man's relationship with the stars. No longer will we look up to the sky and wonder. Now we will look to the sky—to the Moon—and know that there is another civilization there, a civilization able to build fantastic cities and accomplish great feats of engineering."

The gathered reporters murmured, some not quite understanding what they were hearing. Finally, a stringer for the New York World asked, "Are you saying, Professor, that you have seen Moon men?" He meant it as a serious question, but his colleagues thought it a joke and laughed along.

Annoyed at the laughter, Lawrence continued, "Not precisely. Using the Great Refracting Telescope, I was able to detect quite clearly buildings and a causeway in the vicinity of Petavius Crater on the Moon's southern hemisphere. I have seen the creations of the Lunarians or 'Moon men', as you call them. From this distance, it would not be possible to see the beings themselves. I have made detailed sketches of what I have seen which I will have reproduced and sent to observatories around the world. Because of the position of this crater near the Southern Polar region of the Moon, it is best viewed three days after the new Moon, that is, twenty-nine days from now on August 18, 1890. All capable observatories should prepare to observe Petavius Crater at that time. Then, my observations will be confirmed."

"Professor, can you show us your sketches now?"

Lawrence wanted to show his sketches, but he wanted to be asked to see them. He dared not appear too eager. He had had colleagues who in their great excitement to announce a discovery, had given the impression of being amateurish and over-zealous, and thus were not taken seriously. He would not make that mistake.

"I will show one. The rest will be disseminated in due time." He flipped through a leather portfolio and pulled out a leaf of paper. Holding it up to the assembled reporters, he explained, "This sketch shows the central city. As you can see, there are numerous buildings, some taller than what Mankind is presently capable of erecting. There are indications of roads and perhaps a type of rail system connecting the buildings. Finally, evidence of smoke or steam wafting over the city, indicating that there is significant industry taking place."

The reporters hung on his every word, and strained to see the features in his drawing. They could scarcely believe the amount of detail that Lawrence had drawn, yet the sketch was somehow more artistic than technical in its presentation. Lawrence remembered the details flying out of his pen as he redrafted the hasty sketches he had drawn while looking at the flickering images through the eyepiece. He thought that it had been so easy it was meant to be. He smiled. In less than a month, he thought, the astronomical world, no, the entire world itself, would no longer look down on him as the caretaker of a far-west observatory. They would recognize him as the talented scientist he knew he was.

Airship

By Janice Thompson

How far I've flown I neither know nor care.
Much as this open deck my plans are bare.
Of star or compass I have nary need,
But follow as these downy cloud tops lead.

The chilly breezes toying through my hair
Cascade across my skin and jacket flare
While on the bottoms of my booted feet
The engine taps an unrelenting beat.

I acquiesce to gentle bob and sway
Beneath balloon and rigging bloated shape.
Awaiting now the nearly risen sun
I scan the vast expanse and see no one.

And yet, I hear a rumbling of some sort
Then luminescing clouds off to my port
Combusting deep with ever brighter tones
Now booming louder, louder, nearer, NO!

Bombastic airship, cannons bursting now,
Ejected straight at me from out its shroud.
A maniac, that pilot, heaving hard
Just missing our collision by one yard

His tortured face, the horror in those eyes,
For near destroying me, so I surmised,

Until I saw his passing stern ablaze.
Then mammoth winged beast in brutal chase

Erupting, fierce and howling, scales agleam.
The hot concussion of its down-spent wing
That final moment as it thrust away
Forced ship and I and all the world to sway.

Then came the screams, the pounding and a moan
As crew and cargo floundered down below
Caught in the violent swinging disarray.
The flaming ship and dragon sped away

To disappear in yet another cloud.
Our vessel's motion finally calmed down.
Those lightly injured put the ship aright.
And unspilled rum was quickly spent that night.

Now star and compass were of urgent need.
This damaged vessel and the injuries
Required that we find a ready port
Equipped to lend us aid of every sort.

I searched in haste upending fore and aft
For sextant, compass, and the proper map,
Then finally we found the guiding star
And made for help that wasn't very far.

By dawn I bid the floating docks goodbye
With only half a crew and resupply
But, now where'er I travel through the sky
I keep the navigation tools nearby.

Adelaide's Trial

By BJ Sikes

Adelaide turned the mechanism inside the small clockwork heart. It gleamed in the light. The machinist had used gold, platinum, and copper to create the device and it looked more like a piece of art than a machine.

"As you see," Adelaide said to her mentor, "the internal mechanism is a modification of Archimedes' Screw. I predict that it will move blood as readily as it moves water."

The Royal Physician, Monsieur le Professeur Auguste Piorry reached for it. Adelaide hesitated, looking from the clockwork heart to his face, eager and greedy. She passed her creation to him. Piorry worked the mechanism with plump fingers. It caught as he turned it.

"No, stop," she gasped and snatched the piece away from him. "You'll break it. It moves like this."

He grunted and grabbed it back, glowering at her from under his eyebrows. He peered at the metal heart, turned it in his hand, and snorted.

"Adelaide, what makes you think this contraption would work? There is no way of producing a pulse; this mechanism will just pump continuously. And how do you intend to power it? I do not see a power source."

Adelaide smiled a tight, smug smile. She knew the theory inside out and couldn't wait to see his look of awe once he realized its brilliance.

"There is no need for a pulse; the blood will flow smoothly without it. And as for power, it has a self-winding mechanism. Let me show you." She unscrewed a small plate on the side of the clockwork heart, revealing a tiny fan-shaped rotor attached to an even tinier spring. "There. Do you see it? That rotor winds the mainspring."

He scowled at it and harrumphed. "Adelaide, that is ridiculous. How could it possibly function inside a person? You are wasting my time with your foolish tinkering."

Adelaide's face burned and she swallowed hard, trying to stay calm. This was not going as planned.

How can he be so blind?

"Monsieur le Professeur, you must see. It will function like a Swiss clock, except that the mainspring is wound by the action of this small rotor. The rotor will move as the patient moves. Consequently, the patient will wind her heart as she walks."

He snorted again but his frown wasn't as deep now. Adelaide replaced the plate onto the side of the metal heart. She still wasn't sure that this mechanism would work once installed into an actual person but the theory was sound. She had relied on the Master Machinist to turn her concept into reality and her medical training told her she was on the right track.

Piorry shook his head as Adelaide put the machine back together.

"You are asking me to risk the life of an aristocrat with your outlandish theory? A self-winding heart? What if it fails to wind itself?"

She glanced up at him, interrupted in her re-assembly. The heart felt heavy in her hands.

What if I'm wrong? What if this doesn't work and I kill someone?

Her uncertainty must have shown on her face and he pounced on it.

"Adelaide, I want you to abandon work on this preposterous contraption. You need to return to your research on the modifications we discussed for the Queen's new heart."

Adelaide pursed her lips and took a deep breath. She knew the logic of her Archimedean Heart was sound. His modifications were the real tinkering. A waste of time.

"Please, Monsieur le Professeur, the theory is sound. It will work and it will save the life of one of our Aristocrats. So many are dying young from a weakness of the heart. This invention could put an end to those premature deaths. Just last month, the heir of the duc de Guyenne succumbed after his heart gave out. Monsieur, he was only twenty years old. We—France needs this innovation."

Piorry picked up the heart and examined it, not saying a word. She waited, breathless with anticipation, trying not to fidget.

"You are convinced this contraption will work?"

Adelaide nodded.

"Very well. You may attempt to transplant this device into a patient. We must identify an appropriate candidate. Not the heir to a duchy. Someone minor, perhaps a girl from an obscure family. I will inform you when we find someone. In the meantime, continue to refine this mechanism. It should not jam so easily." He thrust the clockwork heart at her and departed.

Adelaide restrained herself from clapping her hands and giggling.

୫୬

"Are you comfortable, *ma chère*?" Adelaide smiled down at the young girl on the surgical bed. The girl's eyes showed white around the irises and her lips trembled, but she nodded. An attempt at a smile crossed her lips.

"Marie-Ange, you will sleep throughout the procedure. You will not feel a thing, I promise."

Spectators packed the surgical theater despite the deep chill of the room. Adelaide willed herself not to glance toward the Queen and her courtiers. Her own heart pounded and her stomach felt hollow. She pushed wisps of hair off her face.

Marie-Ange looked small and young in the stiff white linen of the surgical gown.

Don't think about her vulnerability; remember her weak heart. She needs this operation.

She was so pale, a young girl of fifteen years old with a failing heart. Marie-Ange would be dead before she was eighteen without intervention, but the transplant might kill her, even if she survived the surgery, and even if the heart functioned inside her torso.

If, if, too many ifs.

The hollowness in Adelaide's stomach became nausea, and she swallowed bile.

Royal Physician Piorry, had already informed the girl's parents that this procedure was experimental and that their daughter might not survive. They accepted their daughter's prognosis with little reaction. They had several other children, and perhaps this daughter was not so precious to them as their son and heir. Still, the father was in attendance; his permission to allow his daughter to undergo the operation was a political coup for the family. If the heart worked and the girl survived, the Queen herself would be the next patient to receive the Archimedean Heart.

Adelaide felt sorry for the pale, unloved child before her. She had the makings of a beauty and could someday grace the Queen's Court.

If she survived.

"Are we ready to begin?" Piorry's voice oozed as he leaned over Adelaide. She nodded and smiled again at Marie-Ange, attempting to reassure her. The surgical assistant wheeled the anesthetic cart closer and placed the black rubber mask over the girl's face. Marie-Ange made a panicky sound, like a wild animal in a trap. Her eyes filled with tears, but she lay still.

"Shh, shh," Adelaide soothed her. "It's all right; breathe deeply and go to sleep, *ma chère.*" The girl inhaled the gas. Her breathing steadied and her eyes drifted closed.

"Not too much gas. She's very light," Adelaide cautioned the assistant.

Piorry was busy chatting with the members of the Court, informing them about this brilliant new device that would save so many lives. Adelaide grimaced at his back then turned her attention back to the sleeping girl. She lifted a brass baton from the tray of instruments. It glowed at the flick of a switch. Adelaide held it over Marie-Ange's chest, checking the girl's heart rate and respiration. The light flickered and Adelaide frowned.

"Less gas," she told the assistant who nodded and complied, turning a dial on the machine. Piorry sauntered over to the surgical table.

"Our patient is asleep. We will now begin the procedure," he declaimed for the benefit of the audience. He flourished his arm at Adelaide. "Mademoiselle, pass me the scalpel."

Adelaide and Piorry opened up the girl's chest and there was a little shriek from a lady in the audience. Adelaide stifled a sigh. Surgery as theater was not her preferred way to work.

Was the sight of blood that surprising? This was an operation. What did they expect?

Piorry announced each step in the procedure as Adelaide operated. They packed the inside of the girl's chest with ice to slow the blood. Adelaide gnawed at her lip. The chance of frostbite was worrisome, but she didn't know how else they could slow the blood enough so that the girl wouldn't bleed to death when they switched out the hearts.

The Royal Physician flourished the Archimedean Heart. It glinted in the light and the audience reacted with gasps and murmurs. Adelaide tried to suppress her triumphant smile at the sight and sound of her creation. The screw inside the metal heart was turning, wound by the gentle shaking when Piorry had presented it to the audience.

The ornate metal heart looked incongruous nestled in Marie-Ange's chest. The girl's own heart looked pale and shriveled next to it. Adelaide, her hands steady, opened a connection between the clockwork heart and the girl's blood vessel. Red blood gushed out, splattering Adelaide. Piorry cursed under his breath and took a step backward to avoid the gore. Adelaide took a deep breath and clamped the leak.

Time for the next blood vessel. Move fast, this one is under even more pressure. Now would be a good time for Piorry to actually help me.

"Monsieur," she murmured, "you must hold the clamp firmly here or she will bleed out." He shot a startled glance at her but shifted closer, clamping as she directed. They raced to switch the blood vessel connection from its original heart to the clockwork replacement. Adelaide heard the swoosh of the screw as the blood moved through the metal heart.

Yes! It's working. Now to remove this useless piece of flesh.

Removing the old flesh heart was a delicate process and she couldn't rush. Blood drenched her to the elbows by the time she finished. As she closed up the girl's chest, she thought that Marie-Ange's face seemed to have a touch more pink in it.

Piorry dabbed at the few droplets of blood on his sleeve with a sponge and flicked it onto the tray of instruments, then stepped back from the operating table. He bowed toward the Queen and addressed her, beaming.

"Your Majesty. The operation appears to be a success. My latest creation will revolutionize augmentation as we know it, saving many lives and strengthening our nation."

Adelaide dropped the instrument she was holding.

HIS creation? Did he just take credit for my invention? The one he told me was preposterous and would never work?

Her hands shook and her mouth thinned with rage. She glowered at his oblivious back.

"Monsieur le Professeur Piorry, you are to be congratulated on your magnificent achievement," the Queen said, a wheeze in her soft voice. "We look forward to the day when you perform a similar procedure upon Our own person."

He bowed again even deeper this time.

"Indeed, Your Majesty. It would be an honor."

The Queen drifted out, trailing a parade of courtiers behind her. Piorry smirked as they departed, and then followed them out. Adelaide remained behind to care for their patient—her patient—despite his claim. The nausea in her belly had turned to fire and she shook with silent fury.

Courting Adventure

By Emily Thompson

Vivian Swift was lost in thought as she moved through the forever shifting crowds of New York City. Her mind worked furiously on the problem of whether to attend Miss Barkley's tea on Saturday, or Madam Willoughby's luncheon. She couldn't leave one early to attend the other without offending Madam Willoughby, but Miss Barkley and her usual guests were far better company. Vivian frowned at the thought of yet another dreary luncheon, or indeed another aimless tea even in the best company. Surely there were better, more productive ways to spend one's days than prattling on endlessly while also being constantly concerned with one's manners or—

Vivian's umbrella suddenly caught on a passing gentleman's hat, knocking it clear off his head. Vivian gave a cry as the hat fell, her nerves tightening like a hangman's noose. Her hand shot out to catch the hat as her embarrassment brought a flush to her cheeks. She nearly dropped her umbrella in her frantic motions, but managed to rescue the hat in midair.

"I'm ever so sorry, sir," she began, inspecting the hat to see if it had been damaged by her umbrella.

"My goodness!" the gentleman exclaimed.

He chuckled lightly as Vivian's eyes darted over the passing crowd. To her relief, she saw no scorn nor annoyance on any of the faces around them, and the crowd hardly seemed to notice that she and the gentleman had both stopped in the middle of the sidewalk. They all moved around them like fish in a tight school, around a particularly uninteresting rock. The gentleman smiled back at Vivian, while she raised her umbrella to shield them both from the lightly falling snow. She did her very best to hide her own anger at herself, or the fact that her heart was now pounding, and she offering him back an equally polite smile.

"You have good reflexes, my dear," he remarked, taking his hat back when she offered it. "Why, your hand shot out like a rabbit!" he added with another chuckle. Vivian refrained from correcting him that it wasn't her reflexes, but her terror and her own oafish action that moved her hand so quickly. "Oh, no harm done, no harm done," he insisted when she tried again to apologize.

Clearly much better at being a gentleman than she a lady, he refused to let her take any blame at all as he bid her good day and hurried on after his own business. Nonetheless, Vivian's nerves refused to be silenced so easily. She slipped out of the throngs that moved up and down the street, standing before a shop window as if to examine the display. The shop owners had clearly tried to cheer up their little window by installing a few glaring electric lights outside, to illuminate the display. With the heat inside fogging up the glass, the added lights only reflected off the glass, obscuring the display almost entirely and turning the window into a mirror.

This optical trick allowed Vivian to stare back at her own reflection as she endeavored to collect herself. Despite the tugging winds, the rambling crowds, and the drifting snow, her black curls were still perfectly in place, gathered together in a knot under her lilac hat. She gently adjusted the angle of her hat with a gloved hand, noting that yes, the two different fabrics—from separate shops—appeared to be identical. She also saw that her understated but carefully applied makeup remained flawless. Although the edges of her silver skirts that peaked out from under her jacket had been inevitably sullied from the snowy streets, all else appeared perfect.

Vivian took a deep breath, staring back at her own encouraging appearance. She had grown increasingly distracted in recent days, for reasons she couldn't fathom. She seemed to be forever forgetting things, confusing dates and appointments, and most recently walking into people. Of course, she'd wondered if she were perhaps too harried by the business of her own life, but all of the other young society ladies of New York attended just as many balls and parties as Vivian did. All of them were either recently married or soon to be, and many were dealing with all of the arrangements of a coming wedding, just as Vivian was. Why couldn't she cope when all of her acquaintances could? Surely she was better than that. Surely.

She shook her head, forcing herself once again to stop obsessing. One more glance at her reflection promised that, although her nerves might be in tatters, she at least appeared outwardly steady, confident, and elegant. Grateful for the tightness of her corset, which held her back straight when her mind slipped to other things, and to her own natural height that gave her a perpetually lofty air, Vivian finally gathered herself enough to leave the comfort of her own company. She turned from the shop window and fell back into a quick pace to make her appointment.

Arriving at the tea shop, Vivian removed her jacket and left her umbrella in a stand by the door. Hers was not the only one for once, as more ladies seemed to realize that using an umbrella in the snow did wonders to rescue one's hat from the weather. She hung her damp jacket on a peg by the door and scanned the busy tea shop for Grace's round, rosy, and forever-cheerful face. Spotting her friend at a table by a window, she hurried closer. Grace gave a pleased squeak at the sight of Vivian approaching, and rose from her seat to offer a smile and an embrace.

"Oh you look just stunning, as always," Grace exclaimed with amiable jealously, pulling back to admire Vivian's silver and lilac dress, and the soft, black-velvet shrug around her shoulders.

"Oh, come now," Vivian replied bashfully. "But you look just darling in peach, Dear," she added quickly, as they both took their seats at the table.

Grace beamed at the praise and gave a shrug. Vivian had always admired Grace's sweet, natural, and unassuming charms. In a simple peach gown with pink silk flowers on her hat, her golden hair worn long and gently curled, and no make-up beyond a blush of pink on her round cheeks, Grace struck Vivian as warm, inviting, and beautiful in ways she had never learned to be herself. While Vivian could manage to make herself flawless for a time—through a great deal of effort—Grace was always so comfortably pretty and naturally friendly that people seemed unable to resist the urge to be delighted by her.

It was no wonder she'd been one of the first of Vivian's friends to be married. She'd had her pick of all the most eligible bachelors in New York, and had had the luxury to choose a man she actually liked and still got along well with. Vivian had had her suitors, but choosing her own fiancé had been a chore. She hadn't been taken with any of them. They all appeared in the same uninteresting gray to her eye, and it was hard to even tell them apart. In the end, she'd chosen the young man who had the best prospects and hoped that romance might come later. What more could she ask for, anyway? It wasn't as if she were some daring heroine out of an adventure story. And she knew well that wishing for things like adventure or heroics never led to anything but disappointment.

"Vivi, dear?" Grace asked, drawing Vivian's attention back to the present.

"Oh!" Vivian gasped. "I'm so sorry," she said, realizing that she hadn't heard much of what her friend had just said. She'd only vaguely realized that the waiter had appeared and served them both their tea, but Vivian hadn't yet even sipped at her own cup.

"Are you feeling all right, Darling?" Grace asked, worriedly. "You were very distracted all last night as well."

"Oh yes, I know," Vivian moaned, remembering the party that she had barely survived. She used to love parties, but these days she found herself growing tired far too early, and also staring off into space—obsessing, or worse, *daydreaming*—for long moments when she should be socializing. It didn't help that no one else ever had anything interesting to talk about. "I'm all right," she said to calm her friend, reaching out to pat Grace's hand. "I just haven't been sleeping well, I suppose."

"You should have a nip of brandy before you go to bed," Grace said as if declaring an order. "I always do when I can't sleep. It puts me right out, I assure you."

"I'll have to try that," Vivian replied, smiling. "But I'm so sorry, what were you saying, Dear?"

"I said," Grace went on patiently, her anxiety rising quickly, "that I'm being courted by a shadowy association! They want me to join them."

Vivian glanced down to the peculiar letter Grace was holding up to show her. The envelope was black, and the writing on the front was in silver ink. The upper left-hand corner bore a delicate drawing of a raven, a crow, or some other dire looking bird. Grace placed the envelope on the table between them.

"Good heavens," was all Vivian could manage to respond with.

"Exactly," Grace agreed. "Why, it's just the most extraordinary thing!"

"But who is it?" Vivian asked, before finally having a sip of her tea. "The government?" she asked, half-joking.

"No, apparently, it's the Rooks," Grace said, tapping the drawing of the bird on the corner of the envelope.

Images of clandestine meetings in black shadows, secrets, assassinations, and international espionage in faraway corners of the world sprang instantly to Vivian's mind. Grace had been right to call them *shadowy*. While no one outside of the Rooks knew exactly what they got up to, or even how many members there were, most people had heard of them in passing whenever anything frightfully mysterious or adventurous was happening. The newspapers often credited them with strange, unexplained goings-on, world-wide.

"Now, I know what you're thinking," Grace said to Vivian, drawing her attention back again. "What would these unusual people want with me?" she asked, gesturing to her own innocence with a look of surprise.

Vivian nodded, showing her own surprise, and trying not to say anything her friend might take offense at. The image she had of the Rooks would demand someone of poise and elegance. Grace, as lovely as she was, simply didn't seem their type.

"Well, the letter said that the Rooks are looking for Sighted people to join them."

"Oh, I see," Vivian said, suddenly recalling the one thing for which she was the most jealous of her friend.

Of course, many people these days had come forward and announced to the world that they possessed Sights: special abilities of understanding or enhanced senses that defied conventional human limitations. If Vivian had had one of her own, she too would have been happy to proclaim that she did. But even so, Grace seemed to feel anxious about letting the existence of her own Sight be widely known. As close as they were, it had taken many years for Grace to confide in Vivian that she possessed one of these special gifts at all.

Apparently, ever since she'd been a little girl, Grace had always understood every word that was said to her, in any language of the world. She'd discovered this when her politically minded father had invited a number of foreign dignitaries to a special dinner at their Hampton estate. Grace had told Vivian that she'd thought it strange that the men had spoken in perfect English when asking their translators to say just the same phrases to the others. It had taken her a while to even realize that she'd been understanding their native languages—none of which she had even heard before in her life—just as easily as she understood her own.

"But I don't know if I could do something like that," Grace went on with a shudder, staring at the letter distrustfully. "Imagine, using my *Sight* all the time!" she added in a disgusted whisper. "Why people would surely think me so very strange..."

"You're nothing of the sort!" Vivian said swiftly. She resisted the urge to proclaim that having a Sight was a blessing—a guarantee of an interesting life—and not something to hide. Vivian knew Grace well enough to know that she would never fully agree with her on that point.

Grace offered her back a grateful smile, but didn't otherwise respond.

"Well," Vivian said, unable to let the point go entirely. "I'm sure your Sight would be most valuable to the Rooks. I hear that they deal with many foreign peoples. It would be convenient to have someone with them who could understand everyone."

"Oh, I'm sure it would," Grace said, still looking concerned. "But could you honestly imagine me in that sort of situation? I mean, *me*?" she added, hand on heart and eyes wide. "Traveling the world, translating secrets and goodness-knows what else, surrounded by mysterious men and *violence*!" She gave a shiver, clutching herself tightly. "Oh, it's too much!"

"There, there, Darling," Vivian said, reaching across the table with an open hand.

Grace wasted no time in taking the offered hand, holding it tightly as she took deep breaths. Concerned as she was for her friend, something began to stir in the back of Vivian's easily distracted mind. While Grace was clearly frightened by all the things she'd just said, each point listed had sent Vivian's heart aflutter with unexpected excitement. Could such a life even be possible for a respectable young lady of society? Vivian had heard that there were just as many Rook women as there were men. Of course, this point had been mentioned to highlight the scandalous nature of the Rooks, but just the same, might it be true?

"You don't have to accept their invitation, do you?" Vivian asked.

"No, I don't," Grace said, shaking her head. "The letter said that they only want people to join them out of their own interest and ambition, not by any sort of force. Something about that being the glue that holds them all together," she added off hand.

"Then don't let this trouble you," Vivian said gently.

"Oh, but I haven't told you the worst part!" Grace gasped, looking to her friend desperately. "Paul said I should consider it. Can you imagine!"

"He did?" Vivian asked, astonished to hear that Grace's husband would even suggest such a thing.

"He did," Grace confirmed emphatically.

"What did you say?"

"I didn't know what to say," Grace said, shaking her head.

Vivian gave her hand a gentle squeeze.

"He said it's a fantastic opportunity," Grace went on, emboldened somewhat. "It's the sort of thing that only happens once in a lifetime. He said I should be sure of what I want before

I decide anything. And if I truly wanted to join them, then—can you imagine!—he said that if I really wanted to, I *should* join!"

"Here, have a sip of tea, Dear," Vivian soothed, noticing that Grace was breathing hard in her excitement. "I'm sure Paul would never mean for you to join if you didn't want to."

"I don't!" Grace exclaimed, clutching her teacup in both hands now, as if for dear life. "Why would I? Why would any respectable young lady want to join some nasty old group like the Rooks, Sight or no Sight?"

Vivian glanced down at the black envelope. Perhaps it was the strangeness of even seeing a black envelope. Perhaps she was growing overtired from all of her distracted moments and poor sleep. Perhaps it was nothing at all but her imagination, but for a single instant, Vivian felt a strong, enticing, gravitational pull toward that letter on the table. If she'd been any other woman, she would have taken the letter for herself, then and there, and dove headlong into danger, intrigue, and adventure.

"I'm sure I don't know," Vivian said, tearing her eyes off the letter to look at Grace.

Although Grace appeared heartened to hear Vivian agree with her, Vivian's heart was pounding now. She knew it was partly from the heady rush of her own thoughts, and partly in fear of them. Surely she didn't truly want to join a mysterious, nearly secret organization, throwing away her entire life, just to put herself into danger. Surely.

"The letter said that if I wanted to join I should apply at an address here in the city," Grace said, staring at the letter with a furrowed brow and uncharacteristic tension. "And if I don't want to join, I need only refrain from responding."

"Then you shouldn't respond," Vivian said. "Just forget all about it."

"You're right," Grace said, making her decision. She picked up the letter and thrust it at Vivian across the table. "If I had a match, I'd burn it now, but I simply don't want this vile thing in my possession for another instant. Please. Take this away from me and destroy it!"

Vivian stared at the offered letter with alarm. She couldn't join the Rooks, herself. She simply couldn't. She had no Sight.

Granted, not all the Rooks were likely to have Sights. Hadn't Grace said that they mostly wanted their members to *want* to be with them? But her family would never forgive her for abandoning her social standing. And what of Trevor? Maybe she didn't love him now, but surely she would learn to, and they might well be happy together.

"Of course, Dear," Vivian said, realizing that she really should take the letter to support her friend. The rigid black paper felt heavy in her hand, as if it contained more than it appeared to. "Think nothing more of this business," she added with a smile, slipping the envelope into her handbag. "I'll dispose of this for you later."

"Oh, thank you, Darling," Grace said, appearing greatly relieved. "You're a dear friend to me. Yes. Now. You have a wedding to plan, don't you?" Grace said, slowly returning to her natural, bubbly and carefree self.

As the conversation turned on to wedding plans and occasional society gossip, Vivian had to work very hard to keep her mind on the present. Throughout the entire tea, the black envelope whispered to her of fascinating mystery, daring intrigue, and glamorous adventure. By the time she and Grace parted, Vivian felt exhausted from the sheer effort of not thinking about the letter in her handbag.

After walking away from the tea shop, she stole away into an alcove—out of the falling snow—and slipped the envelope out of her handbag. She paused only for an instant, staring at it and feeling the world turn beneath her feet. She marveled at how remarkable it was that this little thing could cause her to feel more violently alive than she had ever felt before.

Surely, she couldn't return to her ordinary life now that she had gotten a glimpse of what was open to her. Surely.

Two Days in June, Part I

By Sharon E. Cathcart

5 June 1832

Enjolras kissed his pretty Marianne goodbye and pulled on his trousers.

"I'll be back with supper," he said, as she pulled the blankets over herself.

"After your meeting, of course." Even her pout was adorable.

"Yes, *chérie*, after the meeting."

"Bring that useless Grantaire with you," Marianne called after him. "Otherwise, I'll never hear the end of it from Olympe."

&&

General Jean Maximilien Lamarque was dead, taken by the cholera. He'd died in the old hospital; Lariboisiere had not yet been built when the epidemic hit. You may know that hospital; it is still in use today. It is in the 10th arrondissement, although they didn't call it that at the time.

Henri Grantaire could scarcely credit it; it seemed as though Lamarque would go on forever. So much larger than life he'd been; hell, Grantaire had served under him in '30, right next to Jean-Claude Enjolras. Little they'd all known; even Lamarque had said they'd been in the wrong, putting Louis-Philippe on the throne.

Grantaire's feet dragged along the rue Saint-Denis to the tavern. He'd agreed to meet Enjolras there, as well as some of their fellow students from the Sorbonne. How old Grantaire felt when he considered the youthful enthusiasms of Bahorel, Combeferre, Courfeyrac, Feuilly, Joly: all of them were children in his eyes—even the well-spoken Jean Prouvaire, with his idealism. The eldest of the group, Lesgle, was a duke's heir; the entire lot was vehemently anti-royalist. Really, it was their only common bond.

They called themselves the Friends of the Abaissé, an adjunct of the Society of the Rights of Man. To Grantaire's cynical eyes, they were just another Sorbonne fraternity: wealthy young men playing at philosophy and high-flown ideals of revolution and war without having the slightest idea of the true cost of either. Each time they agreed to meet at the ABC Tavern ("I'll see you at the Abaissé"), they reveled in their own cleverness at making a pun.

If Combeferre was the group's guide and Courfeyrac its center, as they'd all often opined, Enjolras was its Chief. When the other men spoke of their mistresses, Enjolras claimed that la Patrie—the Republic—was his only woman.

Of course, Grantaire thought that was another glorious pun. Enjolras' love was the plump, delightful Marianne, whose parents had named her for the spirit of the Republic. She shared a flat with Olympe, who had nearly as much a hold on Grantaire as his beloved wine.

Wine. Yes, he needed more wine. Perhaps a lengthy toast to the people's general would be in order once he got to the tavern.

⃝⃠

Bahorel bought another round of wine for the group; it was his turn, after all. At least Grantaire was late; that meant the bottle would last longer. The veteran-student was always drowning his sorrows.

Combeferre and Feuilly were playing dice, while Courfeyrac and Prouvaire loudly debated a point of philosophy. It looked to be just one more night in the dingy tavern on the rue de la Chanverrie.

Until Grantaire entered, his face solemn as a judge, followed by an equally subdued Enjolras.

Grantaire picked up the nearest glass—which happened to be Bahorel's.

"A toast to fallen comrades, my friends," he intoned. "General Lamarque has gone to his reward."

‼ℭ

Before we learn more about our friends on this particular evening, first we must know about how they arrived at this place. Grantaire and Enjolras are the elder statesmen, although not the eldest of the group. They are the seasoned veterans...the ones who fought under Lamarque just two years previously in order to put Louis-Philippe on the throne. At the time, they believed in their cause.

But now, that Louis has proved as dissolute as many others of the same name. The people of Paris are starving; there are no animals to be seen, as pets and zoo animals alike have been eaten. The same thing happened during the Reign of Terror; starvation kills ethics just as surely as it kills the hungry. Crime increases when people grow more desperate.

And Louis-Philippe does nothing to help the hungry.

Grantaire and Enjolras discuss these problems frequently during their visits to Marianne and Olympe ... to the disgust of the young women, who would like their beaux's attention to be undivided. Unlike the monarch, the two men cannot look upon suffering and remain silent. And so, they began to talk of revolution.

‼ℭ

Let us first look to Henri Grantaire. He and Enjolras have known one another since childhood, after all, and are nearly as close as brothers.

But do not presume they were equals in the nursery. On the contrary, young Henri was the son of the majordomo. His father served the Enjolras household.

Henri was a quick boy, but not always quick enough. His father was swift with physical punishment, most particularly when he though the boy was putting on airs above his station.

And how might the little Grantaire be doing this? Why, by befriending the solitary Jean-Claude, scion of the bourgeois household that gave the elder Grantaire his living.

Henri had noticed the solemn boy, who seemed to be near his own age. A shy offer to pet a precious dog on the young master's part soon led to sharing Henri's rolling hoop, the two boys running after it. Their laughter echoed across the lawn, with a joyful dog barking counterpoint and nipping at their heels.

Jean-Claude begged his father to allow his new friend to sit in the nursery during sessions with the tutor. Thus, the butler's boy and the gentleman's son had identical educations.

For his part, Grantaire was always the more grounded of the two. He had an eye toward the practical. He saw life in all of its ugly reality.

It is no wonder that he took to drink at a relatively early age. Wine and brandy dulled all manner of pain, whether from the bitter reality that he would never be more than a servant's son to the physical pain of his father's fists landing yet another blow.

Perhaps you are thinking that Grantaire's father should have been grateful for the generosity shown to his son. However, you must also remember that pride is a very peculiar thing. A man does not always like the idea of his son surpassing him on the world's stage. Such a son might look down on his father.

And so it was that the elder Grantaire determined to keep young Henri humble, by any means necessary.

It did not help that Henri looked so much like the mother who died giving him life. Fair-haired and blue-eyed, the lad had been the recipient of the scullery maids' sidelong glances since his days in short pants.

For contrast, look upon the dreamer, Jean-Claude Enjolras. As dark as his young friend is fair, this lad prefers his books and his dog to rowdier sport. It is because of this that his father, a well-to-do draper, encourages his friendship with the less-polished Grantaire boy. Life must be lived, not dreamed about in a classroom.

So it is that the unlikely pair become the very best of friends and are soon inseparable. Each of us has had just such a childhood friend; even when the slings and arrows of life move us apart for a time, we always come back like metal to a lodestone. So it was with Grantaire and Enjolras.

As they got older, their antics grew apace. Grantaire it was who took Enjolras to a Montmartre crib for his first encounter with a whore. Grantaire had, by that time, had nearly every scullery maid belowstairs. At least one had been dismissed with a big belly and no reference.

Enjolras was delighted by the pleasures of the flesh to be sure, but could never hope to be his friend's equal in debauchery. This young Enjolras, it must be said, saw himself as destined for greater things.

The boys' tutor was wont to complain that young Jean-Claude had his head more frequently in the clouds than in his lesson books. Yet, each assignment was completed, on-time and correctly. The schoolmaster deemed it a puzzle.

Enjolras steeped himself in history books; deeds and exploits of the past were his true religion, no matter how many times he attended mass in the family chapel.

It was in this vein that, his head filled to the brim with heroes, Enjolras went to war at the tender age of eighteen. Grantaire, not to be left out if drinking, wenching and fighting were in the offing, followed suit.

Two years on, this same Grantaire and Enjolras study at the Sorbonne. Enjolras reads the law and Grantaire philosophy. They have seen more of life than their fellow students ... far more than they wanted to see. Grantaire most often views life through the distortions of a wine bottle as he tries to forget the fetid stench of the battlefields.

As for Jean-Claude Enjolras, he puts on his elegant suit of clothes and goes through his day. What cannot readily be seen is the fervor for justice and equality that burn in his heart. Each tale of his country's revolutions has made him determined to see better times for all of his countrymen.

It is this same belief in equality that saw him offer to let the butler's son pet his beloved dog.

As I said, there are seldom any cats or dogs to be seen nowadays. As with the zoo animals in 1789, there has been too much hunger in the streets. The starving cannot afford to be sentimental over pets.

And so it is that Enjolras' soul is aflame with a fanatic desire that none should know hunger or want. The child of privilege has seen far too much of both, between the pages of his books and on the battlegrounds.

So, too, one General Jean Maximilien Lamarque had seen too much. When Louis-Philippe could not be bothered to keep his promises to France, Lamarque spoke out. Once a supporter, Lamarque became an outspoken critic of the crown.

And of what did he speak? Lack of meaningful work. Lack of homes. Lack of food.

And what did the well-to-do of Paris say to this lack?

Nothing.

To Enjolras' view, it was almost as bad as Marie-Antoinette's legendary, albeit inaccurately quoted, *let them eat cake*.

There was no cake, and little bread, to be had. An income from Enjolras *père* kept clothes on the younger man's back and a roof over his head.

And Grantaire? Each month's modest pension from the king's army bought a garret room and cheap drink.

How, then, do these youths have mistresses like Marianne and Olympe—beautiful young women who might easily seek wealthier company?

Both girls sew for a dressmaker. They are fortunate that the lighting is good and the hours fair for the wage given. Not all are so fortunate.

Olympe's own mother, after all, had sold herself to make ends meet after the child's father abandoned them.

All too common a tale in this place and time.

And where did these four meet?

In the gathered crowd during one of Lamarque's speeches. The moment Marianne's blue eyes fell on Enjolras, she declared herself smitten, and nothing would do but that she must sidle closer while dragging Olympe in her wake.

From that moment, Grantaire declared himself Olympe's slave. She returned his regard joyously.

Many a night saw the four of them together, dining in the women's rooms before retiring to their respective bedchambers.

Each night, after their lovemaking, Marianne prayed that Jean-Claude would ask for her hand. Being a lawyer's wife was a step up for a grocer's daughter.

Each night, that same Enjolras would talk of France's future—but never his own, with or without Marianne.

It seemed that he could only envision the former.

Olympe doesn't worry so much about a future with Grantaire. She worries more about getting through until tomorrow. This is her mother's legacy. Her father left no legacy, of course. Perhaps this is why Olympe takes such an epicurean view of her lover, and of her life.

⬥⬥⬥

And so, these are the major players upon our little stage. And what, you may well ask, does our stage look like?

The winding, narrow streets of the Latin Quarter inform our tale. The cat's-head cobblestones lead to stone buildings, some elegant dwellings and some mere tenements. The students live in the latter, for the most part; even Baron Pontmercy's heir has humble rooms, so that his fellow students will not know him for an aristo.

But this is not young Pontmercy's tale, and so we will leave him there.

As we have already observed, there are no pets left in Paris; there is, however, another kind of animal. There are droves of hungry children, the grubby little *gamines* whose parents send them out to beg for a crust of bread ... if they have parents at all. Many of them are expert cutpurses and pickpockets, melting into the dank, narrow alleys with the booty taken from unsuspecting passersby.

As with any large city, the backstreets are filled with whores and mountebanks, wigmakers buying desperate women's hair, dentists buying anyone's teeth ... in short, the usual sorts who prey on those most in need of kindness.

At least the wigmaker and dentist give coin instead of taking it.

There are also the priests of nearby Notre Dame, providing a bowl of soup and small loaf of bread to each hungry Parisian who stands in line, until the provisions run out.

And so the stage is set, and our actors gathered.

ⅎↃ

But wait: there is first one more person with whom we must be acquainted. That is Robert Enjolras, second son of that aforementioned family. Though Napoleon's law says that all children inherit equally, there are still some who hold to older ways. Thus it is that this same Robert goes for a soldier. Had there been a third son, he would have been for the church; however, Divine Providence has seen fit to send only Jean-Claude and Robert to monsieur and madame Enjolras.

So, young Robert moves through the ranks swiftly, riding the back of a bought commission. At the time of our tale, he is a captain of the National Guard, every bit as passionate and handsome as his elder brother.

And now, my friends, let us return to the tavern. Young men with old souls are plotting!

ⅎↃ

"A toast to fallen comrades, my friends. General Lamarque has gone to his reward."

Grantaire drains Bahorel's glass and smacks his lips in satisfaction as he returns it to his dismayed companion.

"What do you know of the funeral plans?" Combeferre inquires. "Surely there will be a procession, with catafalque and all."

"Indeed," Feuilly joins in. "The people of Paris will want to pay their respects."

"We must find out," Enjolras speaks with authority. "For we may well use this somber occasion to make a change for the better, all over France."

Grantaire sees the familiar light in his friend's eye and shakes his head.

"Innkeeper," he calls out genially. "More of your wine, and good meat pies, for all. Plotting has ever been hungry work."

With that, he throws some coins on the table. The innkeeper's daughter snatches them up when she brings the requested items, barely acknowledging Grantaire as she slaps greasy trays on tables.

And so it is that the night wears on, in discussion of weapons, gunpowder and treason. Revolution has ever been thus.

℘℘℘

Of all of those clear-eyed idealists, Grantaire is the one with a secret: he wishes he were a father. Where others of his number might give a cuff and a "Be gone with you, brat!" to the filthy gamines who steal to stave off starvation, Grantaire is the one who shares his bread. Grantaire is the one who provides a penny here and there, though he has little enough himself.

Though he has never known serious need, he has known what it is to look upon those who have more and to feel the pain of lack.

But for the grace of God, thinks he, I could be one of those ravening little boys eking out their living on the streets by any means necessary.

Grantaire thinks, from time to time, of marrying Olympe ... or of throwing both caution and precaution to the winds and getting a child on her. Either scenario will cause her to lose her situation with the dressmaker, though. And, in times such as these, perhaps it is best not to bring another babe into the world. There are mouths enough already crying for food. Thus, this particular desire remains unspoken.

Grantaire wonders whether he truly recalls hearing a story of a man jailed for stealing bread ... or if it was an illusion found in the bottom of a wine bottle.

He shakes his head to clear it and heads out into the night, handing a coin to a lad of about six years in age and sixty in countenance and demeanor. He is around the tavern nearly as much as the students.

"It is late for you to be about, little Gavroche," Grantaire tells the boy. "Go buy your bread and cheese, and hide away safely."

"My thanks, monsieur," the boy replies. "This will feed me and the other two boys I'm helping. My babies and I thank you."

With that, the gamine melts into the darkness of the Saint-Michel slums as Grantaire makes his way homeward.

For his part, Enjolras goes neither to his home nor the waiting arms of Marianne. Instead, he makes his way to a certain army barracks. There he speaks with the handsome young captain he calls brother and learns of the plans for Lamarque's funeral procession. Now he knows the route, the hour...all.

He also knows that Robert will be amongst the honor guard.

Whether this is an ill omen or good, only Divine Providence will tell.

ℕℛ

Enjolras arises from Marianne's bed far earlier than either of them desire. His bodily needs have been slaked; neither of them knows of a certainty what the day will bring, and it may well be their last time together.

The guns have been hidden in the tavern; today they will be unpacked and handed to men who, except for Enjolras and Grantaire, have never shot at anything other than game animals … if even that.

May God have mercy on all of their souls, prays Jean-Claude Enjolras, as he prepares to lead men into battle once again.

From the Ground

By Justin Andrew Hoke

"I can say with most certainty, that we were never meant to live in the sky."
    —T. D. Bishop, Farmer/Council Member

We broke from the caves when we no longer feared the dead of night, and now we reach for the sun as it creeps away from us daily. A world born from fear has ignited a passion to reach for the black that chases our wheel away. Each day by day we take to the effort to climb. We climb to expand. We expand to increase our reach.

Our reach will know no limit as we feed the machine of *all-kind.*

Today we strike the ground to build from nothing: the era of Man. All who carry a shovel own the earth they move. From the silt comes a song of angels, telling the heavens to prepare for our arrival. Foundation will give way to frame, to form, to atmosphere, as we grace the sky with our presence and build a nation above the cumulonimbus.

For when we reach them, the clouds shall anoint us as ambrosial.

When we ascend, we will take the air of Gods in our breath and speak more gospel than we have ever felt. When we move the waters against the heaviness that once tied us down, we will mock gravity as it becomes less than trivial. The force that has held us to this pestilent soil for too long, will become unworthy.

We shall leave it behind and make new souls in the freedom of the mesosphere. Our hands will move mountains, our feet will grace the pother of our efforts, and our backs will rest knowing that we have earned what we have so deservedly taken.

The earth shall know who owns it and those of us that live above it will look down from our rule!

Grace will come upon us with ascension. In the night we will strive to touch the black, to show it we are not afraid. It will not consume us for we are unbreakable, unlike the breach of heaven. We will clasp the stars in our hands and make waves upon the universe as it becomes our domain, for the result will prove we are more formidable than those that claim to have made us.

We shall prove our worthiness to be more than God.

To become His keeper ....

Putting on Airs

By Lillian Csernica

The carriage rolled down the cobbled avenue. Dr. William Harrington observed the gentle twilight of mid-February with quiet contentment. London still laboured under a blanket of sooty snow, but here in Kyoto flowers were already blooming. Madelaine leaned against her mother, one fingertip stroking the carved wooden cicada that hung by a string from a wooden stick. Spinning the toy around the stick produced a sound remarkably similar to a cicada in the heat of summer. Mother and daughter both wore dresses of forest green wool, a fine compliment to their dark hair and fair skin. Constance wore her hair swept up beneath her bonnet. At nine years old, Madelaine was still young enough to wear hers in a single long braid. Harrington wished he could capture the moment in a painted miniature.

Harrington's black wool topcoat, gray trousers, navy waistcoat over a high-collared white shirt, and wine-colored cravat were quite proper on Harley Street. The heavy clothing did prompt a bit of envy toward Japanese men with their option of wearing a *yukata*, the lightweight cotton kimono worn in the spring and summer months. Harrington still needed some comfort and tranquility after the ordeal of Madelaine's fever and the bizarre events of New Year's Day. Two months without further supernatural contact had helped Madelaine recover. For Harrington, many questions remained unanswered.

The carriage reined in before the gate of Dr. Harrington's home. The driver opened the door and let down the step. A cat yowled. Furious barking erupted, startling the horses and making them stamp in their traces. Harrington stepped down from the carriage. Across the avenue, the thin, bony figure of their neighbor, Mr. Carruthers, hauled back on the leash of his aging bloodhound. The dog strained forward, almost jerking the poor man off his feet.

Again the cat yowled. The bloodhound yipped, a thin, broken sound of pain. Madelaine jumped down from the carriage and grabbed a small branch fallen from one of the pines lining the avenue. She ran in front of the bloodhound and started swinging at the shadows.

"Bad cat! *Get away!*"

Harrington rushed to snatch Madelaine up in his arms. He caught a glimpse of yellow-green fire burning in the shadows.

"Came out of nowhere." Mr. Carruthers knelt beside his cowering bloodhound. "Black cat, big as a collie! Poor Bartholomew." He dabbed at the dog's nose with his handkerchief. Blood stained the cloth.

"Constance," Harrington said. "Take Madelaine inside." He beckoned the carriage driver and gave him several coins. "Go to the office of Dr. Chambers, the veterinarian. Bring him here at once."

"Hurry, man!" Carruthers wrapped Bartholomew in his coat and tried to lift the great dog up in his arms.

"Here now, let me do that." Harrington picked up the bloodhound, staring into the shadows. What he'd glimpsed looked nothing like any cat he'd ever seen, not even a black panther once shown at the London Zoo.

₧₧

The following afternoon, Harrington found Constance in the parlor dressed for tea time in a lovely dark blue plaid. The tea table held an abundance of scones, cucumber sandwiches, shortbread, and other dainties.

"This seems quite a feast for the three of us, my dear."

"Mrs. Thompson sent a note asking if she might bring another couple. They're new to the British set here in Japan."

Alexander Thompson, Undersecretary for Technological Exchange, had been present for the events of New Year's Day. When Harrington ordered a steam-powered wheelchair for the Abbot, he'd no idea Thompson would henceforth think of Harrington as a colleague. The maid showed the Thompsons into the parlor. Short, stout, and balding, dressed in a brown tailcoat, gray waistcoat, and black stovepipe trousers, Thompson made a comical pairing with his wife Eleanor, a slender woman gowned in garnet taffeta.

"Dr. Harrington!" Thompson said. "So good to see you."

"Undersecretary." Harrington smiled. "And Mrs. Thompson! I'm delighted you could join us."

Mrs. Thompson's smile gave her rather plain face a sudden sweetness. Behind her stood another man. Mrs. Thompson guided him forward.

"Do allow me to present Colonel Peter Anderson, a civil engineer on Mr. Thompson's staff."

The colonel was a tall, solid man with a head of thick russet hair and impressive side whiskers. He wore charcoal gray jacket and trousers with a red waistcoat. At the colonel's side stood a petite Japanese woman. Her glossy black hair displayed rather too many ornaments in its elaborate style. Her *yukata*, a fine yellow silk sewn with red and purple dragonflies, clashed with the other ladies' quiet elegance. Surely the colonel hadn't married a courtesan?

The colonel gripped Harrington's hand in both of his. "Quite honored to meet you, doctor. I understand the workings of machines, but it takes a true genius to fathom the workings of the human body."

"You're too kind, colonel."

The Colonel said something in Japanese. His wife bowed, making the ornaments in her black hair tinkle like tiny wind chimes.

"Myoko speaks no English, I'm afraid."

"Please," Constance said, "do make yourselves comfortable."

While Constance got everyone settled on the sofas and served tea from the silver tea service, Harrington studied Myoko.

"Colonel, I understand you're new to Japan," he said. "May I ask how you met your wife?"

"Certainly. I was in the Imperial Gardens, inspecting a damaged bridge. When I looked up from my work, I saw Myoko sitting nearby on a stone bench, under the shade of her parasol."

"Love at first sight, colonel?" Mrs. Thompson asked.

"Yes," Colonel Anderson said with a faint, slightly foolish smile. "Yes, I suppose it was."

"Forgive me, doctor," Mrs. Thompson said. "I must make a small confession. When Mrs. Anderson learned you have a little girl, well ...."

"Perhaps I should explain." Colonel Anderson sat forward. "The Japanese love children. To meet a little British girl, one as clever and sweet as your daughter is said to be, would be a rare pleasure for my wife."

Constance glanced at Harrington. In that glance he read disapproval, of both Myoko and her request. He shared her feelings, but Mrs. Thompson had put him in an awkward position.

"In the face of such praise, we can hardly refuse, can we, my dear?"

Constance rose and hurried out. She returned with Madelaine, who looked quite charming in a simple dress made of the same dark blue plaid Constance wore. Nurse Danforth made a discreet third.

"Madelaine." Harrington beckoned her. "You remember Mr. and Mrs. Thompson?"

"Yes, Papa."

"It's so good to see you up and about, young lady," said Thompson.

"Thank you, sir."

"This is Colonel Anderson," Constance said, "and his wife."

Myoko studied Madelaine, dark eyes narrowed. To Harrington, Myoko didn't seem all that pleased.

"*Anata wa neko ga suki desu?*"

"*Hai,*" Madelaine replied. "*Neko wa dai suki desu.*"

"Well done, young lady," said Colonel Anderson. "So you like cats very much, do you?"

"Yes, colonel."

Myoko reached into the sleeve of her *yukata*, then held out her hand to Madelaine. Madelaine drew back against Harrington.

"It's all right, dear," Mrs. Thompson said. "Mrs. Anderson just wants to give you something."

Madelaine took a slow step toward Myoko. Harrington wondered at Madelaine's reluctance. Myoko opened her fingers and dropped into Madelaine's palm the tiny figure of a cat curled up as if asleep, carved from the deep red-brown of boxwood.

"*Arigato gozaimasu.*"

Myoko smiled. "*Doh itashimashite.*"

Something about that smile put Harrington on guard.

"Madelaine," he said, "May I see your gift?"

When Madelaine turned to face him, the little cat rolled across her palm. She closed her fist to keep from dropping it.

"Ow!"

Madelaine opened her fist. The tip of each tiny wooden ear had pierced her palm. Harrington had seen a few such carvings. The makers took pride in the smooth, glossy surface. To leave a splinter would be unthinkable. He took out his handkerchief and gripped the carving between finger and thumb. As he pulled it away, a drop of blood welled up.

"Papa," Madelaine said, "I don't want any tea. May I go to my room?"-

"Of course, darling. Nurse Danforth?"

"Yes, doctor."

Madelaine clung to Harrington's sleeve. "Papa ...."

Her eyes rolled back. She collapsed. Harrington caught her in his arms.

"Madelaine!" Constance cried. "William? What's wrong?"

Harrington stood up. "Do excuse me."

Nurse Danforth hurried ahead of him, sliding open the door to Madelaine's room. Harrington laid Madelaine on her bed and pressed his ear to her chest. Rapid heartbeat. Short, shallow breaths. He lifted one of Madelaine's eyelids. Her pupils were dilated.

"Papa, the cat monster ... Mrs. Anderson ...."

Hallucinations. Delirium. Harrington's own heart began to pound. Not this, not now, when Madelaine had only just recovered! Better light and a magnifying glass might confirm what he suspected. Based on the information available at this point, he could make only one diagnosis.

For reasons unknown, Myoko had tried to poison Madelaine.

"Prepare an injection of morphia. The smallest possible dose."

"Yes, doctor."

Nurse Danforth prepared the hypodermic syringe. Harrington injected Madelaine.

"Stay with her," Harrington said. "If her breathing changes, call for me at once."

"Yes, doctor."

Harrington snatched up a small lacquer box from Madelaine's dresser, poured out her little treasures, dropped the carving inside, and tucked the box into his jacket pocket. He ran back to the parlor.

The colonel and his peculiar wife were gone.

"Go, Constance. Sit with Madelaine." Harrington turned to Thompson. "Where is Mrs. Anderson?"

"She just walked out. The colonel followed like some lovesick schoolboy." Thompson frowned. "Mrs. Anderson looked quite pleased with herself."

"I'm sure she did."

Mrs. Thompson gasped. "What are you saying? The colonel's wife meant to do your daughter harm?"

"At the moment, it very much looks that way," Harrington said. "Some investigation is in order. I will decide tomorrow whether or not to contact the authorities."

⅚⅙

The next morning Madelaine appeared weak but stable after a restless night full of nightmares about cats. That made Harrington all the more determined to consult the Abbot of Kiyomizudera. He sat with the Abbot in the temple's private reception room along with Mr. Fujita, the young Japanese man who acted as Harrington's official translator.

"Yesterday we had an unusual guest, a Japanese lady married to a British engineer. Something about her frightened Madelaine. She gave my daughter this." Harrington took the small lacquer box out of his jacket pocket and removed the lid so the Abbot could see the cat carving inside. "Please caution the Abbot not to touch the carving. The points of the ears are very sharp."

Fujita translated. The Abbot took the box from Harrington's hand and studied the carving. He spoke.

"What happened when your daughter accepted the *netsuke*?" Fujita asked.

"The tips of its ears punctured Madelaine's palm. Shortly after that, she collapsed. She showed symptoms of being poisoned."

Fujita translated. The Abbot replied.

"Did your daughter say anything that would explain why this woman sees her as an enemy?"

The question startled Harrington, but it made perfect sense.

"At the time I thought Madelaine was delirious from the poison. She kept trying to tell me Myoko is really a cat."

The Abbot clamped the lid down on the lacquer box. After a moment's silence, he spoke.

"Harrington-*sensei*," Fujita said, "the Abbot will prepare *ofuda* for the protection of your household. He will also burn the *netsuke*."

Harrington's heart sank. He'd hoped the events of New Year's Day were a once-in-a-lifetime experience. "Please, Fujita-*san*. Ask the Abbot why the gods and monsters of Japan keep attacking my family."

Fujita translated. The Abbot replied at length, then made Harrington a full formal bow, his forehead almost touching the *tatami*.

"Harrington-*sensei*." Fujita spoke in a soft, reverent voice. "The Abbot wishes to apologize most sincerely."

"Apologize? Whatever for?"

"You have brought your Western knowledge here to protect the health and well-being of the Abbot. You have become one of his guardians. It is the fate of all guardians to do battle."

Harrington left the Temple carrying three *ofuda*, long strips of parchment which held sutras written in heavy black *kanji*. The

Abbot had given Harrington very specific instructions about using them.

∞

Upon Harrington's return home he hurried to Madelaine's room. Nurse Danforth rose from her seat in the corner.

"Good evening, doctor."

"Good evening."

"Maddy? How are you feeling?"

Madelaine said nothing. She lay there, listless and dull-eyed. Harrington checked her pulse, respiration, the responsiveness of her pupils, and her temperature. All showed a pattern consistent with the effects of datura, but none were severe enough to cause him serious anxiety. Fortunately for Madelaine, Myoko had underestimated the amount of datura needed, along with failing to choose the most effective method of administration.

"Has Madelaine been active at all today?"

"Madelaine did ask for her work bag and some sewing materials."

"Did she complete the work?"

"Mama took it all away from me." Madelaine's plaintive tone startled Harrington.

"Why would your mother do such a thing?"

"Papa, I *must* complete my work tonight. If I had it here in front of me I could show you why."

"Well then." Harrington went in search of Constance. She sat in the parlor reading a book. "Constance, Madelaine was making something this afternoon. You took it away from her. She wants to show it to me."

"It would be best if she did not see the—the object again."

"I will be the judge of what is best for her, both for her physical well-being and her mental health."

"No good will come of this, William. Madelaine is far too caught up in all this nonsense about gods and monsters."

"The sewing, Constance. Now, if you please."

Constance laid aside her book and left the room. She returned with a bundle of fishing net and thrust it into Harrington's arms.

Harrington excused Nurse Danforth for the remainder of the evening. He sat on Madelaine's bed and together they spread out the fisherman's net across her lap. She'd sewn shrine tokens to the tough fibers, tiny wooden plaques painted with animals from the Chinese zodiac and small brocade bags tied up with white cord.

"Papa, what did you do with the little cat carving?"

"I showed it to the Abbot when I visited the Temple today."

"What did the Abbot say?"

Harrington paused, weighing his words. "The Abbot gave me a special prayer to put on our front gate. Only good things can come into our house."

"Is it on the gate now?"

"Not yet. I wanted to look in on you first."

"Thank you, Papa. Don't put the prayer on the gate just yet."

"Why not?"

"Do you remember when you promised to believe what I told you about Japanese fairy tales?"

"Yes, darling. How could I forget?" They'd spent New Year's Day on the veranda of the Kiyomizu Temple. The Abbot sat trapped in a steam-driven wheelchair while the Japanese god of chaos threatened Harrington with total destruction.

"I have a plan, Papa. If you will help me carry it out, I believe we can catch the monster that hurt Mr. Carruthers's dog."

"With this?" Harrington touched the net. "Will it be strong enough?"

"Oh yes, Papa. That's why I used temple charms."

"How did you get so many? And where did the net come from?"

"Sato-*san* and Hochizuki-*san*."

"The gardeners? They know about this?"

"They were eager to help, Papa. This creature has been killing birds, other cats, even a baby deer. It must be stopped."

Harrington stared at Madelaine in pure amazement. He'd trusted her on New Year's Day. He'd trust her now.

"Very well. How shall we proceed?"

ॐ

After the entire household had gone to bed, Harrington took the chair from Madelaine's bedside and set it by the open window where he could keep watch. The sounds of voices and carriage wheels subsided. Lights in nearby houses began to go out. The waxing moon rose, throwing silvery light into the garden and casting inky shadows. By the stiffness in Harrington's legs, he guessed two hours had passed, perhaps more.

Out in the garden, something hit the ground with a soft thump. Paws dug at the sand spread in a thick layer under Madelaine's window. Harrington shut his eyes and listened, every nerve alert. He'd embedded a hook in the largest chunk of sea bream. Fishing line ran from the hook to the trap's trigger, which would respond to the slightest tug.

The small dish that held the sea bream scraped against the sand. The creature was eating. A sudden click made the four corners of the fisherman's net jerk upward from beneath the sand. In the net thrashed a large black cat. Its furious yowl split the night.

Madelaine flung aside the bedclothes and stumbled over to the window.

"Maddy," Harrington whispered. "This looks like an ordinary house cat."

"This, Papa, is a *bakeneko*, a cat monster. They're vain, bad-tempered, and they like to play tricks."

The cat glared at Madelaine with eyes like weird green flames.

"Bad cat! Putting on airs, pretending you're a lady!"

The cat hissed, straining toward Madelaine with claws bared.

"The Abbot knows about you!"

Clouds drifted across the moon. Shadows covered the cat. When the moon came out again, the net sagged under the weight of the larger shape it now held. Harrington leaned out over the sill.

Beneath him lay Myoko, stark naked. Harrington spun around and pushed Madelaine back from the window.

"*Tasukete, kudasai!*" Myoko cried. "*Tasukete!*"

"What is she saying?" Harrington asked.

"She's shouting for help. She looks human now, doesn't she?"

"Yes. *Quite* human."

The door slid open. Nurse Danforth hurried in, tugging a robe on over her night dress. "Doctor! Whatever is that noise outside?"

"Get me another blanket, please."

"Yes, doctor." Nurse Danforth took one from the chest at the foot of Madelaine's bed.

Constance appeared in the doorway. "Madelaine! What are you doing out of bed?"

"Mama! I caught that nasty cat who hurt Bartholomew!" Madelaine turned to Harrington. "Be careful, Papa. They're very clever."

"Don't worry, Maddy." Harrington patted the three *ofuda* in his jacket pocket. "I'll take care of Miss Meow-ko." He took the blanket from Nurse Danforth. "Stay with Madelaine. Keep her away from the window."

"Yes, doctor."

Harrington left by the kitchen door. Out in the garden, he spread the blanket out next to Myoko. When he reached for the net, Myoko hissed at him. He slapped her across the face.

"You hurt my little girl. You could have killed her!" Harrington composed himself with an effort. "Be very grateful I do not believe in cruelty to animals. Otherwise I would gladly stuff you in a sack and drop you in the river."

He unhooked the four corners of the net and rolled up Myoko in both net and blanket. Using two drawing pins, he secured the first of the Abbot's *ofuda* to the blanket, locking Myoko into her human form and limiting her powers. Harrington carried her into the garden shed, set her down on some bags of fertilizer, then shut the door. Another drawing pin and the second *ofuda* sealed that door.

Out of the shadows behind the shed stepped a monk from Kiyomizudera. The monk offered Harrington an envelope addressed in Fujita's handwriting. Harrington tore open the envelope to find a single sheet of writing paper.

Dear Harrington-sensei,

Please allow the monks to remove the cat monster. The Abbot will see to it the bakeneko *does no further harm.*

Your humble servant,
Fujita Masayuki

How had they known the trap would catch Myoko tonight? The Abbot must have sent a message to Madelaine, or vice versa. Harrington stepped aside, waving the monk toward the shed.

The monk bowed, then clapped his hands twice. Through the gate at the back of the garden walked two more monks. They carried a palanquin, something like a long wicker basket slung between two poles. The first monk opened the doors on the side of the palanquin, entered the shed, and came out carrying Myoko. He tucked her inside the palanquin, closed the doors and tied off the handles with red cords. The three monks bowed to Harrington, took up their burden, then departed through the back gate.

Harrington leaned against the garden shed. He took from his pocket the third *ofuda*, the one meant for the front gate. The Abbot said Harrington had become a guardian. If that was true, he'd do well to follow in Madelaine's footsteps. Her knowledge of folklore, her talent for machinery, and her sewing skills had protected the entire neighborhood from the murderous habits of the *bakeneko*.

Wild Card

By Dover Whitecliff

Unlike arena fighting, intelligence work generally doesn't involve any. Intelligence that is. It does involve more work than is strictly necessary, especially collaborating on foreign soil. But this time I found myself in Te Raro. City of Lights, Vices, and Guilty Pleasures. Absolutely no comparison to that courier job to the Uyat. No slurping down grubs or pulling off sand-leeches in this place.

It took a bit of work to keep from grinning like a bloody idiot in front of the bellboy when I peeked into the bath and saw a tub big enough to swim in. And the bed — royal size with six (SIX!) pillows. I could smell fresh almond cookies from the suite's entry hall as I walked in and spotted them laid out in a perfect flower pattern on the night table's doily. Pure, unadulterated joy. Until.

I stared dubiously at the eight aithergrams in bright yellow envelopes laid out on a polished silver salver. Oh the joy of working in someone else's sandbox. The bellboy anticipated my question before it was even a thought.

"Those started coming in about twelve hours ago, Miss. Right after we confirmed your reservation. Will there be anything else, Miss?"

"No. Thank you." I handed him a tenner and he left, closing the door behind him. Well, if it's your duty to clean the jacks, best do it sooner than later. Eight aithergrams. All addressed to Kenna Wolfesdaughter. Not She-Wolf. Not Lupa. A proper greeting then. Eight. The number for air, for vision and far-seeing. A clue. How quaint. I picked them up and read them top to bottom.

Some seemed friendly: SORRY I MISSED YOU. SEE YOU AT DICKSON'S.

Some sounded like warnings: CEASE YOUR SCURRILOUS SCRIBBLINGS OR ELSE!

And some were just bloody odd: AARRRGGGG! LOVIN' THE FUDGE! THANKS, MATEY!

Now what am I supposed to make out of that?

Qin-To being the most civilized of nations on three continents evidently meant their intelligence agency operated on the principle of form over substance. I flipped through the aithergrams again. Took them out of the envelopes. Sniffed them for lemon juice in the hopes of some sort of simple solution or invisible ink. No such luck. Oddly enough, some of the words were blurry. Almost like the aithergraph had been jiggled and parts of the messages double printed during transmission. Qin-To, self-professed center of the greatest in all modern wonders, wouldn't tolerate a faulty aithergraph in any of their cities. Would they?

Right then, let's take it from the top, reading only the offsets: "Sorry I missed you. Obey my instructions. Discover the ides of dogs. The password is 'Aarrrgggg! Matey!'."

"By all the sacred Elements, please tell me this is a joke." I dropped the aithergrams on the posh sheets I obviously wouldn't be enjoying any time soon, walked to the window, and stared at the city laid out below, banging my forehead on the slanted glass in disgust.

Nothing for it, Girl. Out you get. Just keep thinking about chocolate stout and truffles and the midnight ice cream buffet.

I pocketed the key, left my room with one last longing look, and went in search of dogs. And pirates. In a land-locked city. The things I do for my liege lord.

I gave myself a once over in the polished brass doors of the lift and wondered just what was under the eyepatch. Mr. Black Heart Pin hadn't exaggerated when he'd said my new mechanical eye had all the latest enhancements. I still had no idea what it looked like nigh on three months after Nigel's bomb had taken my real one in the Solstice Games. Every time I tried to see with it, my head split from pounding. I always slammed my eyelid shut before I got a good look. Well, at least with the scar and the patch I'd fit right in with pirates. Aarrrgggg, Matey, indeed.

And once I delivered the programming card Fa's boffins had extricated from the guts of the IKAROS wings, I would have a whole month until they reined me back in to provide for Fa's security at the Great Exhibition of Duoros. Te Raro was mad in the midst of preparation for the Exhibition like nothing I'd ever seen. Even the hoopla surrounding the Sword Dance held a dim candle to the excitement buzzing everywhere I looked.

A gong announced the lift and I stepped in. Odd feeling going slantwise down the outside of the Tetra in a glass bubble with the gaslights flicking by every few seconds. The Arclight that crowned the capstone of the casino pierced the night sky and washed out any chance of seeing the stars, so I turned my attention to the builders and their giant Mechanicals preparing the empty lot across the boulevard they called the Kodo. 'Lot' didn't do it justice really. The Tetra could have fit into the space twice over. I could even see the start of the foundations for the Grand Pavilion that would dwarf everything nearby next to the mooring yards where the dignitaries and all and sundry would disembark for the debauchery to come.

Every bit of Te Raro overloaded the senses. Size? Half a turn of the glass had passed by the time I navigated gaming tables to the door. Sound? Jingling and ringing of the pachinko boxes and clockwork fortune wheels swelled to their own symphony beneath shouts and laughter. Smells? Steaming bao and caramel apples. Plumeria and ginger. Wet stone and smoke. I dodged the steam carriages to cross the Kodo, aiming to be just another bumpkin in the herd.

The gargantuan bronze angora statue dwarfing the incoming guests to the Gratia Artis Hotel gave me a still pool of onlookers to blend into while I pried up a map of the city from a dusty corner of my mind. Pirates and dogs. Where would they be? A flash of light on the statue startled a memory out of the shadows. My first visit to 'Raro. My coming of age. Not a party or my first pint of the stronger stuff. No, Kyree had signed me up for an out-of-class exo-suit bout to entice our target out of her suite and down to the arena so Fa could liberate I-don't-remember-what national secret from her possession.

Not often a bantam's first fight out of the juniors was with a middleweight in the biggest arena on the continent, but I managed to pull it off by the skin of my teeth. When the photographers flashed their bulbs and Kyree held my hand up for the crowd out front of that statue, I had still been breathing hard and grinning through a bloody nose and black eye near swollen shut. Kyree, who towered over me still, had only come up to the smallest clawed toe on the angora's foot.

A Good Time Boy pushed past me.

Pay attention, Girl. Pirates and dogs.

I turned to make my way through the gauntlet.

"Tickets for tonight's show, miss?"

"Our boys will take care of you, missy—free samples this way!"

"Find the ball and win big—step right up and take your chances!"

In the spin and chaos and gaslight, it was easy to forget being in 'Raro for an actual purpose, but not so easy to quash instincts pounded in by a relentless Kyree or honed by an even more relentless Fa for half a lifetime. And there's nothing like that hair-on-end tingle you get when a predator is stalking you. But stalking to kill or stalking to corner and converse, that was the question.

Three in the crowd defied the ebb and flow of humanity stopping to gape at this or that. That narrowed it down.

Which one? The tall one in the tuxedo? The woman in the ao dai *with the cobalt hair?*

Both moved gracefully, hunting cats herding prey, watching everything without watching. Either could pose a serious threat. Well, until they spotted each other and melted into an embrace. They danced past the bouncer's velvet rope and disappeared between two shallow pools teeming with the water birds that gave the Ciconia its name. That left only number three.

Please no. Not that one.

While it's true that a slap-you-in-the-eyeball pink and orange flamingo dancing down the Kodo in polka-dot bedroom slippers while handing out calling cards for a bawdy house would go largely unnoticed by the locals, I wouldn't exactly consider it de rigueur fashion for tailing someone. I figure I must have cheesed off the Gods of 'Raro something fierce considering every damn thing about this job aimed toward embarrassment. No doubt in my mind Kyree or Briar would find out somehow some way, and stories of the Great Flamingo Hunt would follow me to my grave.

Now what? Not like I could body slam an ersatz casino mascot in front of the paying customers. And one thing was certain sure: leading the flamingo to my contact was not an option.

Think fast, Girl.

I pretended to gawk at a volcano fountain erupting with crimson lights and flame, then, when the flamingo was close enough, I sauntered on, making my way through the crowds choking the Bridge of Whispers and into the Illyrian Resort with its festooned boats and singing oarsmen ferrying kissing couples hither and yon, keeping my eyes open for a place to have a quiet conversation.

There.

I sidestepped into an alcove behind a marble column, and counted to twelve. Pink fluff hove into view and I struck, grabbing the flamingo round the neck and twisting its wing behind its back. It was taller than I was, and I made a guess at where the neck was; hopefully, I was in the right spot. Not that a flamingo's squawk would be noticed in this place.

"Is there a reason you're following me?" I pulled my elbow tighter, trying to feel for body parts under the fleece and foam.

"Mmmrph." I kept pressure on the wing and let go the neck long enough to yank off the flamingo's headpiece and drop it.

"You were saying?"

"I'm from—ow—from Headquarters." The flamingo, really a mop-headed effete with a weak chin and pouty lips, would have kowtowed if I hadn't had him in a hammerlock. "An honor to finally meet you Lady Kenna, an honor." I let his arm loose. He tucked the feathery headdress under his arm and tried to kiss my hand.

Oh no you don't.

I turned his attempt into a death grip handshake. "Your exploits are legend." He winced, but continued pumping my hand up and down. "Quite the pleasure."

I extracted my hand with some difficulty. "And you are?"

"Garrick Winslow. I'm your liaison here in Te Raro. Station Q is small, what. We had word you were coming of course. I'm here to help you with the wild card. Sorry about the flamingo, but it was the easiest way to follow you without being noticed."

"Without. Being. Noticed."

He actually blushed.

"Yes. Well. We're a backwater really. This is the first bit of excitement we've had in some time. I am *so* looking forward to working with you."

Working with me? You want excitement, Winslow? I'll give you excitement—far away from me.

"Good timing, Winslow. Someone's on to me. From the airship. Purser called him—"

Name. Name. I need a name. Ah! The aithergram.

"Dickson, I think." I made a show of peeking around the column, looked down the Kodo, and picked at random. "Damn all. I thought I lost him in the Tetra. There. Do you see him? Tall. White moustache. Deerstalker and cape. I think he may be after the card. He won't be expecting you. Lead him a merry chase to buy me some time."

"But. But. The wild card." He sputtered. "Shouldn't we hide it?"

"I'll keep it safe. Meet me at the Frozen Bar at sunup. Go. Now." I grabbed the flamingo headdress and jammed it back on Winslow's shoulders, pushing him out into the crowd to be swept away.

WHOOM! The blast ripped my thoughts away from the flabbergasted flamingo. That sounded just like—a cannon. WHOOM! This time followed by rollicking music. Rollicking *pirate* music. How could I have forgotten? Briar would say something snarky to that, something about getting hit in the head one too many times.

I weaseled my way through the throng to Buccaneer's Cove. Two model ships manned by scantily-clad, incredibly clean pirates (you expect filthy, pockmarked pirates in 'Raro?) battled each other, lurching to and fro on tracks beneath the lagoon to the blast of air cannons and pyrotechnics.

A herd of younger males ignored the ships and crowded around a street performer, just come of age by the look of her, posing for photographs in a short, blue-spangled skirt, crimson corset, and stomping boots, an interesting take on one of the heroes from the marvelous dreadfuls. Keeping the oglers at a respectful distance were a semicircle of knee-high foo pups, sparks illuminating their lightning-stone manes. On a whim, I counted them. Fifteen. Ides. I suppose foo pups counted as dogs, all things considered. The alpha curled his lip at me. I growled back. He lolled his tongue and barked. Their mistress turned her gaze on me, took in the eyepatch, and arched an eyebrow expectantly.

Fine. Have it your way.

"Aarrrgggg, Matey." My best bucca-sneer.

"Come with me." She tossed me the leashes. "Sorry boys. Short break. Back in a bit." She blew her admirers a kiss. The foo pups cleared the way, pulling me along after them to Sarn's Palace.

Funny what people in 'Raro thought the palace at NorFort looked like. Last I was there, I don't remember seeing a fountain statue of Maralissandra Alstashevana Trientanis, Sarn of Sarns, Savior of the Nation, posing half-naked with arm raised high and water spewing every which way from the tip of the Dragon Sword.

"You're the She-Wolf that the Commander goes on about?" She asked when we'd reached a quieter hallway.

The Commander? From Rannport? How did he fit into this?

"Sometimes."

"I thought you'd be taller."

"I get that a lot."

She laughed and flashed a smile, opening the bronze and crys-glass double doors to the penthouse.

"Mum! Lupa's here!" A yell loud enough to make any teenager proud. To be fair, the ongoing party nearly drowned her out.

"Pool!" came the answering call. We skirted the throng to an opulent balcony, as yet uncrowded, probably due to the hunting cat staring through the glass at the party goers like a platter of amuse-bouches. My escort reached up to scratch beneath its diamond collar, and it rested its chin affectionately on her head. I felt the purr through the soles of my feet, boots and all.

The foo pups arrayed themselves in front of me and started a glare-off with the cat, who gave one imperious look and then turned back to watching the guests and licking its chops. My escort slid the glass door shut behind us, flopped onto a lounge chair at the edge of a pool that seemed to drop off the edge of the building into starlight, and proceeded to ignore us in favor of pulling a top-end musicon from her reticule and fiddling with the dial until the right tune poured out. *Over my Head* by No Moss. How appropriate.

"Lupa, so good to meet you. Did you have fun with the aithergrams?" She erupted out of the pool like a force of nature, full of life and exuberance, curly red mane dripping sparkles of light. Her laugh was downright infectious.

"Aarrrgggg, Matey?"

"Couldn't resist. I love pirates. And Dr. B was right. You do look the part with that patch. He sends apologies by the way. Says the headaches will ease up as you get used to your eye. Says to try it at twilight—not too dark, not too light. Good time to practice." Dr. B? Mr. Black Heart Pin? The Commander? Just who were these people? Definitely not my Qin-To counterparts.

"What should I call you?"

"Madame E. I thought you might appreciate something more straightforward. Easy enough to intercept your contact's transmissions, trim it to eight from twenty and double print the important bits. Agent Xiung is still in the Clockwork Graveyard waiting for you to rifle through a thousand pages of the Chang Sen Codex in your night table drawer to decipher the double-layered cryptique." Madame E grabbed a towel big enough to cover the bed in my room in the Tetra. She smiled. "He won't miss you for another two or three hours at least, and he can't help you anyway."

"He can't?"

"The Service can only determine the probabilities on a punched card. The card you retrieved in the Solstice Games hasn't been punched. It's a wild card."

"So it could do...anything?"

"Exactly. But the number combinations on a wild card can be interpreted by the right person. Maybe even in time to learn what they're planning and stop it."

"Do you know where I can find the right person?"

"Only one in all Qin-To. Pascal Lovelace. Top of his class. I went to finishing school with his sister. Lovey sees patterns in things no one else can. He still can't figure out how you beat him last spring." Wait. Beat him? Not Inarion Blue?

"Lovey?" I had to concentrate to replace the image of a spotty, gangly squit with the pug-nosed, muscled, exo-suit middle-weight it had taken all my wits and a considerable amount of luck to get the better of. "Blue's real name is Lovey, ah, Lovelace?"

"He hates it when I call him that." She laughed. "So I do it all the time. But he's the one you want. There's just one problem."

"Problem? What kind of problem?" This didn't bode well.

"Lovey can take in all the combinations on that card and tell you what they're up to, no doubt about it, but he isn't exactly easy to get to."

"Where is he?"

"Tell me, Lupa." She beamed enigmatically. "How do you feel about doing time?"

"Prison." *Fa is going to skin me alive.*

THIRTY DAYS LATER

Minotaur in the Mist

or

Never Trust a Tomb Robber to Tell You Everything

By T.E. MacArthur

Platanos, Chania Region, Island of Crete
December 23rd, 1893

"So, this is just another, ordinary curse?"

"No, no. Only the ghost of a limb-rending, man-devouring Minotaur."

The Colonel half smiled. "Ah, nothing to worry about then."

Miranda Gray had to admit, she was getting used to the Colonel—despite her better judgement. He was refreshingly witty, if incredibly dangerous. "You're concerned that we're off chasing a wild goose when we should be serving Queen and country," she said as the sharpshooter ate a handful of dates.

"I couldn't care less if they want us for another assignment, but if they do offer it, I wouldn't want to have to say 'no'."

"They won't throw you back in prison. You're rather useful."

"You don't know the Minister."

She looked up. "I know that he says you killed his brother." She was prying with purpose.

The Colonel looked down at his hands, then out at the setting sun. "My employer did the deed, but I'm not entirely ashamed to say I was involved. We were in the midst of a brilliant plan. I make no promises about being a good, decent man."

"I never asked you to."

A long silence followed, punctuated by the cry of a bird in the distance.

"Davies said "the 'Bull of Heaven' and the 'Heart of the Sea.' That's what we're looking for, Colonel."

"Ah yes, he was sharing his knowledge with you, before you were interrupted."

"I almost had the information." Gray shook her head. "The Bull of Heaven is a reference to an oriental legend—and by that I mean ancient Mesopotamia, and not Crete. Still, the Bull was very important to the Minoans."

The Colonel stood up and walked to the railing by their table. A light breeze blew through the sleeves of his shirt. It was likely the Colonel was not used to being so—naked. Yet the acceptable attire for Britain, Germany, and Switzerland was too heavy for Crete, even in winter.

"Then we're looking for a statue or a monument representing a bull? And in the exaggerated light of a Perigee-syzygy Moon, we'll be shown the location of the Heart of the Sea? All this is based on the word of a disreputable tomb robber and the diary of a crazy 16th century privateer? Madame Archaeologist, I feel as if we have this treasure already."

She couldn't help laughing. "Absurd, isn't it. Well, my dear Colonel, I've chased after crazier goals with less evidence." She got up from the table, leaving behind a perfectly good cup of wine. Holding the journal of Sir Charles Bellingsfield, explorer in the 1590s and rumored mad man, she leaned against the railing next to the Colonel. "We do have some advantages over Davies."

"He got here two days ahead of us."

The Colonel was understandably tense. Was he imagining Malcolm Davies, the professional tomb robber, holding a knife to her throat, then escaping into the river? When he'd learned the details, he was infuriated—though not in a romantic way. She knew better. He, of all men, knew she wasn't helpless by any stretch of the imagination. He once said that he found her to be intriguing and stimulating as a colleague. He genuinely respected her intelligence. It seemed he preferred the company of brilliant people, even the wrong sort of people. It was his experience that he made up for such failing by being the expert that he was. Gray certainly appreciated his skills.

"He knows, in theory, where he is going. But, he doesn't know everything. Davies hadn't translated all of Bellingsfield's journal, but I have. All we need now is to find the Minoan Bull of Heaven."

"No one seems to know what that is. You've asked every scholar and archaeologist you know. Arthur Evans doesn't even know," the Colonel grumbled.

Gray turned her back to the railing and watched as a waiter began clearing some of their dishes. "Perhaps we're asking the wrong people."

She smiled at him and he watched her boldly approach and chat with the waiter. It was a waste of time, of course, yet her ability to converse so easily with academics and natives alike ...

The waiter pointed to the horizon, to the northeast.

"Truly?" Gray said, her expression astonished.

The waiter nodded, smiled, and accepted her gracious gratuity.

For several moments, the Archaeologist and the Colonel stared at one another incredulously. "No," he finally said. "Not that easy."

"Apparently so. And that makes me nervous."

Before she could explain, a clay pot of flowers mere inches from the Colonel's head shattered and a shot rang out. Both of them dropped to the floor, and Gray looked back into the restaurant to see the entire café staff do the same. "That was meant for you, Colonel."

"Not fair! Bloody unsporting." The Colonel withdrew a short revolver from his coat pocket, just in reach where his jacket hung on the back of the chair.

"Can you see who shot?"

"Someone's running away over there."

"Damn good eyes you have, Colonel."

"Necessary for the occupation, Madame."

"It's simply a thought on my part, but I believe this is a sign that we're on the right track."

"Break open the Champagne?" He hadn't realized how hard his heart was pounding. "What *did* the waiter tell you?"

Gray looked over the railing quickly, then settled back beside the Colonel. "See the two mountain peaks over there? That's it. Not a statue, not a monument, but the mountains themselves. Two equal-sized peaks with a curved saddle of land in between."

"Doesn't look like horns to me."

"Not from here, but, in direct alignment with the moon over there ..."

The Colonel nodded. "I never like it when it's too easy."

"I suspect your intuition is correct. Still game?"

Well, that's a damn silly question.

౭౦౦౩

Chania Region, Island of Crete

The Perigee-syzygy Moon on the Winter Solstice was predicted to appear 40% larger than usual. Ancient people had been astonished by this phenomenon—and it was easy to understand why. As the enormous moon rose over the horizon, it appeared a dull orange, from the dust stirred up by the wind. It loomed in the distance, moving slowly, like a stalking panther, casting unusually strong light.

Gray felt a chill crawl up her spine, and it wasn't from the winter night air. Shadows began to change and move. Skeletal trees cast images of demonic creatures growing and menacing the countryside. Scrub bushes shivered. The air smelled of decay.

The Colonel, air rifle in hand, climbed up the path that led directly to the saddle between the two peaks. They could easily make out the Bull's horns with a little imagination. He waved to her, and Gray quickly moved up to join him. On her back, she wore a simple pack with basic archaeological equipment and Bellingsfield's book. In her hands, she carried a low-lit lantern and a Bisley-grip, .45 Long Colt.

At the top of the saddle, the two sat for a moment, waiting.

"Think Davies is around here?" she whispered.

"I'm counting on it, Madame."

Gray turned to look down at the sea toward the west. A broad pillar of light cast by the moon onto the waves began crawling across the ocean, drawing in toward land. "Watch there," she pointed. "Normal moonlight wouldn't have made such a clear indicator."

The Colonel looked over his shoulder repeatedly, making Gray wonder which he was thrilled by more: the rare mystical secret about to be revealed or the chance to kill Davies.

Slowly—too slowly—the light dragged itself across the water and onto the top of the cliffs.

"There," Gray said in an excited whisper. "The Heart of the Sea."

Just at the edge of the light, a hole in the clifftop was revealed. An odd, shape, broken at the top. "That? That's not a heart."

"Don't look for what we think is a heart symbol. *That* is closer to the shape of a real human heart, as they knew it, and any damage I'll wager is from two-thousand years of erosion." She adjusted her pack. "Shall we go?"

"What the hell. I'll go first. That's my job."

Not that I couldn't, she thought with some frustration. Though, he was right. It was his job to protect her. As he began his decent toward the cliffs, some 500 feet away, she waited—looking for any indication that Davies and his men were nearby.

At the top of the cliffs, looking out over the well-lit ocean, the agents peered down into the so-called Heart. Up close, the hole was rather imposing. Until one was right on top of it, it was impossible to see the ancient steps cut into the rock, spiraling down. Down into the dark. Very clever, those Minoans.

"Still want to take the lead?" she teased.

A howl rose up from the hole. Horrible, almost deafening. "What the hell was that!"

"Wind, my dear Colonel." She wasn't entirely sure.

"That was not wind, Madame Archaeologist."

The howl rose again, sounding every bit angry, bitter, and vengeful.

She had to admit, it was terrifying. Exciting! "Fine, it's the ghost of the Minotaur waiting to kill us. Feel better?"

"Oh, so much better." He swallowed. "I prefer knowing what I'm up against." He gripped his rifle and began climbing down the stairs. Once inside, the howl surrounded him, warning him off one more time. "Better you than a hangman," he whispered into the dark.

"What?" Gray was leaning into the hole with her lantern.

"It might be a hundred feet to the bottom. I don't suppose old Bellingsfield told us what to do when we get there?"

"No. His journal never made it that far. He left it aboard ship when he disembarked for this exploration. Never came back."

"Well, there's an epitaph if ever I heard one."

"Yours or mine?" Gray was sorry she had to put away something, in this case it was either the gun or the lantern. She couldn't climb with both her hands occupied, and the gun lost out to practical illumination.

The stairs, what little remained of them, spiraled down to the bottom of the hole. What waited was astounding: no great frescoes or palace columns, as Arthur Evans had found, but simple clay pots—perfectly intact. The seven, 4-foot-tall amphorae were sealed with tarred cork, and painted with exquisite black geometrical shapes. Each had a different animal: an octopus, a fish, a dolphin, a bull, a bird, an ibex, and a snake. There appeared to be nothing behind them indicating a doorway, but there was something suggestive of a lock. Gray held her lantern up to examine the lock closely.

"Have we found the treasure room?" The Colonel began pointing his rifle up the stairs. He had his job to do, and the Archaeologist was in her element. He knew to stay out of her way.

"If all we ever find are these amphorae, I say yes. These are in perfect condition and I can't see that any have been opened. Treasure to an archaeologist. But I don't think this is all."

"Why put them here?"

"A guess? One of them has the key to this lock—if it *is* a lock."

"Don't you know?" he said, lightly mocking her.

"Archaeology is about educated guessing; plenty of digging at nothing but dirt, and readdressing ideas once more evidence is collected." She set her pack down and pulled out a trowel. "It may sound strange, but we don't find things as often as you might think." She lightly prodded the lock. "It's not all excitement and riches."

As if responding to her commentary, the howl blasted through the hole, causing both agents to cover their ears.

"One thing's for certain," the Colonel said, watching as Gray added the opposite end of a thin brush to her strange lock-picking efforts, "there's no Minotaur down in this hole. He'd never fit."

"True, but we don't know what's on the other side of this lock. This may not even be a lock."

"A trap?"

"One can only hope. This is a tad obvious, don't you think?"

"Always encouraging."

She thought for a moment that she'd seen something above. Perhaps it was her imagination.

The Colonel appeared to have seen it too. "What is your educated guess about what's in those amphorae? If only one has a key ..."

"Who knows? Perhaps at the time they held poisonous snakes, or dangerous insects. Maybe even acids. Anything to punish the wrong choice. Hence my picking the lock instead."

"Because, of course, only the right people would make the right choice."

The howl made both of them stop for a moment. It sounded right next to them.

"I do wish that thing would shut up," the Colonel snarled.

"I was thinking the very same thing about you, Colonel," a voice called from above.

Gray didn't even bother to look up. "Let me guess."

"You invited *him* to this soiree." The Colonel aimed at the figure climbing down the stairs.

"He invited me, remember? Anyone with him?"

Davies, dressed less opulently than usual, stopped and held out his own lantern. "You insult me, *Nefer*—oh beautiful one." She glared at him from her dirt-smeared face. "I have no reason to bring anyone with me. You are the best at what you do." He crouched on the step near eye level with the Colonel. "You're the one who insisted on bringing baggage with you."

It must have been tempting for the Colonel to put a bullet between the man's smug eyes. But, instead, the Colonel looked to Gray. Between them passed an easy, unspoken agreement. It might serve their purpose to have Davies on hand, and not skulking around behind them. Gray rolled her eyes and went back to her lock.

"Besides, my dear lady, I am not interested in sharing my portion with too many."

"And what portion is that?" she asked, pushing on something that seemed to push back.

The hole shook, and dirt fell on them from above. Both Davies and the Colonel braced themselves on the stairs. Gray pressed her back against the far wall—watching.

The area around the lock shattered and fell inward toward the tunnel that now lay beyond the hole. The crash echoed for a good minute before it was silent again.

Her first thought was that one of her compatriots might be injured. No. All were well, if confused and surprised. Then the amphorae: had they survived? They were important. They were beautiful. One appeared cracked, but not exposed. The others were safe.

The howl erupted from deep inside the open tunnel, louder than ever.

"That came from in there," the Colonel noted, redirecting the muzzle of his rifle. Even Davies was startled, and drew a pistol. "There's no wind in there."

Gray stared for a moment and searched for words. "I'm sure there's some natural explanation. We are on a cliff side, after all."

"Are you sure, Madam Archaeologist?"

"Well, Mr. Davies, if I'm wrong, we won't be worrying about it for very long, will we?"

Davies never took his eyes off the tunnel as he crept toward the entrance. "Do you believe in ghosts or Minotaurs?"

"Prior to now?"

Shaking his head, less in disagreement and more to clear away any doubts, the Colonel pushed Davies out of the way and held his rifle at waist level.

"Don't get in my way, Colonel. I want my treasure, and *Nefer* wants her codex. I don't know or care what you want." Davies pushed back and took the lead with a lantern.

Stepping up to the Colonel, Gray whispered in his ear. "I doubt there's any treasure, but he's right, I do want the codex Bellingsfield used to translate Linear A. It's worth far more than any golden baubles. It's knowledge."

He nodded. "He'll get tricky if he doesn't get anything for all his efforts. He's my problem. You just find your codex."

The howl warned them one last time. The Colonel had been right; that was no wind in that tunnel. "Ever bag a Minotaur?"

He let her pass him, into the tunnel. He was now on rear guard, probably the more vulnerable and dangerous position on an expedition. "There's a first for everything." The tunnel was much hotter inside. "Remember what I said about things being too easy?"

Ghost Bets the House

By AJ Sikes

Ghost flicks the cards from his hand, one by one, sliding them up and out with his thumb in time to the riverboat's rocking. He watches them hit the green felt. First the Ace, then the King followed by his lady. Then the Knave and the ten.

"That's a lotta heart," the other gambler says from across the table. "Wonder where a black man like you goes about gettin' so much heart."

"Aw, go on, Macky," says a light-skinned woman standing by the table. "Ghost played square. I was here watchin' him the whole time."

"Yeah," Macky says. "And who was watchin' you?"

Macky puts a hand on the table and keeps the other one out of sight. Ghost knows what's going to happen. Same as happened the last time he pulled down big on a riverboat. So he scoots back from the table, reaches to a handrail, and pulls himself to standing. Macky tracks him with his eyes, keeping that one hand hid beneath the table.

"Want to sit back down, Ghost?" Macky asks. "Seems you owe me the courtesy of a chance to win back some of my coin."

"Seems you're mistaken," Ghost says to Macky, flashing a look at the woman standing beside the table. He catches her slight nod and knows Macky didn't see what passed between them.

Ghost lifts his hat and nods to Macky. "Much obliged, Mister McClintock," Ghost says. "I thank you for the game."

He turns to leave and hears the chair scrape across the deck as Macky rises. Ghost also hears the clicking of the hammer on Macky's little Derringer.

"You're a cheat, and I want my money back," Macky says.

Ghost keeps walking, waiting for the sound he knows is coming.

"I'll shoot you in the back," Macky says to him. "I don't care."

For a second, Ghost half thinks Macky would shoot him in the back. Then he hears a solid *thwunk* and a body falling to the deck. The little Derringer clatters against the planking, too. Ghost turns around slow and sees the woman standing with a blackjack in one hand.

"Thanks, Jenny," Ghost says, tipping his hat and tossing a coin at her. She catches the dollar and slips it into her bodice to nestle against the others Ghost knows she has tucked away.

"My pleasure, Ghost. You got enough now?"

"Believe I do," Ghost says, but can't deny the nagging doubt he might be wrong. "Least I hope I do."

"Well good luck," Jenny says. "Get that girl back to her momma."

Ghost tips his hat to her again and leaves the little upper deck saloon. He hears Jenny grunting behind him and the sound of shoes being dragged across planking. A little ways down the deck, Ghost pauses and listens. Another grunt comes his way, followed by a loud splash.

"Rest in peace, Macky," Ghost says, thinking about the thirty splashes that preceded that one. Thirty men from Bacchus' krewe. One game for each of them. One loss for each man, too. And now Ghost's pockets are full enough he can attend Bacchus' game and get Namah and her mother and brothers out of New Orleans.

ဆၣ

The casino house looks like any other old plantation manor in New Orleans. Tall columns, fluted and flecked with moss and mildew, and chipped where Union bullets struck all those years ago. Back when the Southern Territory had the crazy idea to call itself the CSA and then really throw caution to the wind and open fire.

"Should have just settled it all with a game of cards," Ghost says to the night. He walks up the steps and shows his face to the boys there. Two of Bacchus' tough roosters, one white and one dark and each with a neck as thick as Ghost's leg. They stand aside, the sneers on their mugs hanging heavy like the air on a Louisiana spring day.

"I hear you been playin' well, Ghost," the white one says. "Word is, none of your games ends without you makin' a killin'."

Ghost pauses his step and stands across the threshold, one foot in and one still out. He turns to face the white man and gives him the one good eye he has left. He puts everything he has into the stare, aiming for as high a caliber as he can get. But with just one eye left, the trick falls flat and the heavy just keeps on sneering.

"Maybe try it on the dealer," he says. "If you make it to the table."

Ghost lifts a finger to his hat brim but switches to a different finger on the way. The doorman's sneer turns to snarl, and his partner chuckles.

"You asked for that one," the Negro says and laughs some more.

Ghost leaves the simple twins at the door and continues inside Bacchus' gambling house. In front of him, a high stair leads up from the foyer to a landing and balcony that circles around to the right. Ghost knows that right now Namah is up there somewhere being preened and polished for the game.

For a solid minute he stands there, breathing in the luxury and perfume. He smells the wine and hooch, the fancy feast laid out, all the scents of fine living and foul minds. He hates the gambling house, what it stands for and what it is. He hates it and always has. But most of all he hates Bacchus for making him party to what went on here, what has always gone on here.

Off to the left is the main parlor where the guests grab their nosh and mix drinks with dances and try to keep off one another's toes. To his right, under the balcony, is the doorway to the gaming room. A thick blue velvet curtain hangs in the entrance. Ghost hears the clicking of shuffled cards, the hoots and laughter, and once or twice a little groan.

It's time to change the way the cards fall in this town, he thinks, and steps through the heavy curtain.

ဆာ

The tables are laid out in a ring around the pit boss, a heavy with light skin and a dark suit, a perfect match for the one at the door, except this one has a brain in his head. Ghost holds back from sending him a finger. He knows the man and isn't ready to die. Not yet. So he waits while the pit boss approaches. He shows the man his billfold.

"Like to get in on the deb table tonight," Ghost says.

The pit boss raises an eyebrow and looks over Ghost's shoulder. Ghost waits like he did on the riverboat, knowing what's coming. On cue, Mr. Bacchus rolls his voice into the conversation like a boulder down a hillside.

"Ghost, I understand if you suffer from reduced vision these days. But surely you must see the error of your ways."

Ghost turns slow and keeps his hands clear and in sight the whole time. "I'm not here for any trouble, Mr. Bacchus. Just looking to get into the game. My money's good, isn't it?"

"Indeed, if it is money, it's good."

The pit boss holds out Ghost's billfold and Bacchus lifts it in his meaty fingers, weighing it like a slab of beef ready for the scale.

"So you're here to conduct business?"

"Yes, Mr. Bacchus. Just business, that and nothing more."

"Okay then, Ghost. But a condition. You see that man there?" Bacchus says and points to the table on the far edge of the room. Ghost turns his face fully to the side, bringing his good eye to bear. He sees a tall bird, the kind with more money than sense, but plenty of the latter still. Enough to earn him the money to charter an airship across territory lines from New York to New Orleans so he can play at Bacchus' deb table.

"What about him?" Ghost asks, half sure he knows the answer. He isn't wrong.

"Get him to go all in. That's the condition, Ghost. You can play, but if you fail to get my guest from the Eastern Seaboard to empty his pockets, then it'll be your pockets that end up empty. Your clothes, too.

"And," Bacchus adds, "your veins. Are we clear?"

"Sure thing, Mr. Bacchus. We're clear."

Ghost accepts his billfold back from his former employer and doesn't bat his eye when he sees the century note Bacchus palms and tucks into his jacket.

ℴ)Ↄ

Ghost takes his seat at the table. The house opens the match with an even money bet on a simple game of high card pull. Ghost and Mr. New York are joined by six other men, all with finer suits and hairstyles than Ghost has ever worn or ever will. He knows an act when he sees it. These birds are all planted by Bacchus, other attempts at getting the gentleman from the Eastern Seaboard to throw himself into the pot head first.

One by one the players take cards from the deck. One by one they turn them over. Ghost flips a Jack. New York shows a King. The others all flip low cards. The deal passes to New York and he calls for a hand of stud.

"Let's keep it simple for now, boys. Nothing wild but our hearts, hey?"

Ghost smiles at the man while the others sniff or just ignore his nonsense. He deals and Ghost lifts his cards.

Two sevens and an Ace high.

Bets go in and bets go up. Players go out.

Ghost wins the hand with his pair. New York folded at the last, leaving Ghost to call against one of Bacchus' dummies. The guy was sitting on a hand of junk, and if he could have kept from wincing every time he looked at his cards, or just stopped looking at them, Ghost might not have figured his bluff.

But the guy doesn't know cards, and Ghost makes him the first one he takes out.

One by one he eats them alive, just like he ate thirty more of Bacchus' krewe before this night, playing hard and sharp as a steel spike. The kind he'd like to drive into Bacchus' eye one day. Or his own brother's.

But Ghost doesn't spare too much time thinking about revenge. He's here to win, and to make sure the man from New York loses.

Everything.

"Deal goes to New York," Ghost says and passes the deck. The tall bird is down from where he started, but he's still sitting on more money than sense.

And he's still sitting on more than Ghost has in his billfold. The others are all out, but for one, a guy who actually knows his cards. At least he knows them enough not to bet on junk or give away a bluff before the call.

Two more hands and Bacchus' final patsy goes all in. Then Ghost shows his ladies full of fives and Bacchus' man goes out. New York loses with two pair, Aces and tens.

The bell rings and Bacchus steps up to the table.

"Two men left. So the time has arrived to reveal tonight's debutante prize."

Following Bacchus' cue, the pit boss brings Namah into the center of the room. She's finer than when Ghost saw her before. Her dark hair is all finger waves and glossy shine, and her round face is powdered like porcelain. Bacchus kept his promise. She looks the perfect angel, and Ghost knows she's been kept away from anything like corruption.

The shackle on her wrist and the chain the pit boss holds in his hand tell a different story.

New York has the deal. He calls a seven-card game and sends the cards out to play. Ghost checks the hole, sees two faces. Waits for the rest.

He's straightening while New York looks to be full of heart, just like Ghost's last game on the riverboat. Ghost chances a bet, raises once.

New York sees it, raises again. Ghost folds.

They play another hand. Ghost loses again.

New York passes the deal. Ghost calls a five-card favorite, slides the cards off the top. He answers New York's first raise with one of his own, then calls on the next. Ghost wins. Another deal, another win.

And then another. The deal passes and Ghost takes the next hand. And another after that. New York is sweating now. He checks his billfold, flashes eyes at Ghost, then at Namah.

"Will the house—will the house accept collateral to cover a bet?"

Ghost's ears prick up. So do his hackles.

Bacchus steps out of the ring of flappers, dandies, and dolls staring at the cards like they'll reveal the future.

"What type of collateral does the player propose?" Bacchus asks, eyeing New York with a hungry smile on his mug. Ghost waits, his cards face down in front of him. He knows what they are. He doesn't need to look. New York checks his hand, puts it down, lifts it and looks again.

"I—" he says. "I have a shipping concern here. At the port. The … the harbor master can confirm my ownership. It's the *Yak and Quail,* she berths on Pier 13."

Ghost sees a tear hang in New York's left eye when he gives Bacchus a nervous smile and says, "She's a real hauler."

Bacchus smiles. He nods. Ghost watches the man's fat fingers as they peel off notes from a roll in his hands.

One of those centuries is mine.

The bills hit the table. New York snatches them up and adds them to the pot.

"I call," he says and shows his cards. Three men, all in a row, crowns on their heads.

Ghost drops his chin then lifts it, sending an eye full of sorrow in New York's direction. One by one, he slides the cards across the table and turns them face up.

"Three letters, all the same," he says.

New York groans, or croaks. The man makes a sound Ghost has never heard before. And then he cries. He puts his face in his hands and falls out of his chair and cries on his knees.

Bacchus approaches and collects the bills he put down. He slides a key onto the table and Ghost picks it off the green felt surface.

"I do appreciate a man who pays his debts," Bacchus says. "Let this be the end of our rivalry, Ghost."

Ghost stands, says nothing. He walks by New York and goes to Namah. She's got that fire back in her eyes, and Ghost sees that she means to let it out on whoever dares touch her. He presents her with the key and nods at the exit. She takes the key, unlocks the chain that was looped through the cuff on her wrist, then she undoes the cuff and throws it on the floor.

Ghost feels the crowd. He feels Namah following him. She follows him out of the house and down the street to the sedan he won in his first game thirty days before.

Namah's mother and brothers wait in the sedan. They want to jump out, but Ghost told them to stay put, so put they stay. Ghost sees Namah to the car, opens the door.

"Thank you, Mr. Ghost," the mother says from the driver's seat, still clutching the wad of folding money he gave her last night. "Thank you from my heart. Thank you."

Ghost shakes his head. He closes the door and waves them away. Namah wasn't the first girl to stand in that house wearing jewelry that needs a key to come off. She was just the first one Ghost got free in time. She won't be the last.

Ghost has to get another bankroll in his pocket, and he's got thirty days to do it.

Peace Is Better

By Harry Turtledove

"Here we go again, Barbara," Bill Williamson said. "Ready to roll?"

Barbara Rasmussen nodded. From the left rear seat of the Mighty Mo, the sasquatch Governor of Jefferson watched his publicist's blond curls bob up and down above the back of the right front seat. "I sure am," she said. PR people never lacked for enthusiasm. That sometimes made them scary, but they needed it.

"Then we'll do it." Bill stepped on the gas. He stood nine feet two in his stocking feet, though he was much too hairy ever to have put on stockings. The back seat of a car as humongous as his '74 Caddy with the extra-long steering column let him drive for himself, which he enjoyed.

Yreka had been a state capital for sixty years now, but it was still a sleepy little place. Anyway, the government office building lay only a couple of blocks from the onramps to the I-5: Jefferson's backbone and, when you got right down to it, the whole Pacific Coast's.

He put pedal to the metal as soon as he swung onto the northbound Interstate. He didn't worry about 55, or about saving gas. Even at 55, the Mighty Mo's mileage was a joke. The Eldorado's engine was only a little smaller than a World War II fighter's. The beast weighed as much as a Messerschmitt-109, too, especially with him in it.

Fifteen minutes out of Yreka, he and Barbara rolled through Hilt, which was two gas stations and a Burger King. A moment later, Barbara said, "The old border between California and Oregon was somewhere right around here."

"Sure was." As if on cue, they passed a road sign that said WELCOME TO JACKSON COUNTY. Bill went on, "That was Oregon. Siskiyou, where we were, used to be in California. We don't miss Sacramento—"

"Or Salem," Barbara put in.

"Or Salem," Bill agreed. "And they don't miss us."

Another hour put them at Wolf Creek, where they got off the Interstate and onto Jefferson State Highway 71. No one ever called it that, though, not even to make Highway 71 Revisited jokes. "Here we are," Barbara said as they headed toward the ocean, "on the Gable Memorial Highway."

Now Bill was the one who nodded his big, shaggy head. Unless in the rear-view mirror, Barbara couldn't see that, so he said, "You betcha. If ever a politician delivered for his home town, Gilbert Gable was the guy. Without him, Port Orford wouldn't be much bigger than Hilt back there."

If not for Gilbert Gable, who became Governor of Jefferson in 1934, miles of the road across the mountains to Port Orford probably would still remain unpaved. If not for Gilbert Gable, the railroad probably wouldn't have gone through. If not for Gilbert Gable, the big breakwater that turned Port Orford probably would never have been built. If not for Gable and FDR and the WPA and the CCC and the other half-forgotten thickets of Depression-era initials ....

He died in the saddle, three days before Pearl Harbor. The papers called it acute indigestion. Bill had heard from Yreka old-timers that he drank like a fish. Drunk or sober, what he did lived after him. The highway and the railroad and the breakwater let Port Orford play its part in shipping men and weapons across the Pacific to fight Japan.

Thinking about that, Bill chuckled. "If not for Gilbert Gable," he said, "chances are we wouldn't be doing this photo op at the Port Orford Datsun dealership."

"Well, no," Barbara said. "If not for Gilbert Gable, chances are that Datsun dealership wouldn't be there. But it's a good photo op—and Mr. Fujita will be so proud for you to recognize him for all he's done."

"This is Jefferson. Everybody gets along here," Bill said. "That's what I told the Yeti Lama a month ago, and it's the truth. Even if we have to work at it sometimes, it is."

"He knew that before you told him. He wouldn't have wanted to visit Jefferson if he didn't." Barbara paused a moment, then went on in a smaller voice: "He's impressive, isn't he?"

"Yeah." Bill nodded again. He hadn't wanted to admit, even to himself, just how much the holy yeti exiled from Tibet had impressed him. "Me, I sold houses, I got a law degree, I went into politics. I shake hands, I slap backs, I twist arms, I make speeches. I've got a knack for it, like."

"You do a lot of good. I wouldn't want to work for you if you didn't."

"Thanks," Bill said, more because she sounded as if she meant it than for her words themselves. "But the Yeti Lama . . . When he says something, he *means* it. He means it all the way down. He's not a politician, talking to hear himself talk. You have to take him seriously. I don't know that I ever met anybody like that before."

"*Gravitas*," Barbara said.

"Huh?"

"*Gravitas*," she repeated. "It's a Latin word that means what you just said. I learned it a few years ago, watching the Nixon impeachment hearings. Barbara Jordan has it, too, and I'm not saying so because we've got the same name."

"No, you're not. And you're right. She does," Bill said.

On they went. A lot of the cars they shared the road with were little Japanese machines: Datsuns and Toyotas, Hondas and Mazdas. Their sales had boomed since gas went through the roof after the first oil embargo. To Bill, they all seemed the size of roller skates. If he hit one with the Mighty Mo, he could bring it home on his fender like a moose—if he noticed the accident at all.

Also on the road heading for Port Orford were smoke-spewing eighteen-wheelers hauling this, that, and the other thing to the harbor for export. More big trucks heading east carried what came into Port Orford, as well as lumber from the nearby mountainsides and fish and crabs pulled out of the Pacific. Gilbert Gable would have been proud had he lived to see it.

Once they came out of the mountains, the land fell swiftly toward the sea. The Mighty Mo's temperature gauge dropped, too. Bill watched it with relief. The massive car had been working hard. The Gable Memorial Highway joined US 101 a mile or so north of Port Orford. Bill drove south on the 101 almost to the breakwater-protected harbor. He turned left on Seventh and went a couple of blocks to Jackson.

At the corner there, an enormous American flag flew on a tall aluminum pole topped by a gilded eagle. An equally huge flag of Jefferson, pine-green with the gold-pan state seal in the middle, waved beneath it. They fluttered over the land of the free, the home of the brave, and an auto dealership whose sign proclaimed it FUJITA DATSUN OF PORT ORFORD in big red neon letters.

"We're here," Bill announced, pulling onto the lot. A local TV news van had already parked there. The cameraman was checking something on his equipment. The reporter, his hair sprayed so the breeze couldn't get playful, gabbed with a couple of newspapermen Bill recognized. He asked, "What time you got, Barbara?"

His publicist was left-handed, so she wore her watch on her right wrist. She raised it to her face to read the tiny women's-style dial. "It's a quarter to twelve, Governor," she answered.

"Good. Thanks. We aren't late." Bill parked two spaces from the news van. Not showing up on time here would have been embarrassing but not unforgivable. He'd really worried when he went to Eureka to meet the Yeti Lama. He'd made it—and the *Heiwa Maru*, the holy yeti's ship, came into port an hour late. Well, it let him and Barbara grab lunch.

He got out of the car and stretched. The Mighty Mo was as comfortable for a sasquatch as any car was likely to be, but standing up felt good just the same. He smiled at the shiny new Datsuns on the lot, mileage proudly painted on their windshields. He might have been able to drive some of the bigger ones from the trunk. A sleek little 280ZX? Not even that way—not a chance.

The hairsprayed reporter waved to him. "How's it going, Governor?"

"Not bad, Stu," Bill answered easily. "Always good to get out and let the people take a look at me."

"I guess it is," Stu said. "And there's a lot of you to look at." In a different tone of voice, that would have pissed Bill off. But the TV guy didn't mean anything by it. He was just talking to hear himself talk. Bill let it slide.

A car salesman walked up. He might have come right from Central Casting. Hair sprayed even stiffer than Stu's. Porn-actor mustache. Loud wide tie straight out of 1973. Gold Qiana shirt. Plaid jacket made from what looked like the hide of a particularly ugly furnished-apartment sofa. Polyester pants with white belt. White shoes. There he stood, a gladhanding cliché.

"Welcome to Fujita Datsun, Governor Williamson. Welcome to Port Orford. I'm Dave Jenkins." He stuck out his hand. As Bill carefully shook it, Jenkins went on, "Shall I tell Nobuo you're here?"

Like many of his kind, he had a gift for the obvious. But Bill had the politician's gift for putting up with such people. "That would be good," he said, and left it right there.

Dave Jenkins hurried away. He came back a deferential pace and a half behind the dealership's founder and owner. Nobuo Fujita was in his late sixties, short and skinny. His close-cropped gray hair receded at the temples. He wore a charcoal-gray suit, a white shirt, and a sober navy tie.

He looked more like a dentist than someone who sold cars. A dentist, though, wasn't likely to be carrying a sheathed samurai sword. Well, neither were most automobile dealers.

"Thank you for coming, Governor," he said in fluent but accented English. "You do this simple businessman too much honor."

Bill paused a moment to make sure the reporters and cameramen were in place. Seeing they were, he answered, "I don't think so, sir. After all, this is the tenth anniversary of the opening of Fujita Datsun. And you first visited Port Orford a lot longer ago than 1969."

"Oh, yes. That is true." Fujita's smile seemed embarrassed, even rueful. "It was thirty-seven years ago this month: September 9, 1942. I was warrant flying officer in Japanese Navy. The submarine *I-25* surfaces off coast of Jefferson at six in morning, just as it gets light. We have in watertight container on deck a Yokosuka E14Y1—a small floatplane. We assemble pieces from container. We fuel. We put on two 77-kilo incendiaries— big load on small plane. I am pilot. I get in with Petty Officer Shoji Okuda. We take off, fly east to America."

"And you came to Port Orford," Bill said.

Nobuo Fujita nodded, looking back across the years. "I came to Port Orford, yes," he said. "I saw harbor. I saw town. I dropped my bombs. I flew away as fast as I could. Antiaircraft guns started shooting. I was lucky. Only one small hole in left wing before I am out of range. I flew back to submarine. It picked up Okuda and me and plane and got away."

"I remember that. I was seven or eight then," the Governor said. "You set a ship on fire and burned down a warehouse. Everybody started hopping around like fleas on a hot griddle."

"It was small thing, nuisance thing," Fujita answered with a shrug. "On twenty-ninth of September, *I-25* came back. We took off again with more incendiaries. This time, orders were to start forest fire. I dropped bombs in Siskiyou National Forest, flew back, and escaped again."

"It must have been wet. No fires that time," Bill said. "No one here even knew about the second raid till you told us."

The old Japanese man shrugged once more. "It was war. You try what you can. But after war was over, I felt sad—Port Orford beautiful town. In 1962, I ask American embassy in Tokyo if I could see it in peace without being treated as war criminal. They graciously say yes."

"I should hope so!" Bill exclaimed. "Plenty of Americans who bombed Japan and Germany have visited those places." He thought of Hyman Apfelbaum, the Attorney General of Jefferson. He'd flown thirty-one missions over Europe in 1944. After the war, he toured Germany, getting by with his Yiddish. He got by so well, a local asked him if he'd been there before. He told the man no, that seeming preferable to *Only in a B-17.*

Nobuo Fujita shrugged yet again. "You won. We lost," he said bleakly. But then his smile returned. "When I came, everyone was so kind." He hefted the samurai sword. While the reporters scribbled shorthand in their notebooks, the TV cameraman swung in for a closeup. Fujita went on, "This was in my family four hundred years. I gave it to mayor of Port Orford to show I was sorry to attack town."

"But now you have it back again," Bill said.

"Now I have it back again, yes," Fujita said. "I worked for Nissan—parent company of Datsun cars. I learned English. When they told me they wanted dealership in Port Orford, I remembered friendly people and lovely country. I came in 1969. When I got here, kind mayor returned sword to me. I will be here for rest of my life. I am U.S. citizen since year before last."

"That's wonderful, Mr. Fujita. That's an American story. That's a *Jefferson* story," Bill said, looking into the TV camera. "You bombed Port Orford a long time ago, but now everybody here's glad to have you for a neighbor. A month ago, the Yeti Lama told me he wanted to see Jefferson because this is where everyone gets along, regardless of race or size."

"Yeti Lama very holy personage," Nobuo Fujita murmured.

"He was right," Bill said. "I'm nine feet-something, you're five feet-something, but so what? Once our countries were at war, but so what? Now we're at peace. And we'll stay that way, too, because peace is better."

"Peace is better," Fujita agreed. Bill Williamson draped a large, companionable arm over his shoulder. The still photographers snapped away.

The Traitor Moon

By Katherine L. Morse and David L. Drake

Dr. Sparky McTrowell stared glumly into her half-finished cider and then out the window of the Thistle & Heath Pub at the waxing moon. It had been nearly two months since she had received the news she had been awaiting for twelve years. It felt like she had been waiting a lifetime. Every sound and color flooded back to her of the moment she heard the news.

"Got 'im!" exclaimed the notorious airship pilot shaking the telegram in her fist.

"'Got whom, my dear?" Chief Inspector Erasmus Drake asked his fiancée as he looked up from his copy of The Sword Exercises Arranged for Military Instruction.

"My father's murderer," she replied flatly.

He was as utterly astonished by this statement as she was nonplussed. "Murderer? I thought he drank himself to death."

"Adam McTrowell was driven to drink by the thieving snake as surely as if he had poured every shot of whiskey himself."

"And does this thieving snake have a name?"

"Annunziato Venator," she growled, spitting out each of the ts and brandishing the yellow sheet of paper that read: GAMBLERS FRIEND #1 CONFIRMED EDINBURGH.

Reliable as ever, Angus Sutherland had identified Nunzio accurately. The Italian's flight instinct had proven more formidable than Angus' determination. Nunzio had gotten away clean by the time the telegram arrived.

Drake and McTrowell had cornered him outside Pitlochry nearly a month before, but he'd just wriggled out of their grasp by the light of the Harvest Moon, callously burning down a barn to cover his escape. Her Royal Majesty required Drake's services back in London, so he had returned while she spent the month laying a "trap line" across the highlands. She visited every town, village, pub, and farm from Moray Firth to the Firth of Lorn. Down one side of Loch Ness, Loch Oich, Loch Lochy, Loch Eil and Loch Linnhe, and up the other spreading the word that there was a reward for reliable information on Venator's whereabouts. But she didn't really want to trap him there; she wanted to drive him farther north. Although the lands now belonged to Clan Sutherland, it hadn't been a generation since it was Clan Mackay land, and the McTrowells were Mackay. She wanted him trapped in her homeland.

So now she was cooling her heels, literally, in the October cold in a pub in Inverness, perched at the crossroads, literally, of all the possible paths her quarry could take. Drake would arrive in the morning on the first train from Edinburgh. She had thought about going down to meet him in London and bringing back the air yacht, the *Peregrine*. A few days in the comfort and relative warmth of London would have been welcome, but she feared she might miss the signal that Venator had been found. If he slipped through this net, she knew she would never get another chance. So she waited and shivered and sipped her warm cider with only the approaching Blood Moon for company.

She stared at the eerily crisp shadows cast by the lunar light. She knew Venator was going to ground during the day and moving at night to avoid being seen. This behavior was conspicuously aberrant compared to the rest of the populace, but it would only help her find him if she could actually pick up a crumb of his trail. She knew the pattern to observe; she needed a sensor, or rather a net of sensors.

৪৩

Sparky stood on the platform, glaring furiously at her pocket watch as if it were the little gold device's fault that the train hadn't arrived yet. She positioned herself in the center of the platform to maximize her view of the disembarking passengers. Her diminutive height increased the challenge of spotting someone amongst the milling passengers and fading light. There, a brown bowler! No, it was a young man the right height, but skinny as a rail and barely old enough to shave. She looked in the direction of the locomotive. Surely Drake wouldn't have drawn attention to himself by traveling first class. And clearly he would have sent word if he weren't able to come. Despair snuck into the corner of her mind. Something more important in London had his attention; she was on her own; this wasn't his battle.

As she turned to re-enter the stationhouse she caught the flash of a leather coat in frantic motion at the back of the train near the cargo carriages. He was unloading a familiar set of crates and wooden components from a suspiciously unmarked rail car with the assistance of a handful of extraordinarily muscular young men. They were all wearing clothing obviously intended to look like civilian laborers, but they had all chosen clothing so consistent as to all be uniform in their appearance. She wanted to run to Drake, but kept her gait smoothly nonchalant so as to avoid drawing attention to the industrious activity. One of the "laborers," the one with the widest shoulders she'd ever seen on a man, handed the last crate down to Drake. The two shook hands. As the young man turned to climb back in the carriage, he spotted McTrowell approaching. He saluted crisply, re-boarded the train, and slid the door closed. The train whistle screamed and the train chugged away.

Erasmus collected Sparky into his embrace. "I brought you a present."

Trying to choke back a threatening tear, she replied lightly, "How could I not love a man who brings me our air yacht when I need it most? We really need to refurbish this thing. It's starting to show the miles."

"I know how it feels," he replied roguishly. He patted the nearest crate, musing, "I would have flown it up here, but that is your job. And I was not sure where I could land it without attracting attention."

"I don't even want to think about how many favors you called in to get the Royal Aerial Marines to deliver it."

"Her Majesty sends her regards," he whispered in her ear, "and asks that you keep this matter out of the broadsheets."

"You are the most brilliant man ever," she grinned.

"Yes, of course, my dear. But what have I done today to remind you of that fact?"

"The Scottish Highlands are vast and craggy. Searching them on foot or horseback is too time-consuming. I've been stewing about ways to track Venator. I had an idea and you've just brought me the last thing I need to make it work." She stood on her tiptoes to kiss him gratefully on the cheek. "Let's get this thing out of sight, and find an herbalist and some horse blankets."

“”

"What are you staring at, dear?" Sparky asked without taking her eyes off the controls of the Raptor-class air yacht as they ascended across Loch Shin. She was amazed at how well the small craft still handled despite all the crazy adventures she and Drake had already had in it. And it still came together neatly and air-worthy as ever despite being hauled up from London on the train.

"Those animals—over there—they look like yaks," Erasmus pointed below the *Peregrine* to a small herd of the shaggy creatures grazing languidly.

"They're Highland cattle, but the Scots sometimes just refer to them as hairy cows. You'd want a coat like that too if you had to survive the Highland winters."

"How do you suppose they would look at night covered in that foxfire concoction you brewed?" he quipped.

"Just about the time I think I really know you, you surprise me with the things that come out of your head," McTrowell chuckled.

“”

"Darling," Sparky implored Erasmus, "could I convince you to stay here out of sight with the *Peregrine*? I'm afraid you're just a little too British for these parts and I don't fancy explaining the airship."

The Chief Inspector considered the potential perils of the situation. He handed her his police whistle. "Use this if you get in trouble. And I mean *my* definition of trouble, not yours." He affected a stern and concerned expression to emphasize his point.

She reached up under the tartan arisaid covering her blouse and skirt, and tucked the whistle into a pocket. "Yes, dear."

∞೦೫

Sparky rapped sharply on the cottage door. "Hello, is anyone home?" she called, putting on her best impression of her Auntie Catherine's accent.

The old man who opened the door eyed her suspiciously. "What do you want, lass?"

"My name's Spar ... er, Czarina McTrowell." She waited for the significance of her last name to sink in. "I'm searching for the man who murdered my father."

"He's not here," he replied, raising a quizzical eyebrow.

"I apologize if I implied that he was. He's been seen in these parts, hiding in barns during the day and moving at night. I, um, a scientist friend of mine devised a way to track him. If you'll just put this in your barn just inside the door where it will be seen?"

"How is this blanket supposed to catch him? Is it some kind of trap?"

"No, but ... when he uses it and then moves on, he'll leave a faint trail that glows in the moonlight. We'll follow the trail."

"We?"

"My fiancé and I."

"One man and a small slip of a lass like you don't seem hardly enough to catch a murderer."

"It will have to be," she replied stonily.

The cottage's occupant stood staring at her without taking the proffered blanket. "What did you say your father's name was?"

"Adam McTrowell."

"McTrowell, you say?" He nodded and took the blanket. "Do you have more of these? I could give them to my neighbors and save you some time."

"Oh, thank you! That would be very helpful."

"And this murderer will leave a glowing trail like a will-o'-the-wisp?"

"Exactly."

ℝ℞

"We were fortunate that so many of your clansmen were willing to help with the distribution of the horse blankets," Erasmus commented to Sparky as they launched the Peregrine for the sixth time that day in the dim fading light of sunset. The wind at the edge of Scoury buffeted them with bitter cold and challenged their handling of the little airship. "I had expected the task of distributing them to take at least two days. Shall we return to Inverness for some well-deserved sleep?"

The airship pilot replied through chattering teeth, "We should get back south toward Loch Shin. The full moon is tonight. If he moves, we can catch him."

"You are exhausted. Are you sure flying at night in your state is safe?"

"Tonight we own the night and the sky. Annunziato Venator doesn't stand a chance."

He could see it was futile to try to dissuade her.

ℝ℞

"There!" Drake shouted, pointing at a tiny dot on the ground that looked like a firefly from the air. Sparky banked the Peregrine to come back toward the faint glow.

"Do you see any more?"

"Yes. Stay on your current heading," he replied. "Wait, what is that?"

"I can't look now. What does it look like?"

"It's a light following the trail, but it looks like a flame, maybe a torch." The Chief Inspector watched for a moment longer. "Dear, I think you had better bring the Peregrine around for another pass. You need to see this."

Sparky did as Erasmus suggested, flying as slowly as possible. Tempted though she was, she dared not descend for fear that the sound would alert her prey. The ethereal scene that unfolded below looked like a dance of insects. The firefly's luminous trail flitted with relative purpose. The path of the torch more resembled that of an ant or bee. It followed the firefly at a discreet distance before veering off to another faint light, probably the cottage of another clansman. The ant was joined by another. The pair of ants picked up the firefly's trail again. Half an hour later, one of the ants veered off, collecting another before rejoining the pursuit.

After an hour of this dance with the ants gaining more forces, the firefly's light disappeared. Venator must have ducked into another barn. The ants closed in. The firefly reappeared, glowing more brightly and really flying this time. Venator had not been clever enough to realize the trap of the horse blankets soaked in foxfire, but clearly now understood that he was being hunted. McTrowell opened the throttle on the Peregrine. Drake was puzzled, "Are you not going to follow the pursuit?"

"I know where they're driving him," McTrowell replied through clenched teeth.

"Where?"

"Kearvaig at Cape Wrath."

"Well, you Scots are certainly a poetic lot."

೫೧೪

The Chief Inspector surveyed the assembled clanspeople, the light of their torches and the full moon reflecting off the polished blades of freshly sharpened claymores. He had no doubt they intended to truly make it a hunter's moon. "My dear, this is not the way."

"These are my people and we will have our due."

"He has committed at least a dozen crimes since we flushed him out of that barn a month ago: the stolen horse, the barn burned to cover his escape last month, even the dead dog. I will walk right into that shieling and arrest him." He produced his manacles to emphasize his point.

She looked at his restraints and shook her head. "That is the law; it is not justice."

"I am a sworn officer of Her Royal Majesty. I cannot stand by and let this transpire."

"Then do not. Walk away."

"You know I cannot."

"If it will assuage your conscience, I can have my cousin Graham here," she pointed to a mountain of a man who was testing his skills with his broadsword as easily as Drake would wield a foil, "carry you away."

They stared implacably into each other's eyes by the light of the Blood Moon.

The Rise of the Dragonfly

By Anthony Francis

"If she's expelled, I resign," Dean Navid Singhal said. The Chancellor's eyebrow raised, but Navid stood his ground. "The cadet was acting on orders, and besides, this is Liberation Academy. We'll not hand out discharge papers the moment a student awakes in hospital."

"No, no, of course not," the Chancellor said, lifting her glasses and drawing a hand over her face. "Any accused must have a chance to acquit themselves; therefore, a disciplinary hearing must be called—if it *should* be called. Acting on orders, you say?"

"Yes," Navid said, his steely gaze betraying none of his nervousness. "I asked Cadet Willstone to investigate some, ah, malfeasance, and her unauthorized flight has the hallmarks of her bold style. Unfortunately, prior to her report, the crash rendered her unconscious—"

"The crash put her in a *coma!*" the Chancellor barked, dark eyes boring into him. Rumor had it she'd been a nun—and her legendary glare could make even a Dean feel like a scolded schoolchild. "Why, sir, did you send a cadet investigating in the first place?"

"Ah, that," Navid said—and smiled confidently. "I'm not at liberty to say."

෨෬

Jeremiah Willstone's eyes opened slowly. A wood slat ceiling sloped away overhead.

After a few relaxed breaths, she looked around. She was in a gown, in bed, in hospital. Perhaps a dozen beds in the ward, less than half filled, mostly with older patients, sleeping silent, many with spiderwork scars over them—Lichtenburg figures, the kind left by early blasters.

She knew this. This was a veteran's ward—a *coma* ward.

Jeremiah sat bolt upright. The room swam. Comas could last for *years*. Frantically she searched for a mirror, and found one in the shiny surface of a Mechanical nurse rolling towards her, seeking in the distorted reflection of her face the answer to the question: "How long?"

"You have been un-con-scious for thir-ty days."

"A month!" Jeremiah said, horror tingling down to her very toes. She was fighting self-replicating monsters that could possess everything from a rat to a person—godknows how large a colony could have grown in a month! She hopped down. "I must report to Navid at once!"

"Please re-lax. You may be weak. You might fall," the Mechanical said, firmly taking her arm just above the elbow and trying to guide her back to bed. "I have call-ed a phy-si-cian. She will be here short-ly."

Jeremiah grimaced, quickly glanced over the Mechanical, then reached up with her free arm, feeling just above its elbow joint. She found what she wanted, clamped her fingers, squeezed and twisted—and the Mechanical's entire forearm came away in her hand.

"Hold this," Jeremiah said, plopping the forearm in the Mechanical's other hand. She whirled to action, as was her habit, but the room decided to join in, and Jeremiah grabbed the Mechanical for support. Quickly, though, she found a satchel she presumed was hers. "Ah."

"Please do not in-jure your-self," the Mechanical protested.

"I'll risk injury," Jeremiah said, extracting her cadet blues, "to save the world."

80Q3

Mere moments after the Chancellor's departure, Navid's door burst back open, Professor Dyson storming in without the courtesy of a knock—therefore catapulting him into the middle of a most confidential conference ... with Navid's most extraordinary former student.

"She looked *infuriated*! You're playing a dangerous game, Navid," Dyson said, striding forward, even as his voice lost steam. "Mark my word, you've brought the Chancellor's eye down on you, and it ... will have repercussions ... throughout the department ..."

Dyson's mouth fell open, and Navid smiled, savoring the moment. Then, introductions.

"No doubt it will. Professor Dyson, good to see you. We were just discussing whether to take you into confidence," Navid said, extending his hand towards his other, more spectacular visitor. "I believe you've already met *Commander* Willstone ... back when she was a cadet."

Dyson stared openly at a future Jeremiah, decked out in a full gold Expeditionary tailcoat ... with great brass dragonfly wings protruding from her back. Wordlessly, she let the brass wing covers fold back ... and the great faery wings unfurled into a gossamer rainbow.

"Ah yes," Commander Willstone said, smiling sidelong at Navid: she had to be loving this. "Professor Dyson, Foreign Biology, ah, 301, wasn't it? Taking your class has served me in good stead, though it did leave me with a touch of xenophobia. Still, good to see you again—"

"Time travel," Dyson said, staring at her outstretched hand. "Not possible."

"I assure you," Navid said, glancing at a wizened finger on his mantle, "it is."

"Willstone, I just saw you in hospital not *two days ago*," Dyson said. "As a cadet—"

"And shall see me as one again," the Commander said. "Come out of there—*cadet*!"

ꙮ

Jeremiah froze. There was *no way* that brass-winged impostor could have seen her in this priest-hole Navid had shown her; yet even in the camera obscura projection from the pinhole, the strange creature seemed to be staring *straight at her.* Reluctantly, Jeremiah stepped out.

Dead-on, the thing was worse: a not-mirrored mirror, older—and those wings!

"What were you doing skulking back there, cadet?" Navid said sternly.

"Sir, practicing discretion, as you advised, sir," Jeremiah said, on autopilot, her eyes taking in the both of them, jealously noting their close collegial distance around Navid's desk! Clearly her mentor trusted this ... this *doppelganger* more than *her!* "I—I don't understand—"

"Stay calm, Cadet," the impostor said, raising her hands, even as she stepped forward and brass wing covers bobbed, but, God, that face, more lines, wings of faery fire, erupting from that tailcoat, and *they'd called her Commander*—gently, her twin said, "Please, little Dragonfly—"

Hearing a name she only wrote *in her own diary*, Jeremiah integrated all the facts at once. Her little stunt *had* washed her out of the Falconry—but in some desperate future, she had found another way to get wings—by betraying her body to Foreign monsters!

"*Trrraitor!*" she screamed, drawing her *Kathodenstrahl* and firing in one swift motion. Her future, Foreign-infected self caught the aetheric beam with one hand, then, raising the other, aglow with the horrible light of some Foreign power, she released—

∏

—a bolt of energy, which caught the cadet amidships. She crumpled, *Kathodenstrahl* falling from her hand, but the elder Jeremiah darted forward, catching her younger self in those wing covers, cupping them like a cradle, slowly lowering the cadet to the ground.

The *Kathodenstrahl* sparked as its tubes cracked, and Jeremiah cursed.

"Blood of the Queen," she said. "Don't remember breaking that one—"

"What in God's name happened to you," Dyson said. "Some Foreign infection—"

"Symbiosis, with the Burning Scarab," Jeremiah said. "Advanced creatures, if I do say so myself." Examining her own younger head, she smiled. "Good to see you at last, Dragonfly." At Navid's puzzled look, she said, "I rarely get a chance to look at myself."

"What about in the mirror?" Navid asked curiously.

"Mirrors don't reflect X-Rays or aetheric flux," Jeremiah said, turning her younger face back and forth with a strange wonder. "They're no good, at least to my Scarab eyes. I've never really gotten a good look at myself ... at least, not from the outside."

"Scarab eyes? That's deeper than symbiosis," Dyson said. "Sounds like *parasitism*—"

"Whatever it sounds like, I didn't know it was in my future," Jeremiah snapped, even as she carefully cradled her younger head in her older hands. "Gentlemen, I'm afraid I must attempt a memory purge. Fortunately ... I know this brain inside and out."

And before Navid could speak, power surged between Jeremiah's fingers. Her younger head twitched, her cadet body bowed, then relaxed into her older hands—but the whole room seemed to flicker, shifting subtly, becoming unfamiliar—an eerie sense of *jamais vu.*

"Did you perceive a shift?" Dyson asked, turning. "As if everything rearranged—"

"Temporal heterodyning—erasing those memories changed something. Commander!" Navid slammed his fist down, wincing at the jolt to the prosthetic finger he'd gained on *his* time travel misadventure. "You're far past cadet! Must I *continue* to chide you for recklessness?"

"A calculated risk. A small temporal shift is better than a nasty paradox," Jeremiah said. They helped her lay her younger self out on the sofa, then turned to business. "Sir, we've tracked another incursion of the gear plague, gathering here, or perhaps about a month back—"

"I had you investigating it," Navid said, "but you, for some reason, stole some wings—"

"And crashed them," Jeremiah said distantly. "I ... recall. That's why I washed out—"

"You did it for the cause," Navid said. "What did your younger self have to report?"

"I ... don't remember," Jeremiah said. "Oh, bugger me! I think I just erased it!"

"We could check in on her compatriot," Dyson said. "The Lady Westenhoq—"

"I have a better idea," Jeremiah said, standing. "Why don't I check in on *myself?*"

"Jeremiah," Navid warned. "Recall *you* warned *me* about meddling with the past!"

"I'll be discreet." Jeremiah tapped a date on her springback bracer. "Back in a flash."

໓໕

The hooded figure advanced on the fallen cadet's prone form. Within the steel mask, what was left of its face smiled. *Yes, yes, this was the one that they'd sought earlier, the human with the strange signature, the mechanic with the needed skills, the cadet they suspected—*

With a dazzling flash, a *second* copy of the cadet appeared, shouting, "Not so fast!"

—of being a time traveler. Within the steel mask, the figure said: "Oh, bollocks!"

The cadet, in full Expeditionary garb, leapt forward over her fallen self, planting her legs astride those broken wings and unslinging a long thermionic weapon with a great brass bell on the end—a blunderblast! The hooded figure darted aside, firing its shockgun—

—but the blast was absorbed by copper shields, filigree ovals flipping before the cadet even as gossamer blossomed behind, no, not shields, *wing covers*, so familiar, that filigree, even as wings charged with power—the aetheric power of that Foreign scourge, the Burning Scarab!

"Bollocks! Bollocks! Bollocks!" cried the running figure, as blasts rained from behind.

80C8

Professor Dyson stepped out of Navid's office to find the Chancellor—and the Baron.

"Good God," he said, as shocked as a first year stumbling out of a bar to find a proctor.

"God?" growled Lord Christopherson, Fifth Baron Abinger, a very tall man—and the Academy's biggest donor. "God has little to do with my ill niece laid out unconscious in hospital for a month, or tottering out of bed straight to the man who put her in danger in the first place—"

"Which you know because you tracked her locator here, I take it," Dyson said, glancing at the Chancellor. They'd hoped to sneak her back to the infirmary, but—"Sir. Your 'ill niece' is a capable and remarkable woman, and as for putting her in danger, *she's* the one who—"

"Listen to me carefully, man," the Baron said, leaning down over Dyson, pointing an enormous finger in his face. "Foreigners have *eaten* our family. We lost her sister. Her mother. Her aunt, my wife! Not even a grandmother or a cousin! Jeremiah is literally *all I have left*!"

Professor Dyson's mouth remained hanging open: the huge man had a valid point.

"Wait here, your Lordship," the Chancellor said. "I'll get to the bottom of this."

80C8

Minutes later, Navid found himself wondering whether a man could literally wilt.

"—only to find Cadet Willstone laid out like a doll!" the Chancellor roared at him, glaring with those blazing black eyes, hand waving at the aforementioned unconscious cadet. "I find myself forced to question your relationship with this young woman—"

"That's egregious," Navid said. "The Comm—beg pardon, the Cadet and I do have an unusually close relationship, but it is completely—" and then Commander Willstone appeared in a bright flash, a strange gadget in her hand, and Navid finished: "—absurd."

"The blackguard eluded me, but he dropped this," Jeremiah said, handing the gadget to Navid, even as he stared in horror at the Chancellor, who in turn stared at Jeremiah's wings. Jeremiah said: "This is probably better handled by my younger self—"

"Younger self," the Chancellor muttered, and Jeremiah whirled, her turn for shock.

"Oh my!" she said. "Sir, I must protest! The more people you bring into confidence—"

"The more dangerous it becomes," Navid finished for her, inspecting the strange gadget. "I won't make a habit of it—oh my." He ran his finger over the engraving he'd found, then glanced at the Commander's wings. "Better handled by your younger self, indeed—"

"Younger self," the Chancellor repeated. "And no twin, sister, cousin, or even aunt—"

"I...do have an aunt, ma'am," Jeremiah corrected kindly. "Right now, about your age."

"Right now," the Chancellor repeated, blinking those piercing black eyes. A pounding came from the secretary's office, and the Chancellor shook her head and hissed: "I understand! But right now, the Fifth Baron Abinger is about to break down that door to get to you!"

"My uncle?" Jeremiah squeaked. Her wings twitched. "He can't see me like this!"

"Go," Navid commanded, hiding the gadget. "We have the matter well in hand."

Jeremiah stabbed at her bracer and disappeared in a flare—right as the Baron burst in.

The giant man stood frozen in the doorway. "Did ... you perceive a golden flash?"

ℰℭ

Groggily, Jeremiah blinked to awareness: on a couch, in Navid's office. Professor Dyson and the Chancellor were there, *oh, bugger me*, she'd cocked this one up with that theft. *Wait ... hadn't there been a crash? Hadn't she been in hospital?* She muttered, "What the devil—"

"Well," Navid began, as if answering a proffered question not her own.

"Mya!" cried her uncle, pushing his giant frame between Dyson and the Chancellor.

"Uncle!" Jeremiah squeaked, quite a high register, most unsoldierly! "I—uh—what?"

"What? *What?* The Falconry *grounded* you, yet you stole a set of wings and promptly *crashed* them, ending up in a coma for a *month*, that's what!" the Baron roared. "If there's any sense to the turning of the world, you'll be promptly expelled—and I will take you home!"

Jeremiah stared at her uncle in horror. It was all true. What had she to say?

"Chancellor, I repeat what I said," Navid said. "If she's expelled, I resign."

"I concur," said Professor Dyson. "I would also be forced to tender my—"

"Then *I'd* be forced," the Baron growled, "to pull *whatever strings I had to—*"

"If she's forcibly withdrawn," the Chancellor said, eyes flashing, "I resign too!"

Sudden silence. The Baron glared at the Chancellor with the snarl of a tiger.

"Precisely what medicine do you all have me on?" Jeremiah said suspiciously.

"*Sirs and ma'am*, what medicine am I on, *sirs and ma'am*," Navid corrected.

"Oh! I," Jeremiah spluttered. She *was* still a cadet! "Sirs and ma'am, I—"

"She missed a month of term," the Baron said icily. "By the rules of the Academy—"

"By the rules," the Chancellor said, "I have a great deal of discretion dealing with—"

"It's not unheard of," Navid said, "for students to undergo an accelerated program—"

"Transfers, for example," Professor Dyson said. "I will step up and tutor her myself—"

"You...ridiculous...*educators*!" the Baron roared. "You may think war is a classroom problem, and applaud solutions based on cleverness, but I fight on the front lines of the war for the planet, and a general cannot afford to encourage recklessness that leads to *failure*!"

Jeremiah swung her feet off the couch and planted them on the floor.

"Failure, sir?" Still unsure whether she was hallucinating, Jeremiah had lain patiently, listening to her fate being decided; but the word "failure" was a backbreaking straw. The room swam, but she stood to attention. "Sir, I dispute that, most strongly, sir. My mission was a success."

The four were silent, but then Navid asked sharply, "But you failed to—"

"Capture my quarry, sir?" Jeremiah said—and cheekily raised an eyebrow. "Sir, when I first encountered these creatures, my fellow cadet Erskine's life was in immediate danger—but I recruited one cadet, two proctors, and sounded a campus-wide alarm. With no-one at risk, I'm curious as to why you thought I planned to take on an unknown force alone—sir."

"I—" Navid said, his mouth hanging open. "Cadet, I—what *was* your mission?"

"Reconnaissance," the Baron said. The giant man gritted his teeth, alternately glaring at Navid—and looking at Jeremiah in wonder. "You didn't know what you were facing—so stole some wings and darted over to check? You still could have assembled a full sortie—"

"Sir, there was no time, sir," Jeremiah said, stiffly at attention, not looking her uncle in the eye. "Sir, I had devised a means of tracking the creatures, but when the Lady Westenhoq applied my scanning profile to our locator network, our foe fled the city like rats, sir—"

"The scanning profile *you* devised," the Baron muttered. "And they fled—"

"So we lost them," Navid said. "Our foe went to ground—"

"Sir, no, sir. I suspected diversionary tactics, so I directed the Lady to analyze their movements, and she found a likely leader. I decided to fly a mission to scout out this hypothesized general and implant a tracking module—and I succeeded. Sir."

The room was silent for a moment—and the Baron spoke.

"You thwarted a Foreign Incursion," the Baron said. His body puffed with pride—but his eyes brimmed with unshed tears. "Discovered a Foreign foe, cleared the city of it, tracked down the leader, and are now planning to run him to ground ... even though it nearly killed you."

"Sir, I," Jeremiah said—then met his eye. "Uncle, I'm trying to honor my—"

"And have done so," the Baron said, drawing a breath. "Well done, Cadet."

Resigned, he turned on his heel; moments later, the door slammed behind him.

"Don't worry, I'll deal with him," the Chancellor said, following the Baron. She paused at the door, glanced back, then shook her head. "The less I know about this affair, the better. Carry on, gentlemen—and gentlewoman—of Liberation Academy; carry on."

"Well, Co—Cadet," Navid said, holding up a strange gadget. "I'm told your memory might be addled—but you were bringing this to me when you had your accident. You'll quickly see you're the right person to follow this lead. Care to resume the hunt— with a bit more care?"

"Sir, with gratitude, sir," Jeremiah said, taking the shiny gadget; she didn't recognize it, but it was engraved with a curious clue, something she did recognize: the name of Erskine, her fellow cadet—and lover. "Sir, with gratitude—I'm back on the case."

The Honorable Eddy

By Kirsten Weiss

May, 1849
San Francisco

There's a lot I'll do for my country—face hostile Indians, battle sinister occultists and mechanical contraptions, even lay down my life. But the Honorable Eduardo Alberto Del Castillo Cabeza de Vaca had me about beat. As the benevolent emperor of the tiny South American kingdom of Neruda, the gentleman had determined that his country's fortunes would improve if he returned with a ship full of gold from the California hills.

The United States government lost an ambassador during Neruda's last revolution. The body still hasn't been found. In a moving letter, the current US ambassador to Neruda pleaded he might have a fighting chance at returning to the States alive if we kept Eduardo safe and happy. All we had to do was keep the Emperor from pitching into a ravine or being slaughtered by irate miners.

Since my partner, Agent Sterling, and I were in San Francisco, preparing for a journey east, we got stuck with the job. Or rather, I did. The Honorable Eduardo had taken an instant dislike to my partner. Eddy didn't like competition when it came to the gentler sex. He didn't much care for gold prospecting either, preferring to dally in San Francisco's less salubrious entertainment establishments.

And so I found myself, watching another sunrise above a cluster of masted ships. Eye blackened, lip fat, and attire rum-soaked, I dragged the Honorable Eduardo back to his honorable hotel. The Honorable gentleman did not hold his liquor well, and during these periods, enjoyed insulting the female relatives of his fellow drinkers.

Now, I'm the sort who prefers the quiet life. Give me a laboratory and some gears and I'm set for the night. Don't get me wrong, I'm not one to shy from a good dust-up, but this was my fifth brawl in as many nights, and if I lost a tooth on one of these adventures, I'd have no chance with the ladies at all.

This had to stop.

My partner thought my predicament funny. Getting no sympathy from that quarter, I hauled my carcass to Mrs. Watson's boarding house and to the one person more desperate to leave the boomtown than I.

Miss Sensibility Grey sat at breakfast, her dark hair piled on her head, an uneaten plate of ham and eggs congealing on the blue checked tablecloth. We were fixed to travel together to the States along with her minder, Miss Algrave. I was looking forward to nights beneath the stars with both the fair maidens. And Sterling.

"Good morning, Miss Grey." I dropped my hat onto the long table.

"Mr. Crane." She set down her mug of tea. "Good gad. Have you been in an altercation?"

"Nope, in a fight." I grinned. I knew what *altercation* meant, and she knew I knew.

She snorted. "You and Mr. Sterling are too quick to engage in fisticuffs."

"Ah, but I wasn't with Mr. Sterling."

She looked up.

"Are you going to eat those eggs?" I asked.

"No." She shoved the plate across the table to me.

I dug in and waited for her to ask about my bruises.

One of Miss Grey's sweeper mechanicals bumped into my booted foot, chirped, and turned, bustling off.

Miss Grey sipped her tea.

"Aren't you curious?" I finally asked.

"I assume you were injured in the course of another secret assignment, which has delayed our journey from San Francisco. Again."

My problems with Eduardo were the latest in a string of delays preventing Miss Grey from taking her place in Washington as a government scientist. "Frisco hasn't been that bad, has it?" I asked.

"I have no workshop, and most of my tools and mechanicals have been shipped east. If I leave the house, people hiss at me on the street."

In short, the poor thing was bored. And why wouldn't she be? Trapped inside this boarding house for months, waiting to move on, no problems for her agile mind to tackle ... I resolved to lay my difficulty at her feet.

"Unfortunately," I said, "you're right, though the mission's not that secret. I'm stuck protecting a very important person from South America, and he's been dragging me through every gambling hell and, er, establishment in San Francisco. The worst of it is, there's no end in sight. We're supposed to deliver him to the gold country, but the man doesn't want to leave town. I think he's figured out gold mining requires actual work."

Miss Grey straightened her already impeccable posture. "Are you telling me that one man's whim tethers us to San Francisco?"

"That and the US Government."

"To perdition with the US Government! What sort of man is he?"

"Rich and spoiled. He runs a bunkum country down south."

"Then you must make him want to leave town."

I snorted. "Easier said than done."

"Is it? I can think of five methods off the top of my head."

I pondered that and shoveled in more eggs. In my time as a special agent, I'd pushed and pulled men into doing all manner of things against their inclinations. Surely I could manipulate one, simple tin-pot dictator. A scheme took shape. "Miss Grey, you have motivated me, and I owe you a debt. Why, the answer's obvious!"

"It is?" She looked at me, disbelieving.

"If you can think of five, I can think of seven ways to encourage the man to move on."

"And what is your plan?"

"I'll scare him off."

"I'm not certain—"

"And in repayment for your brilliant bit of inspiration, I'll bring the man here, so you can get an eyeful." That should liven up her dreary day.

"But—"

"No, no, don't thank me." I rose from the bench. "You've got the Muses beat by a mile, Miss Grey."

"I don't think—"

I hurried off to make my arrangements. Obvious. Obvious! What struck primal fear into the hearts of men? Indian attacks. I'd seen the bravest men go weak at the knees at the mention. Now the local native population was peaceable, and as a thank-you-for-your-good-manners, had been pretty well wiped out between the Spaniards and Argonauts. But Eduardo-By-Your-Honor didn't know that. I had an Ohlone friend who owed me a favor. Showing his war paint in San Francisco would put him at considerable risk, but if I could get Eduardo out of San Francisco … yes, a plan was taking form.

But first I'd keep my promise to Miss Grey, poor thing.

And I did keep it. It wasn't hard to convince Eduardo to pay a visit to the famous lady inventor who'd set San Francisco on fire. Literally. (In fairness, Miss Grey had not set the town on fire, and had been instrumental in preventing the flames from spreading. But crowds can be unreasoning in the face of disaster.)

Late the next afternoon, Eduardo rapped on the boardinghouse door, his chest puffed like a prize rooster's, his dark, mutton-chop whiskers razoring his cheeks.

I swung it open for him and bowed. "Your Highness."

Missing the irony, he swaggered into the foyer, his sword clanking against the coat tree.

I spotted Miss Grey alone, in the parlor, and motioned him inside. A sweeper mechanical bustled about her feet, and Eduardo swooped down upon it. "But this! This is remarkable!

And you must be the oh, so brilliant lady inventor." He lifted her hand and bowed low over it.

Miss Grey's jade eyes narrowed.

"Honorable Eduardo Alberto Del Castillo Cabeza de Vaca," I said, "may I introduce you to Miss Grey?"

"*Mucho gusto*," he said.

"*Igualmente*," she replied and proceeded to rattle off a Tarantella of Spanish.

His brows lifted. "Beauty and brains. But of course, by your miraculous inventions I knew you were a lady of intelligence. I did not realize you also spoke Spanish."

"Though my father was British, I was raised in Lima," she said.

"Ah." He appeared discomfited. "So you're the little lady who burned down San Francisco."

"What an absurd thing to say. I did not burn down San Francisco. It was only a few square blocks and the wharf area, and I had nothing to do with it. Mostly."

His head reared back.

"And you?" she continued. "I would think a ruler's proper place would be in his country, ruling, not gallivanting about the California Territory."

"My country is a poor one, and small. If I can replenish its coffers with gold, I shall be the greatest emperor my nation has seen."

"And your nation has seen quite a few," she said. "Five in the last dozen years, no?"

He snapped his heels together and bowed. "That is true. What marvels you could create for me there. Return with me, Miss Grey. I shall build you a proper lab, the best in the Americas."

She cocked her head, and for a moment I feared she might be considering it. But her good sense asserted itself. "What a gracious offer, but I cannot accept."

"I am devastated." He laid a hand across his heart and turned to me. "We should not interfere with this good lady's work any longer." He bowed to her. "I have heard much of your creations. And if one happened to get loose and set a fire—"

"One did not," she said.

"But if one had, I should forgive it. These Americans, they do not understand true genius." His lip curled. "My offer stands, Miss Grey." Bowing low, he swept from the room.

"See what I'm dealing with?" I muttered.

"Mr. Crane, I do not think—"

"No time. Where the Honorable Eddy goes, I go." I hurried outside and found him striding into a hell, where he bought drinks for all. And that was this fellow's other irritating habit. He was free with silver, but as Emperor, he never carried any. His lackeys were expected to pay for him, and that meant I had to foot the bill. Fortunately, the US Army fort nearby had orders to recompense me, but their patience with the Honorable Eddy was wearing thin.

The next day, I set my plan in motion. I baited him with a hunting party and an aether gun my partner had confiscated from Miss Grey. Eduardo agreed, enthusiastically, and we rode south. He practiced with the aether weapon, shooting branches off the oaks.

Zzzt! Crash!

He was a deuced good shot. I admit I was growing a trifle nervous on my fellow conspirator's behalf.

But my pal, Nightfoot, was a pro. I'd just borrowed the weapon from Eduardo, as planned, when Nightfoot dropped from an oak, shrieking like a dozen outraged braves.

The Honorable Eddy's horse reared, dumping him unceremoniously to the leaf-strewn ground.

Nightfoot was on the Emperor before I could react. It was a good thing we were on the same side. He gripped old Eddy's hair and yanked his head back, the sharp edge of a knife poised at the Honorable's hairline.

"That's no way to treat a friend of the old Chief," the Honorable said in a flawless rendition of the Ohlone dialect.

I nearly fell from my saddle.

Startled, Nightfoot released his grip of the man's hair. And to my horror, fifteen minutes later the two were chatting like long-lost Army pals.

Nightfoot didn't give me away, thank heaven. But he did slap my shoulder harder than necessary when we parted, pledging fidelity.

We rode on, killing a wild pig or three with Miss Grey's device, and then returned to San Francisco for another demonic night of carousing.

The next morning, I staggered to the boarding house, stopping only to lose my breakfast beside a watering trough.

Miss Grey sat at the long table, staring morosely at a rasher of bacon.

Stomach roiling, I collapsed onto a bench across from her. "We're sunk."

"I was afraid your plan wouldn't work." She turned a mug of tea between her slim hands. "What happened?"

I told her the whole, sorry tale. "So those other ideas of yours ... Care to share them?"

She cocked her head. "It might be easiest if I speak to the man myself."

"I'll arrange it."

Well, the Honorable was over the moon about the aether weapon and wanted one of his own. He quickly agreed to another visit to Miss Grey.

He swaggered into the parlor, as full of himself as someone who'd slaughtered three wild pigs with an aether gun can be. "Miss Grey, your reputation has not been exaggerated. You are a lady of true genius. For the defense of my nation I intend to purchase one thousand of your aether weapons."

She smiled. "A significant purchase indeed. But first, can you tell me which nation you intend to purchase them for?"

"On behalf of Neruda, of course!"

"I do not think so, sir. Let us end this charade now. You may well have made yourself an emperor of Neruda, but you are as American as Mr. Crane. And I do not believe the United States government will view your depredations on their courtesy or their purse kindly. Now why have you really come to the California Territory?"

He opened his mouth, closed it.

I stared. "American?"

"Your report of his knowledge of the local Indian dialect only confirmed what I suspected. Neruda is a small nation and an unstable one. Leaders come and go as regularly as the changing seasons. If he is indeed—or was—its so-called Emperor, then I warrant he will not be for much longer. Your government has nothing to gain by hosting him."

The Honorable went white.

I rubbed my face. "But ... but ... the Ambassador's letter!"

She waved her hands. "Ambassadors! What sort of man is appointed ambassador to a country the size of Neruda, where the only resource is an emerald mine?"

I had a sickening feeling she'd tell me.

"I'll tell you," she said. "The sort of person who plans to become the place's next Emperor. That is how you rose to power, Mr. Eduardo, is it not?"

Eddy didn't respond.

"That's not true," I said. "Our last ambassador to Neruda ... disappeared during the revolution." I folded onto a chair and rubbed my temple. It was true. I pointed at the man. "You're under arrest."

"Under arrest?" He gave a Kentucky-bluegrass yelp. "What for?"

"I'll think of something." But here's the rub. No one likes to learn they've been made a fool of, least of all the Army's top brass. Eddy would spend time in the stockade, but my superiors weren't going to look kindly on me either.

"Or ..." Miss Grey began.

"Or?" I asked.

"This gentleman can write a letter stating his intention to catch the soonest ship home, and disappear."

"I ain't going back," the Honorable said.

"Then return to your old identity," she said. "Or take a new one."

He gaped at me. Glared at her. "Got a piece of paper?"

So that's what happened. I thought I saw Eddy two weeks later, wearing miner's clothes and haggling over a mule.

I looked the other way.

The Clockwork Writer, Part II

By Steve DeWinter

I positioned myself in the protective embrace of a storefront stoop on Whitechapel Road across the street from the only place still open at this time of night. Across the street was the same inn that had served patrons for over two hundred years. It was also the place where my twin brother, Joseph, and I were supposed to have our final showdown if my brother followed the clockwork writer's exact instructions to the letter.

At least I assumed this was to be our final showdown. I hadn't seen him in several days. It might have well been years with how quickly he changed in the month since we found the mechanical boy with its ill-fated quill. I know now why our father never mentioned the existence of the doll, if he even knew it was in the attic in the first place.

Nothing the clockwork writer told us to do ended well for others. The loss of a gold bar from the Bank of London resulted in several people losing their livelihood. And since management considered it an inside job, their freedom as well.

My brother had many more questions for the clockwork writer and it quickly became apparent the writer maintained a balance in the universe with each response his quill scrawled on the paper. Each instruction that afforded us prosperity always resulted in someone else suffering for our gain. I stopped asking the writer any questions after the ferry sank in the Thames, drowning dozens of people. I didn't want to hurt anyone else, no matter the personal benefit to Joseph and I through increased taxi fares, which happened to be our family enterprise. It took longer to take a carriage ride through town and over the bridges, but after the third ferry accident in as many days, taxis were the preferred way to go for safe travel over the water.

Joseph didn't see things the same way; he kept asking for more from the doll, and willingly did everything the writer asked of him. When his seemingly innocent action of dropping a steel bar down a sewer drain resulted in the derailment of the recently constructed underground Metropolitan Railway, another threat to our now thriving taxi company, I was determined to stop letting the clockwork writer dictate his actions.

But Joseph refused to listen to me and chose instead to listen to the clockwork writer. As if he could write a better ending for our lives than the hard work we had put into the family business.

It was then I realized that if I couldn't stop the writer, I had to stop the reader. And to do that, I had to ask a question of the infernal apparatus that I never thought I would ask.

I lifted my collar against the bitter cold whistling through the streets of London and watched the entrance to the inn across the way. I held up the most recent note from the mechanical boy who had stared at me emotionlessly from his tiny writing desk as I removed it and read it again. "Tomorrow night, when the clock strikes two in the morning, go where the blind beggar resides on white. Bring a gun."

The note had to be talking about the Blind Beggar Inn on Whitechapel Road. I remembered glancing up at the wall over the fireplace. Grandfather's intricately carved dueling pistols sat on their velvet stands. At least one of them did. The other was missing. I knew my brother had taken it before leaving the note for me to find. He knew I wanted to prevent him from using the mechanical boy and, with the disappearance of one of the pistols from above the fireplace, I knew how far he was willing to go to stop me.

A shadow appeared at the end of the street, and every muscle in my body tensed as I prepared for our final showdown. I took a step out of the storefront before the shadow resolved into a woman of the evening and her escort, both stumbling drunkenly into the inn. I let out the breath I had been holding, only to have it catch again as someone spoke suddenly behind me.

"Turn around. Slowly," a harsh voice commanded.

I slowly spun and Joseph took a hasty step backward as he raised his arm. I stared past the barrel of the hundred-year-old flintlock dueling pistol and into the emotionless gaze of my twin brother. I envisioned the twin of this same pistol as it hung on the wall above the fireplace where our grandfather had them professionally mounted. And where I had left it before coming here.

Had I heeded the final message from the clockwork writer, I would look like the mirror image of my twin brother pointing a loaded pistol at my head. Instead I had refused to follow a direct order, was now unarmed, and about to pay the ultimate price for my disobedience.

My brother's hand was rock steady as he squeezed the trigger without remorse. I watched in slow motion as the hammer snapped forward a heartbeat before the gun's discharge would blind me at the same moment the bullet would end my life.

The gun clicked softly without result. My brother glared at the pistol as if it had betrayed him instead of him betraying me. He aimed and pulled the trigger again. But the pistol failed once more to fire. Then his face scrunched up in pain and he dropped the pistol as if it was on fire. He looked at the skin bubbling up on the palm of his hand and then looked at me in alarm.

I held out a piece of paper to him. "There was another note from the clockwork boy before the one that brought us here tonight. I'm sorry, Joseph. I can't let you keep doing whatever he tells you to do."

He snatched the note from my outstretched hand and read it, his other hand curled against his chest as his face contorted from the pain. He held up the note, waving it in front of my face. "What is this?"

I licked my lips. "It's the formula for a very specific and fast acting contact poison."

He looked again at the last line of the note as he read it aloud, grunting from the pain. "Take the guns from above the fireplace. Coat the flint in wax and dip the handles in the mixture prescribed below. Replace both guns above the fireplace mantle."

His muscles clenched tightly and involuntarily, crumpling the paper in his grip. His only response was to laugh as he regarded his injured hand. I watched in horror as the skin purpled and separated like waxed paper and curled away from the muscle. He looked up at me with a renewed appreciation. "You kept a secret from me. I didn't think you could. Neither did grandfather. That's why he only told me about the clockwork boy. You would have told the whole city and ruined it for us all. Just like father when he took over the taxi company. He refused to use the doll to keep business flowing and tucked it away in the attic. Grandfather entrusted its secret to me. He told me to use it to rebuild the business as soon as I had the chance. We almost didn't get that chance. Father almost lost it on numerous occasions. But I got us back out of debt in only a month."

He coughed, his whole body convulsing as the poison filled his blood. His eyes rolled back and he pitched forward, sliding against the wall.

I reached out to support my brother before he fell. He stood up straighter and pointed at me. "No! Don't touch me!"

I froze in place, wetness forming along the edges of my eyes. "I'm sorry, Joseph."

He slumped against the wall, and then stood up again before I could help him. "You—you did this? To me!"

I blinked away the tears, but wasn't able to bring myself to move towards him. "I didn't want to."

He slumped down the wall again, the blood vessels of his face bursting under his skin and splattering his expression with dark red blotches. "Why? How?"

"I asked him how to stop you without me having to harm you directly. I asked you to stop doing what he said. All you had to do was leave the pistol over the fireplace. You should never have let the clockwork writer dictate how your story ends."

The Shadows of the Moon

By Michael Tierney

In the month since Director Lawrence's announcement that he had observed evidence of a civilization on the Moon, Susan Branham had had no rest. As a member of the observatory staff, she was used to spending her nights at the telescope. Now she had to work during her days as well, fending off inquiries from prying reporters, as well as from curious locals who had made the dusty trip up to the observatory from San Jose. All the while, Lawrence had held court at his home in San Francisco. He had only returned to the observatory once the month had passed and the time to observe Petavius Crater again was approaching. And he's brought along a motley assortment of reporters and curious on-lookers in tow, she thought.

He spoke to the crowd, "Miss Branham is on the staff at the observatory, a very capable young lady, and was assisting me that night. Miss Branham," the director said, "please tell these gentlemen what it was like on the evening that I discovered the city in Petavius Crater."

She stuttered, and finally said slowly, "Yes, that is correct. I assisted the director in preparing the telescope for observing."

"Did you know at the time what a world-changing event you were witnessing?" asked a man writing into a brown bound notebook.

"No, no, I did not. If you don't mind, director, I promised Mr. Simpson I would assist him in calibrating the clock drive for this evening, and I am running late."

"Yes, of course, my dear."

She briskly walked away, lips pursed and tongue pressed firmly to the roof of her mouth. There were many things she'd like to say to the director, none of which were proper for a lady, even a modern woman who worked in science. Since the director had gone public with his so-called discovery, she and the rest of the observatory staff had had to suffer the scorn of their scientific colleagues.

The astronomical establishment, led by the American Astronomical Society as well as their European counterparts (to whom word of Lawrence's observations quickly spread) refuted his claims, stating that particular area of the Moon had been observed for centuries through ever more powerful telescopes, and never had anything like Lawrence's fanciful drawings ever been seen. Besides, they sniffed, the Lick Observatory telescope, while of adequate quality, was manned by an inexperienced staff, and would scarcely be capable of resolving the details seen in the drawings.

Susan bristled at being called *inexperienced staff.* She had studied long and diligently in what would usually be termed a man's discipline, and was finally hired as the only woman on staff at the observatory. She performed her duties faithfully and her work identifying and cataloging double stars had earned praise. *Inexperienced?* She knew that the only person in this whole affair acting inexperienced was the director himself.

୫୬

She remembered that night with a clarity greater than she thought possible. She recalled the director's strange giddiness when they started working. She had assisted him ably, she thought, anticipating his requests as he observed Petavius Crater. She had monitored the skies and had warned him when it appeared that the seeing was deteriorating. Then he started making such wild claims about cities on the Moon. Susan wondered at the time (and many times since) if his hard work at the observatory had brought on a type of nervous attack. She thought that he would ruin his reputation with such assertions. and begged him to be careful, "You are making extraordinary claims and should have correspondingly extraordinary evidence to support them." But his previously jovial demeanor quickly soured. Lawrence accused her of questioning his scientific integrity. He ignored her suggestions to doubly check his observations, and was even so mean as to threaten the loss of her position. She remembered the fevered sketches that he had made. She thought them a fantasy, incorrect interpretations of geological formations. She was relieved when he finally retired to his rooms to finish his drawings.

Relieved, because it gave her the chance to expose the two photographic plates that she had prepared, in hopes that they might provide a better means of recording than the eye and the pencil. Judging the brightness of the Moon through the eyepiece, she estimated the exposure, and opened the shutter just as Simpson entered the dome carrying an oil lamp.

"Mr. Simpson! Safety light, please!"

Simpson quickly blew out the flame. "I'm sorry, Miss Branham," he said from the sudden darkness, "I thought the director had finished for the night."

"He has. But I have not, Mr. Simpson. I am attempting to photograph the surface of the Moon, but I fear your lamp has ruined the plate." She slid the cover back and removed the cased plate from the mount. "I have just one other prepared."

"Again, I'm sorry, Miss Branham. I will leave you to your work", he said, seeming to her rather chagrined.

"Thank you." Her voice softened, "Don't be concerned, Tom. Accidents happen."

When he was gone, she mounted the second plate and exposed it. She then spent a good amount of time looking through the eyepiece at Petavius Crater. The Moon was now moving towards the horizon, and the warm air rising up over San Jose made the image jump and blur. Even when the image was fairly stable for a brief moment, Susan did not see what the director professed to. She saw a crater with a central mountain and a straight ridge running from the center to the crater's lip. Nothing more. Nothing different than could be seen in many other places on the Moon's rough and battered surface.

She had developed the photographic plate she had exposed, of course. It might have been the definitive proof one way or the other. But even with a quick exposure, the features on the image were cloudy and distorted from the turbulent atmosphere that night. Anyone skilled in astronomical photography would recognize it as a rather poor image of a crater on the Moon. Nothing else could be made of it. And certainly not what she saw later when the director's finished drawings were printed in the newspapers: Buildings? Railroads? Factories?

ഇരു

Finally, the day she had been waiting for—and dreading—had arrived. While Lawrence had spent his day leading the parade of wagons and carriages up the Mount Hamilton Road from San Jose, the observatory staff was busy readying the instruments as well as attempting to deal with the crowds of people that were constantly arriving. When she had a chance, Susan periodically stopped in at the office where the telegraph operator had been receiving a series of telegrams from observatories in Europe where the skies were already dark. Cambridge Observatory, the National Observatory in Paris, even the largest telescope of them all, the six-foot "Leviathan" in Ireland, all wired that they could not confirm Lawrence's observations of Petavius Crater. The Astronomer Royal, wiring from the Greenwich Observatory, appended to the official notice, "Perhaps in future, making notice of such observations through the scientific journals would be preferable to announcing them through the popular press."

Susan was not the only member of the staff well aware that the director's findings were not being confirmed; a steady stream of staffers wandered by the telegraph office. When she mentioned it to Mr. Simpson, he only shook his head and said, "I'm not going to tell him. And neither should you. There's no helping him now. The only way any of us is going to survive this is to let him go up in smoke."

"Give them to me, give all of the telegrams to me," she said. "I will keep them and deliver them to the director at the proper time. But I agree with you, Mr. Simpson. He must not learn what the world already knows. It would be better that he discover the truth himself through his own telescope."

After the sun had set in an ultramarine sky, Professor Lawrence ushered the crowd into the great volume of the telescope's dome. He hopped up on the viewing platform. The boisterous crowd of reporters, curious members of the public, and a few open-minded scientists quieted down, hushed by the sight of the Great Refracting Telescope as well as the sense of history in the making.

"Gentlemen, tonight you will all be witness to an event that will, without exaggeration, change civilization forever. For this evening, we will once again be able to see the Great Lunar City of Petavius. Once my assistant and I prepare the telescope properly, and make some preliminary observations, all of you will be able to peer through the eyepiece and see Man's future."

Susan exhaled wearily. She had performed her duties preparing the telescope mechanically, with no joy or anticipation. She remembered the first time she had stepped into the dome, and had been immediately enthralled by the potential discoveries that the telescope could unveil to her. Tonight, she barely looked up from her work. The delight that she once had in uncovering the wonders of the Universe through one of the most powerful instruments of its kind had been tarnished.

"Is the telescope prepared, Miss Branham?"

"Yes, director," she said flatly.

"Why so glum, my dear? Tonight is an occasion that you will remember throughout your career. Very few have the opportunity that you have had working with me. I dare say this will only have a beneficial effect on your professional career," he pronounced.

"Yes, sir," she said, wondering if she still wanted a career.

"How is the seeing this evening?"

"Only fair. Not too different from last time, unfortunately."

"No matter. If I could perceive it last month, I will again. That is for certain. Install the wide angle eyepiece, Miss Branham."

He lectured to the crowd, "I will now begin the process of enlarging, as it were, the image I see through the telescope using eyepieces of increasing magnification. Last month, we required the highest magnification in order to discern the city." Susan assisted him with the eyepieces, and in adjusting the focus of the telescope. Standing next to him on the observing platform, she anticipated his reactions. As she fitted the final most powerful eyepiece to the telescope, he announced, "And now, the time has come..."

Then he went quiet. He fiddled with the focusing wheel and peered through the eyepiece intensely. "Adjust the declination, Miss Branham; Petavius is not quite centered in the view."

She heard him hold his breath for a long time, then he exhaled forcefully. He then snorted in frustration. "This is the highest magnification eyepiece?" he asked, and then more quietly said, "I don't see it."

"Yes, director, the same eyepiece as last month. Is the image clear?"

"Yes, if anything, it's clearer than before." He pulled back from the eyepiece. "Here, you look. My eyes may be tired."

Susan had no expectations that she would see anything other than the geological features of Petavius Crater, but she was a careful scientist and looked anyway. She squeezed onto the observing chair while avoiding coming too close to Lawrence. "I see the crater and its central mountain. The ridge to the crater rim is very clear. You are correct that the seeing is better than last month, director." She covered her left eye and widened her right to get the absolutely clearest image. "I'm sorry, director, I do not see what you would wish me to."

"Let me look again." He pressed his eyes closed to clear them, then gazed through the eyepiece.

"What do you see, Professor?" yelled a voice from somewhere in the darkness of the dome.

"One moment ...."

"One moment ...."

That moment never came.

℥℧

The next morning, after the disappointed crowds had made their way down the road from the mountaintop in the darkness, and the director had retreated to his rooms, the telegrams continued to arrive from observatories the world over, all failing to see anything like what Lawrence had described the previous month. The director of the observatory at Harvard College, a classmate of the Professor's, sent a terse note, "I expected more from a Harvard man, Augie." A telegram had also arrived from the chancellor of the University of California, summoning Lawrence to his office in Berkeley the next day. Susan collected the telegrams in a brown folder, and walked them over to the director's apartment. She knocked quietly, and not receiving a response, pushed them under the door. She heard footsteps and the folder being picked up on the other side of the door.

She was tired. The excitement and stress of the previous day had only increased at sundown, and then she had spent most of the night organizing the visitors' departures. A nap is what I need, she thought. No, it couldn't be a nap, as I haven't slept yet. I just need to put the telescope in order, then I can sleep. Entering the dome, silent and empty again, she put the eyepieces back in their velvet-lined wooden boxes, and moved the observing platform to its normal spot. As she did, she noticed a photographic plate case that had been laid on the shelf under the observing chair. Looking at the label on it, she realized that it was the plate that she had been exposing when Mr. Simpson came in with the unfiltered lamp.

Susan clasped the holder to her chest and looked up at the telescope. She had assumed that the plate was ruined by the light of the lamp, but she really did not know for sure. She could try to develop it. And then what? If it showed the director's Great Lunar City of Petavius, it would vindicate him. If not, she would keep it from him, as she had with the other plate. If it was ambiguous, she feared it would give the director hope that he was right all along.

Or she could just open the case, expose the plate to the daylight, and ruin it forever. No, she thought. She couldn't do that. As Susan stood alone in the center of the dome, she knew she would develop it. She alone could solve the mystery. She would answer the open question, because she knew that science demands that the unknown be replaced by honest answers.

Dragon

By Janice Thompson

All cannons spent, and rudder full aflame
He pulls well hard upon the wheel and cranes
A sweat-drenched brow around to quickly spy
How close they're being followed through the sky.

So close! He thrusts the wheel to push away
The beast would give no quarter to its prey.
Up through the clouds they flew to buy some time,
But nearly hit an airship passing by.

Oh how the startled captain of that ship
Had fought to veer before his vessel flipped
And tumbled out of view, just when, below,
Through thinning cloud the sea begins to show

So down to that abyss he aims the bow
The crew holds fast. It's only seconds now.
The captain heaves the wheel, the stern slams hard
Torrential plumes of water now bombard

The dragon's groping jaws, engulfed, and gone,
Then thrashing to survive with all its brawn
While captain, ship, and crew fly well away.
The fires are out, but damages remain.

Then, all becalmed, they each began to ask
What could have spurred that creature to attack.
They'd happened on its cavern unaware
For on that very spot the charts were bare.

They'd had to swerved to miss it very near.
A subtle bump and they were in the clear
And off they'd hurried, loot-less, knowing well
That none who plunders dragons live to tell.

Then out of nowhere one great beastial cry
Had everybody staring eye to eye.
A second later all the crew aboard
Ran to a cannon, blunderbuss, or sword.

And yet, it was the captain's frenzied skill
Which served to save them all from being killed.
Now each was pressed to mending everything
From makeshift rudder to pectoral wings.

By morning they had managed to regain
Their charted course, though weary and in pain.
In shifts they rested, eager to see port.
How fortunate this trip was fairly short.

Soon, as they disembarked their tethered ship,
Which, floating on soft breezes, bobbed a bit,
A passing stevedore stopped short and stared
At something underneath the vessel where

It seemed to him that something shiny lodged.
The captain looked, and sadly knew what caused
That dragon's rabid chase and anguished wails;
The keel was now embedded with its scales.

Adelaide's Triumph

By BJ Sikes

Piorry sat opposite Adelaide, an ingratiating grin pasted to his puffy white face as he listened to the praises of the aristocrats sitting around the table. His face glowed in the light of dozens of tall white beeswax candles. Adelaide hated him. She wanted to throw something at him. A basket of rolls. One of those ornate golden candelabras. Anything that would wipe the grin off his detestable face.

I admired him once. Even idolized him. The thief!

She hadn't been able to sleep or work since his betrayal last month and her stomach was constantly in knots. Adelaide stared at the fine Palace food on the gold-edged plate in front of her, not touching it. She lifted her solid gold fork and toyed with a piece of the meat dressed in a fine sauce. It could have been a tough bit of yak meat marbled with gristle for all that it appealed to her. She put her fork down and glanced up at her mentor. He was chattering and grinning at the noblewoman seated to his left. This fancy dinner party seemed endless. Her head started to ache and her eyes wouldn't focus. She took a sip of wine and closed her eyes for a moment.

"Adelaide, you haven't touched your food. This veal is tender and flavorful, and the sauce is just divine," Piorry said.

She let a small, tight smile cross her face. She didn't respond further. His grin faltered a bit but brightened as the noblewoman to his left addressed him. She simpered at the famous Scientist-doctor, lush, painted lips pouting, darkened lashes batting.

Adelaide sighed and looked away, accidentally catching the eye of her dining partner.

Seeing his opportunity, he addressed her. She nodded at his platitudes.

Yet another noble begging to be considered a candidate for the Archimedean Heart. As if he were the only worthy recipient.

"Mademoiselle Coumain, you must understand, I am a prime candidate for this amazing new invention. I am otherwise healthy but for my weak heart." Taking in his emaciated form and wan complexion, Adelaide doubted that. "I would take it as a kindness if you could speak to Monsieur le Professeur Piorry."

Adelaide glared across the table at her mentor, the presumed inventor of the Archimedean Heart, and took a long draught of wine. He still had told no-one. She debated mentioning the fact to her dining partner, but then he would probably persist in his request and she was already behind in her other projects. The Queen was waiting for her own Archimedean Heart, although Adelaide was not sure that the monarch's ancient mechanisms would function with Adelaide's new invention.

"Mademoiselle? So you will ask Monsieur le Professeur about my heart?" the nobleman persisted.

Adelaide frowned at the man, her heavy eyebrows meeting. Her nod was abrupt and he drew back, a faint moue crossing his lips. She stared down at the congealing sauce and lumps of meat on her plate. Fighting down a wave of nausea, she stood, her chair scraping across the polished wood floor. The table went silent and a dozen pairs of eyes turned in her direction.

"Pardon me," she muttered and stumbled out of the room.

The hallway outside the nobles' dining chamber was empty and quiet. Adelaide panted, trying to catch her breath and quell the nausea.

Damn this stupid corset. Why did I let that maidservant lace me so tightly?

She leaned against the wall, trying not to bang her head against the ornate picture frame above her. Wisps of hair tickled her nose. She brushed them back without thinking about it. Her breathing was slowing back to normal and she pushed herself off the wall.

Time to go back in, I suppose. I wonder if I could slip back to my room and claim I was not well. I don't think I can face that crowd again.

The door clicked open as she stood debating with herself. Adelaide eyed Piorry as he slipped out of the room. His normally pale face was flushed with exertion and wine. Scowling, he bustled over to where she stood clutching her midsection.

"Adelaide, how dare you leave so rudely? You embarrassed me in front of my guests. I was just about to tell them about the success we had with that young noble ... what was her name?"

"Marie-Ange de Laincel," she said, not meeting his eyes. The nausea was rising again and she struggled to breathe deeply.

"Oh yes, Marie-Ange. Pretty little thing. It was good that she survived the operation. The heart is functioning properly, is it not?"

Adelaide nodded, gaze fixed to the floor. "She's stronger than she looks. The heart is working and she is already walking around."

"Oh? You have allowed her out of the rocking bed? Is that wise? What if her movement is insufficient to wind the heart's mainspring?"

Adelaide suppressed a sigh. Why did he constantly have to question her decisions? She had not made a bad decision during this entire project. She straightened from her slump and met his eyes.

"Sir, she seems to be doing very well with the new heart. All signs show that it is functioning correctly. She will remain in the rocking bed while sleeping to keep the heart wound but she is strong enough to move around now. It is best for the patient to move a little so she does not get weak from being bed-ridden."

"Ah yes, well, let us hope that you are not mistaken. It would be a shame to have to report to Her Majesty that the heart does not work as promised. I would not like for you to be blamed for killing a young noblewoman with a faulty invention." His smile didn't reach his eyes.

Adelaide's heart pounded. He wasn't going to give her credit unless it didn't work, and then she would get the blame? She grinded her teeth but didn't speak.

Piorry's dead-fish smile deepened and he reached forward to pat her arm.

"Now, Adelaide, you must remain courteous to my guests. Leaving abruptly in the middle of my dinner party is unacceptable. The people in that room are close advisers to Her Majesty. If they believe that you are not trustworthy, they may ask for you to be removed from the project."

Adelaide narrowed her eyes and stared at the man who stood in front of her, smirking.

"Removed? How could I be removed from this project? I created the Archimedean Heart!" Her voice rose and echoed in the empty hallway. Piorry grimaced and grabbed her upper arm, squeezing it until she gasped in pain.

"Keep your voice down, girl. I forbid you to speak such foolishness. The Archimedean Heart was created as part of a National Academy project. How dare you try to take credit for it?"

Adelaide gaped at him, spluttering. He gave her arm a shake and she winced.

"Do you understand what I am saying, Adelaide? You are not the so-called inventor. It is a national project. Do you think it would have been possible without funding from the Academy? Your precious Master Machinist does not work cheaply, you know." He released her arm with a jerk. Tears filled her eyes but she kept her chin up, refusing to submit.

"The project may have been funded by the Academy but I am the inventor. I alone did the research and I oversaw the development of the machine," she said.

Piorry's face reddened and without warning, he slapped her. She cried out in surprise.

"Shut up, you stupid girl. Your wild claims will go no further. If you do not cease with them, I will be forced to take action against you." He spun on his heel and walked back into the dining chamber. Adelaide raised a hand to her burning cheek as she watched him go. The door clicked shut. She wheeled around and ran down the hallway, tears flowing down her face.

∾∿

A woman, dressed in a mannish suit stood in the shadows of the hallway outside the dining room, speaking quietly to a Palace guard. The young man nodded and headed down the hallway. The woman stepped behind a statue and waited. The clocks struck midnight. Piorry exited the dining room in a crowd of nobles and stood shaking hands and exchanging farewells. He watched them disperse then scanned the empty corridor, not seeing the woman in the shadows. He stalked off and the woman watched him leave. A grin split her face.

"Ha! After the scene I watched earlier, this could be a fine story for the *Courant*," she said and followed Piorry. He didn't look back as he wound his way through the corridors of the Palace, stepping into dark alcoves to avoid the few courtiers and servants still out this late. The woman shadowing him also halted, keeping out of his sight. He approached the laboratory he shared with Adelaide. The door was shut but light shone from underneath. He let himself in and closed the door. The woman tailing him cursed under her breath. She drew closer, stopped at the door and pressed her ear against it. The young Palace guard joined her, his face flushed with excitement.

ෂ)ೞ

Adelaide looked up from her workbench at the sound of the door, glowering when she spotted Piorry. His customary smirk was gone, a fierce grimace in its place. She shivered at the unfamiliar expression. She hadn't felt intimidated by Piorry since her success with Marie-Ange's heart transplant, but he looked predatory, dangerous. Neither spoke at first.

Piorry, with a voice full of malice, broke the silence.

"I will not have you make me a fool with your absurd claims," he said. His voice grew low and hard, no longer the smooth courtier. "I am the Royal Physician, not you. I am in charge here."

Adelaide raised her chin in defiance.

"You may be the Royal Physician, but we both know that you had little input on the Archimedean Heart. Have you forgotten how you tried to dissuade me from pursuing its development? And now that it has been shown to be a success, you wish to take the credit from me?" Her voice rose. He moved closer to her, and stood across the workbench glaring.

"Adelaide, I have warned you repeatedly. I will not tolerate this insubordination."

She put her hands on her hips and glared back.

"I think it's time I informed Presidente Le Scientist that I am ready to run my own laboratory. I do not need your interference with my work and I refuse to let you take credit for my inventions."

Piorry gripped the edge of the workbench and leaned towards her. His eyes were intent and fierce as he ground out, "I forbid you to speak to him. You are under my control and that is where you will stay until I decide otherwise."

Adelaide slammed down the instrument she was holding. The air seemed to drain from the room, leaving her flushed and breathless.

"I refuse! I am tired of pandering to you. You are a charlatan, nothing but a sycophant, and I will no longer keep up this pretense that you are in charge."

He straightened, his face whitening with rage. Faster than she would have believed possible, he rounded the bench and grabbed her wrist, yanking it up. She shrieked, eyes wide with fear.

"Let me go! You are hurting me!"

"I will do more than hurt you, you insolent girl," he bellowed. He dragged her over to a large, ornate cabinet and flung open one of its doors. Reaching in, he drew out a brass and silver baton and switched it on. It hummed.

"What are you doing with that?" Her voice was high and thin, quavering. "Be careful with that. It produces a strong electrical current."

He bared his teeth in a malicious smirk.

"Yes, I know. Strong enough to stop your heart if I pressed it against your chest." He thrust the baton towards her. She screamed and jerked away, breaking his grip. Picking up her skirts, she dashed towards the door but he was too fast. He grabbed at her dress and yanked her back. She screamed again then shouted,

"Help! Murder!"

He pulled harder and she fell to the floor. Dropping to his knees next to her, he pinned her shoulder down with one hand as the other brought the baton to her chest. She grabbed his wrist to stop him. Taking his hand off her shoulder, he backhanded her, slamming her head against the floor. Adelaide closed her eyes for a moment, dizzied, but kept her grip on Piorry's wrist. With a twist of her torso, she pulled him across her. He tumbled to the ground, sprawling over her. She raised her knee as he fell and he landed hard on it, letting out an *Oof.*

The baton clattered away across the wooden floor. His weight was suffocating her but then he struggled up to his knees, looming above her, panting. She scurried backwards, out of reach, and screamed for help again.

Piorry pulled himself to his feet and grabbed a wrench off the workbench. His face was ugly and mottled-scarlet with exertion. Piorry lunged towards her, snarling, wrench raised above his head. Adelaide tried to rise to her feet but she was trapped, entangled in her petticoats.

They both jumped at the sound of a crash at the door and turned. A strange woman burst into the room followed by a Palace guard.

"Aha! There he is, caught in the act!" she said, a triumphant grin on her face. The Palace Guard rushed at Piorry and grabbed the wrench away. Piorry glared at the guard and opened his mouth to speak but the young man spoke first.

"Monsieur le Professeur, you are arrested in the Name of His Majesty for the attempted murder of this woman," the guard said, gesturing to Adelaide. Piorry shuddered and dropped his head and the guard shackled his wrists together. Piorry didn't resist. Adelaide was still struggling to stand up and the woman came forward to assist her.

"Who are you?" she asked. Adelaide quirked an eyebrow at her.

That's an odd question to ask someone who has just survived a murder attempt. And I've never seen this woman before.

"Who are *you?*" Adelaide replied. The woman smiled, watching the Guard march Piorry out of the room.

"No-one important," she said, turning her gaze back to Adelaide and smiling. "Who was that person who tried to kill you?"

Adelaide looked at the door. He was gone. Her anger drained away and she felt deflated, sad.

"My mentor, Monsieur le Professeur Piorry. He wanted to steal credit for my invention," she murmured. "I suppose his ambition overcame his ethics."

"Ah, a terrible affliction, one sees it so much here at Court. I still don't know who you are."

Adelaide lifted her head and stared into the woman's eyes.

"I am the inventor of the Archimedean Heart."

Adventure Realized

By Emily Thompson

For the very first time in Vivian Swift's entire life, she had reached out to something she truly wanted for herself, and doing so overwhelmed her with a sense of her own ability to enforce her will over the course of her life. She could steer her destiny to follow her own stars, after all.

When she had followed the address given in Grace's letter, she'd found herself in a dark alley. The young man at the unassuming door had let her in once she'd shown him the letter, and he then led her into a glamorous secret cafe at the top of the building, where she could see much of New York through the wide windows. The patrons of the cafe appeared to be from everywhere in the world—men in suits and hats or others in robes and turbans, ladies in silks and furs, some carrying weapons and others with watchful eyes and flawless decorum— and the cafe itself was filled with ferns, stoic black birds in tall cages, and wafting, sweet-smelling smoke.

There she met with the head waiter, who appeared to be a sort of manager for the local Rooks. After hearing her explanations, he accepted her offer to join the Rooks, even though she had no special Sight. Although Vivian had readied herself to abandon her life and all that she knew, she was told that for the moment that would be unnecessary. The Rooks operated all over the world, but New York City was one of their best established locations. Until Vivian rose through the ranks or showed herself to possess special skills in some area, she was asked to remain in New York and work with the Rooks only a few days a week.

Vivian was surprised to find herself somewhat disappointed by this, but did her best to convince herself that it was nice to not have to leave her home, family, and friends. There wasn't even any reason for her to break off her engagement to Trevor, nor for her to miss her usual society balls and parties. Surely this was better than being whisked off into unknown oblivion. Surely.

She completed her basic Rook training—including how to fire a small gun without shooting oneself, which basic operational secrets to keep, when she would be paid for her few weekly hours of work and how to fill out the time sheets— in just a few days. She was then assigned to guard the very same door that she had first approached with Grace's letter in hand. And now, just a month later, she found herself alone in a dark entry way with a tiny pistol, but without any of her initial enthusiasm.

Each day she would ask visitors to the cafe for the month's password phrase, threatening coyly to shoot them if they got it wrong. None of them ever got it wrong, and Vivian was beginning to suspect that she'd forgotten just what she was supposed to do if they did. Nonetheless, the visitors to the secret cafe were frightfully fascinating in themselves.

Men and women in foreign costumes, with a wide variety in their accents, cultures, and attitudes, appeared at her door, bringing a moment of life and adventure in with them, along with a breath of the chilly air outside. But none of them paused to chat, or to tell her anything of their journeys or experiences. And why would they? To them, Vivian was nothing more than a doorkeeper. Their mysterious and fascinating business was all attended to up in the cafe, atop the tall spiral staircase to her left.

Vivian looked longingly up the stairs, to the shifting, soft light and gentle murmurs of voices in the cafe above, and gave a sigh. Why did she still even make any effort to dress well, she wondered, glancing down at her lovely purple gown. A knock at the door startled her out of her thoughts.

She quickly adjusted her purple, turquoise-feathered hat before she opened the door just a crack to find a strikingly elegant and beautiful woman standing outside in the alley. There seemed to be a few other people with her who Vivian couldn't see well through the gap. As she'd done a thousand times, Vivian pointed the end of her little pistol at the beautiful woman.

"Password?" Vivian asked, offering a pleasant smile so that the lady might know there were no hard feelings between them, despite the obligatory weapon.

"What is it, January?" the woman asked of another in the alley with her. Since it was indeed January, the other person must have confirmed so. The woman turned back to Vivian with a charming smile. "Peggotty's lost another button," the woman declared in a gentle Russian accent, giving the correct password.

"Welcome to Hudson's," Vivian said, lowering her weapon and opening the door wide. She sighed again inwardly, wondering why she'd really been given a pistol at all. It seemed silly for her to have one, when she never used it.

A troupe of disparate individuals followed in behind the Russian woman. While two of them looked much the same—both slim young men, ghostly pale, and wearing black—the others with her all looked quite different from each other. There was a blond man dressed in the rugged, earth-toned costume of an adventurer, with sea-green eyes that wouldn't so much as look at Vivian. A young lady who appeared to be covered in shining copper—or perhaps, she was really a puppet made entirely of clockwork? No, that would be like something out of a fairytale!—walked in holding the arm of one of the pale men in black.

Most interesting of all, however, was the last member of the group. He was tall and well-built, wearing a white linen suit—far too thin for the weather, Vivian thought—and his skin appeared to be as white as fresh snow. Vivian wondered if this might be a trick of the light, but all the others appeared normal to her. There were also scrawling black tattooed lines covering his hands, his bare scalp, a part of his face, and the bared top of his chest under his unfastened buttons. And as he glanced to her and offered a light smile, Vivian was startled to find that his eyes were fully gold, with no whites or pupils in them. The blond baboon sitting calmly on his shoulder, and wearing a matching linen suit, and a gold monocle over one yellow eye, tipped its tiny straw hat to her politely.

But just like all the others before them, these remarkable people all vanished up the spiral stairs and left Vivian alone to her wandering thoughts. Vivian leaned back against the wall and let out another sigh. This wasn't at all what she'd envisioned when she'd decided to join the Rooks. If she'd only wanted to ogle interesting people, she could simply stand outside in the alley and watch them pass by. She longed to speak to them, to ask their stories, to have her own adventures! Surely there was more to being a Rook than guarding a single door. Surely.

Vivian's thoughts continued to darken as she listened to the vague sounds from above, and she wondered if she had been nothing but a fool from the very beginning. After all, Grace had a Sight that made her very useful to the Rooks. What skills did Vivian have? She was a society lady, a fiancé to a man she didn't love nor even really like. She had breeding and connections, but now that she'd opened her mind to her true feeling she found that she thirsted for adventure rather than status.

In her own world she was well equipped but bored to tears. In the world of the Rooks, she was little use at all. Vivian shook her head, forcing herself not to cry. Surely there was somewhere she could be, something she could do, that would bring her joy and some sense of achievement. Surely.

With a heavy sigh, Vivian finally realized that the only thing she was truly skilled at was making such absurd wishes. It was in making them come true, however, that her abilities ended. She pulled out a turquoise handkerchief and dabbed at the corner of her eyes before her foolish tears ruined her makeup.

"Are you all right, my dear?" a voice asked from above on the stairs.

Vivian felt a blush of embarrassed heat rise to her cheeks as she looked up towards the voice. The man with the snowy-white skin and the baboon on his shoulder, was now hurrying down the stairs to her, his feet remarkably silent on the metal stairs.

"Yes, yes," Vivian hurried to answer. "I have something in my eye ...." As she sniffed to keep her nose from dripping, she wondered fearfully if her distress was very evident on her voice.

"There, there, now," the man said, his voice deep and soothing, and his words colored by some accent of a faraway land. "You needn't put on a brave face if you're upset."

"Yes, miss," the baboon said in a clear and crisp British accent. "Tell us what's troubling you."

Vivian stared at the rather polite, but still, *talking* baboon in alarm. "Oh, it's nothing, nothing at all," she muttered dismissively.

The man held open a hand, asking for hers with an understanding and patient smile. When she relented and took his hand, she found his touch remarkably warm. She looked up into his golden eyes, noting distantly that while many men were no taller than she was, she did have to look up to meet his gaze. Somehow, just being under his attention felt strange, alien, and yet rather soothing.

"If you won't tell us what's troubling you, then let me ask you this," he said sweetly. "If you could have one wish, what would it be?"

The baboon sitting on his shoulder glanced to him with a knowing grin. That a baboon might be able to do such a thing confused Vivian for an instant before she considered the man's question.

"Oh, I'm sure I don't know," she replied politely.

"Now now," the man said with a smile. "Please answer me. Would you wish for a present? For a solution to some ill? Or would you wish to be taken somewhere fantastic?"

Vivian smiled at his odd questioning. "Somewhere fantastic, you say?" she asked back, jokingly.

"Of course," the man said with a wider smile. "Tell me. If you could go anywhere at all, where would you wish to go?"

"Oh, I don't know," Vivian said, grinning wickedly. She knew she shouldn't, but something about the warmth of his hand, his soothing voice, or the absurdity of it all, made it seem like just the right thing to do. "Well," she said brightly to him, "if I could go anywhere at all, I suppose I'd wish to visit the moon."

The man's smile took on a satisfied warmth, while the baboon gave a delighted tone.

"As you wish," the man said, an instant before Vivian felt the ground fall out beneath her.

Vivian shrieked, reaching out to catch her balance. The man's hand never left hers for an instant, and she caught herself against his solid form, feeling an arm loop behind her back to hold her steady as the feeling of falling subsided and her feet found solid purchase. Frightened, Vivian looked about to see what had happened, but found that she was no longer in the dark little entryway at all.

She and the man now stood on a vast plane of thick gray dust and rock, but she could see mountains in the distance, lit with bright sunlight. This seemed strange because it appeared to be night, and they now stood beneath a black sky full of stars. Looking all around, Vivian slowly came to realize that there wasn't a single road, building, nor any sign of life anywhere around them, and that every inch of the ground and surrounding mountains was the same odd, dusty gray.

"Where's all the cheese?" the baboon asked, looking cross.

"Yes, wasn't there supposed to be cheese?" the man asked him curiously.

"What's happened?" Vivian asked them, realizing that her confusion and fright was beginning to make her body shake while the man continued to hold her steady.

"Oh," he replied, gently rubbing at her back. "You wished to visit the moon. And so," he added, turning and gesturing behind himself, "here we are."

Still confused, Vivian glanced around behind him. A breathtakingly beautiful half-sphere of blue, green, and brown, swirled with feathered white streaks, hung in the stars above the horizon. She nearly spoke up to ask what he meant, when she suddenly recognized a shape on the edge of the sphere. It looked rather like the continent of South America, leaning on its side. She glanced up and winced to find a blindingly brilliant, large, single, point of light in the black sky and stars above their heads. All at once, her understanding fell into place.

Vivian gripped the man's arms and stared up at his face in astonished alarm. "We're on the *moon!*"

"Yes, as you wished," he agreed with a nod and a smile.

"But, we're on the *moon!*" she protested. "I mean, the *moon!*"

He chuckled lightly. The baboon smiled to her amiably. Vivian gaped at the both of them.

"My name is Idris," the man said pleasantly. "This is Jeffery Simian," he added, gesturing to the baboon, who tipped his hat to Vivian again. "I'm a djinn," Idris explained. "I'm always looking for people who know how to make interesting wishes, and I must say you're off to a good start, my dear. Now, would you like to wish yourself back home," he asked, hooking a thumb at the Earth, hanging over just the horizon, "or would you like take a stroll with Jeffery and me on the moon? I've already made it easy for us to walk in this gravity, and also for us to breathe. You would be perfectly safe in my company."

Vivian stared back at the man—rather, the magical, wish-granting, apparently-lamp-less genie—and began to wonder if she'd somehow either lost her mind completely or fallen asleep while on the job. Either way, she didn't seem to be bound for sanity or the waking world any time soon. Wouldn't the shock of finding herself no longer on the Earth have woken her up, at least? But then again, the djinn might just be telling her nothing but the truth. Surely she couldn't be lucky enough to run into a real-life, magical djinn, who wanted to grant her wishes. Surely.

"Idris," Jeffery said, staring back at Vivian worriedly. "I'm afraid you might have rather frightened the young lady. Shall I wish her home?"

"No," Vivian answered, surprising herself. Idris looked back to her with a patient smile. Vivian returned it, taking the crook of his over-warm arm. "My name is Vivian Swift," she said, mastering her decorum. "And I'd love to take a stroll with you on the moon."

"How delightful," Idris replied, clearly pleased with her answer.

As they set out, strolling slowly towards the Earth, Vivian found that it was indeed perfectly comfortable for her to step through the fine, soft, gray dust that covered the moon. Although the air felt chilly to her, it wasn't unpleasantly so, and breathing was no trouble at all.

"Perhaps after this," Idris remarked, "we might visit some place with good cheese. I rather fancy some now that we find there is none here on the moon."

"But maybe there is," Jeffery said with sudden inspiration. "Perhaps all this gray dust is just mold."

"Oh!" Idris gasped, disgusted. "I don't want horrid old moldy moon cheese. I mean, rural France, or Switzerland—goodness, some stout Irish cheddar would be much better than moldy old moon cheese."

Vivian laughed, becoming somewhat giddy with all of the strangeness that had just crowded into her life. "I've always wanted to visit France," she offered. "Have you been there?"

"I haven't," Jeffery answered. "Have you, Idris?"

"I've been everywhere down there," Idris answered with a sigh, staring at the Earth on the horizon. Vivian noticed a note of melancholy in his voice. Seeming to notice her attention, Idris smiled to her and patted her hand, where she held his arm. "But seeing an old place with a new friend can make it seem brand new again. How long do you think you might like to travel with us, Vivian? Because I'm not afraid to tell you that I'd gladly show you the whole world, if you'd wish to see it."

Vivian smiled back to him, her heart beating quickly. Looking into the golden eyes of this djinn, strolling on the moon, she realized that she didn't want to return to sanity, nor wake up again. And if, by some strange twist of fate, this was actually real, she also realized that no part of her wanted to go home. Trevor could marry someone else, she could send her parents postcards from all over the world so that they wouldn't worry too much, and the Rooks could very well find another doorkeeper. Surely, only a true fool would pass up this gift. Surely.

"I would be delighted to see the world with you, sir," she said, surprised by the confidence and calm in her own voice. She smiled, looking off ahead of them at the Earth on the horizon, felt a deep and satisfying calm wash over her, and for once, her mind failed to wander at all.

"Please," he replied. "Call me Idris. You and I shall be great friends."

"Oh, I'm sure we will," Vivian agreed. "Surely."

Two Days in June, Part II

By Sharon E. Cathcart

5 July 1832

Has it really been only thirty days? Marianne asks herself. Thirty days since 300 Republicans, led by Enjolras, stopped Lamarque's funeral in the Place de la Bastille? How well she remembers the day, and her lover's rousing speeches to the gathered crowd. It seemed that the people of Paris would follow Jean-Claude Enjolras to the mouth of Hell itself. After all, they applauded every phrase that came from his mouth and the mouths of the others who spoke on Lamarque's very catafalque.

And yet, that is not what happened at all, is it?

The people, at the end of the day, stayed home.

⁎

The Friends of the Abaissé, along with their newfound comrades, barricaded the narrow streets around Place de la Bastille, and they waited for the people to come.

And they waited.

The only ones who came were the National Guard, twenty-thousand strong on the first day. Among them was one Robert Enjolras who, though sympathetic to his brother, was not sympathetic to the Republican cause. He was sorry he had ever told Jean-Claude the route that Lamarque's funeral cortège would take.

The first night, Marianne took a basket of food to Enjolras for him to share amongst his comrades behind the barricades. The meat, cheese, and wine disappeared so quickly! Hunger was a motivator for many behind the lines that evening. Once the food was shared around, Marianne begged Jean-Claude to come home with her, but he was steadfast.

"The people will come, *ma petite*, I am sure of it."

He would not be moved, and so Marianne went back to her little room to keep vigil.

Olympe reported a similar failure with Grantaire; she had brought him a bottle of cognac and the promise of a night of debauchery. None of that mattered to him ... for once.

And now, here they were, just a little more than a week before the *Fête de la Fédération* ... alone.

On that second day, the National Guard sent twenty-thousand more men than they had the day before. So, facing the Friends of the Abaissé and their few comrades were forty-thousand well-trained, well-fed soldiers.

No one knows for certain which side fired the first shot. Not even the very nice monsieur Hugo, whose wife was a client at the dressmaker; he had been caught behind one of the barricades and felt that his escape had been narrow indeed. He planned, he said, to write a book about the matter one day.

ℬℭ

But, Marianne thought, it does not matter who fired first. At the end of that second June day, ninety-three of the Republicans and thirty of the soldiers lay dead ... among them both Enjolras sons and one Henri Grantaire. The bodies were laid out in long ranks, and both Marianne and Olympe had screamed at the sight of their lovers there. This was the one outcome that none of them had foreseen.

Of the Friends of the Abaissé, only young Pontmercy survives in person. The others survive only in spirit. While this is not his tale, it is Pontmercy who tells Marianne and Olympe what became of their lovers. Of how Grantaire was collapsed, drunk, inside a tavern during the entire battle. Of how, when the soldiers pushed Enjolras into the tavern at bayonet-point, to execute him for being the ringleader of the Republicans, Grantaire awoke at last.

Of how Grantaire arose with dignity, walked to the wall and stood next to his friend as the bullets flew.

The two men who were closer than brothers during life have gone into the next world together. Somehow, young Pontmercy opines, it is fitting.

The result of the whole thing is not what anyone would have predicted. Why? Because soon after those two days in June, the entire thing seems to have been forgotten. The people of Paris are still hungry, and the cruel king is still on the throne.

It has only been a bit more than forty years since the first revolution, in 1789. Neither Marianne nor Olympe were yet born. Marianne remembers sitting by her grandmother's side, learning to sew with tiny, perfect stitches and listening to stories about the Jacobins, the Girondins, the Cordilleras, and so many other clubs whose names she has forgotten. Of how *Grand-mère* learned to make those tiny, perfect stitches after being conscripted, in the *levée en masse* of 1793 with all of the other Parisian women, to make tents and clothes. Of how Robespierre led a terror-filled time, until his life was taken by the same guillotine that had made the streets run red at his direction.

Somehow, she has never before connected that time to this. Never before has she considered that hunger and peoples' rights were the driving causes for both the uprisings of 1789 and the one that took Jean-Claude's life.

Never before has she considered that her charismatic lover was a Robespierre to the Friends of the Abaissé. Nor has she contemplated the similarities between those long-ago clubs and the gathering of Sorbonne students in a dark tavern, dreaming of a better world for all citizens.

And now she grows thoughtful. She wonders whether things will ever really get better for the people of her beloved city. And when the blood of those people will cease to stain the cat's-head cobblestones of Parisian streets.

The Friends of the Abaissé are, like the Girondins and the Jacobins, no more; it is as though they had never existed.

Except for two things.

In Marianne's heart there is now a spirit of rebellion: a belief that better days could and would come if people worked together. The old slogan of *liberté, egalité, fraternité* holds a very different meaning for her now, just a few days before the anniversary of the first French revolution, than it did during those days when Enjolras was her lover. Now it is a burning need to fight for the freedom of all.

And the other thing?

Grantaire's wish is coming true, if only he knew it. In Olympe's belly is his child.

From the Sky

By Justin Andrew Hoke

"We shall prove our worthiness to be more than God. To become His keeper ... and replacement."
—Harold Blythe, Architect/Mayor

We have exchanged the bounty of our Mother Earth to placate the foolish dreams of a prophet. Our hands are dirtied by the efforts of vanity and our faces are smeared with the result of shame. The mutilation that fills our lungs carries a reminder in every cough, in every burn, in every spatter of blood we shake from our tongues.

Our worthiness was never proven, for we were never prepared.

No grace came from killing the ground as we cracked soil for its resources. No treasure was ever to be found in the destruction of our Eden. What did we think we were to gain by leaving the loving possession of the loamy land that we were planted in? We had a world at our fingers, yet we painted the sky in an effort to be sated by the covetous gains of enslaving ourselves to surpass heaven.

The God we shook our fist at did not concede to our *rightful* claim.

We have held on to reminders of our history, but we have cared not to recall the sins that bear the weight of our past. The earthly design of gravity kept us humble. It tethered us to each other and made us respect the atmosphere that contained us!

A balance was broken when we forsake the invisible chains that made us one.

We must now descend: to humble, to learn, to appease the upsetting of balance. Our entitlements only existed in exalting ourselves to the rank of deity. A command so undeserved of a race so uninspiring. Were we to think its upward reach amounted to the wealth of control?

I can say with utmost certainty that we were never meant to rule in the sky.

We are never meant to rule.

Limits exist, yet we've cared not for their warning.

Benefaction will result from our downward mission. It will harken to an era of humbleness toward genius via superiority. We must take our failures in stride and append the grave mistakes stemming from our unnatural greed. This is so we may once again grace ourselves with the humility of gravity.

For when we respect the pull of a force unstoppable, we can recognize the force within.

Blown Sky High

By Lillian Csernica

Constance Harrington took a deep breath. She reminded herself for the tenth time that day the women of Great Britain had followed their husbands to the four corners of the Empire and returned home triumphant. She had followed William to Kyoto, Japan. She, too, would return triumphant.

"I realize beef and pork are not regular features of the Japanese diet," she said to Mrs. Rogers, her housekeeper. "Surely you might at least have found some mutton?"

"No, ma'am." Mrs. Rogers clasped her hands before her. In severe black with her graying hair piled atop her head, she looked every inch the schoolteacher she once had been. "I had a chat with Mrs. Bailey, Lord Beaumont's housekeeper. She tells me it's good form to make sure you have a few Japanese dishes on the table as well."

"I will not serve my guests raw fish."

"No need, ma'am, no need. The cream pan and the honey sponge cake will do."

This was Constance's first garden party in Japan. She'd already compromised on several of the traditional details. That left her anxious about the rest. She wore her dark hair swept up into a modest arrangement, adding a hair ornament decorated with tiny cascades of silk wisteria petals. The silk almost matched the pale blue border trim of her cream silk gown. She wore her aquamarine pendant and earrings. Driven by nerves, Constance bustled around, tidying the centerpieces of blue hydrangea, baby blue eyes and phlox and making sure each place setting was complete.

"Now, Mama?"

Madelaine stood in the shade of the flowering plum tree, holding a basket. She wore blue and gold plaid, with blue ribbons in her long dark hair.

"Yes, darling."

Madelaine carried her basket among the tables. At each place setting, she added a blue *origami* dragon. Constance watched Madelaine's precision with a combination of pride and relief. If Constance could turn Madelaine's mechanical inclinations toward the complex arts of being a truly superior hostess, then perhaps Madelaine could be both accomplished and happy.

A blue pavilion housed the refreshments. The two additional maids Mrs. Rogers hired had the tea and coffee arrangements well in hand, along with the claret-cup and lemonade. Constance looked along the buffet at the food, and her heart sank. One simply could not get a decent loaf of bread in Japan. Rice flour, buckwheat flour, millet flour.... None of those created the texture of good English toasting bread. That and the lack of cold meats meant no proper sandwiches.

A small hand slipped into hers.

"It will be all right, Mama," Madelaine said. "The Blue Dragon Festival is a party for Miss Kannon. Some of these treats must be her favorites."

The traditional Japanese sweets included sandwich cookies made from rice flour and red bean paste, little balls of fried, sweet dough on bamboo skewers, and floral-motif tea cakes. At least the tea cakes brought something of a traditional look to the buffet.

"Madelaine, please," Constance said. "Today could we talk about England? About Her Majesty Queen Victoria?"

"Yes, Mama." Madelaine looked thoughtful. "I wonder what would happen if Her Majesty invited the Goddess of Mercy to high tea?"

Brief pain shot through Constance's temples. Goddesses. Dragons. There had to be some way to cure Madelaine of this mad fixation on Japanese folklore.

In one corner of the garden the string quartet tuned their instruments. Constance caught the eye of the lead violinist and gave him a firm nod to begin. The classical music of Mozart and Haydn soothed her nerves. The kitchen door slid open. Mrs. Rogers came hurrying across the grass.

"Mrs. Harrington, your guests are arriving."

"Thank you, Mrs. Rogers. Please have them shown to the garden. I'll receive them here."

"Yes, ma'am."

Soon the garden was the delightful scene Constance had envisioned: the ladies, in their long gowns and bonnets, drinking tea and chatting with the gentlemen, drifting from one group to another, some taking seats where chairs were set up on carpets in the shade of the pine and plum trees.

Madelaine came running through the garden, leaving Nurse Danforth behind as she weaved between the adults. "Mama, Papa is here, and the Abbot is with him!"

"The *Abbot?*"

Hearing William's voice, Constance glanced back over her shoulder to see him entering the garden with Mr. Fujita, his official translator. The Abbot and two monks followed right behind him, dressed in their peculiar uniform of white pants, a black tunic, and a gold sash wound across their chests and around their waists. Constance hurried forward with a bright smile. William caught sight of her. His moment's hesitation and the sudden broadening of his smile put to rest any doubts she might have had about her appearance. That was small comfort compared to the social disaster looming over her.

Madelaine approached the Abbot, holding out one of her *origami* dragons cupped in both hands. Mr. Fujita stood by ready to be of service.

Constance seized the moment to draw William aside. "William! How could you bring the Abbot here?" she asked in a furious whisper. "Such an important person, with so little ceremony?"

"Please, Constance, calm down. I think the Abbot has had quite enough ceremony for a few days. Mr. Fujita gave me to understand that the Abbot would enjoy nothing so much as a simple garden party."

"But—but I have no idea what the protocol is for this type of visit!"

The Abbot received the little paper dragon as he would the finest treasure. By Mr. Fujita's broad smile and enthusiastic tone of voice, along with Madelaine's blush, there could be no doubt the Abbot was quite pleased.

"The garden is beautiful, the music is playing, and the guests are enjoying the local delicacies." William looked around with a satisfied smile. "I'd say you've done your work very well, Mrs. Harrington."

"Mama!" Madelaine hurried over to Constance and motioned her to bend down. "We need to make a special seat for the Abbot, with a shade over it!"

Further panic gripped Constance. Desperation forced her to take the only course open to her. "Show me, Maddy. You know about these things."

Madelaine walked over to one of the fine armchairs positioned in the shade of the plum tree. She gripped the arm and began tugging at it.

"Really, Madelaine," Nurse Danforth said. "Perhaps some of these gentlemen might help you."

Two of the male guests stepped forward to lift up the chair. Maddy grabbed one of the smaller rugs and spread it on the ground. Her helpers set the chair down on the carpet with its back against the trunk of the plum tree.

"There, Mama. That should do."

Constance bent to hug Madelaine and kiss her cheek. "Whatever would I do without you, darling?"

"You're welcome, Mama."

The Abbot allowed Madelaine to lead him to the armchair. The two monks with him took up their posts on either side.

"Oh my goodness," Constance said. "I must see to serving the Abbot myself."

William's arm came around her shoulders, both a gentle hug and a restraint. "My dear, I believe you were telling me just the other day how concerned you are about Madelaine growing up to be a proper British hostess." He smiled down at her. "The Abbot loves children. If he has any serious needs, one of his monks will see to it."

"Well, if it's really all right ..." Madelaine had become quite a mystery. Only nine years old, yet she seemed to have stepped into the world of Japan much like a native who'd been away only a short time. She knew about the Blue Dragon Festival, and which sweets were appropriate for Spring, and how they must provide the special chair for the Abbot ... Constance still felt quite lost among all the customs and history and new words and old traditions.

William patted her shoulder. "I will ask Mr. Fujita to stay with the Abbot in case any of our British guests would like to pay their respects."

"Yes. What an excellent idea." Constance felt the water closing over her head as she sank even farther out of her depth. "I must go look in on the refreshments and see if we need more of anything."

Constance made her way through the gathering into the blue pavilion, exchanging greetings and compliments. The lemonade pitchers needed more ice. She was surprised to see how many of the Japanese sweets had already been eaten. She hurried into the house in search of Mrs. Rogers and very nearly crashed right into her.

"Here now," Mrs. Rogers said, "you look a bit peaky, Mrs. Harrington." She pulled out one of the wooden chairs at the kitchen table and sat Constance down in it, then poured her a glass from a fresh pitcher of lemonade. "You take a few sips of that, ma'am."

Constance obeyed. "Is it going well, do you think?"

"Oh yes, ma'am. It's all we can do to keep food on the buffet! Everyone is saying how wonderful the garden looks."

Constance drew a slow, deep breath. Perhaps everything would be all right after all.

From the garden came the slow, metallic clank of some large mechanism being wound up. Constance groaned.

"That child!"

She took one more hasty sip of lemonade then rushed out into the garden again. At the far corner, to the right of the string quartet, there gleamed a device of copper and brass rearing up like the prow of a Viking ship. A dragon's head, connected to another device inside a wooden box. Madelaine stood beside it, with Nurse Danforth looking on.

"Madelaine!" Constance called. "Madelaine, do come here!"

William caught up with Constance just as she was about to swoop down on Madelaine.

"Constance, please. Madelaine has just been explaining this to me. It's quite ingenious, and it suits the theme of the party."

"Isn't it enough that you actually *helped* her trap that feral cat? I will not have Madelaine taxing the patience of our guests with one of her ridiculous inventions."

"Constance, we are not in London. The old crones who watch over the debutantes during the Season are not here to start whispering rumors about Madelaine's 'unsuitable interests.'"

"If you understand that much, William, then surely you can appreciate my other concerns. I can't allow our time here in Japan to change Madelaine so much!"

"Constance, I think you'd be very foolish to try and stop a process that's already well underway."

"This is not what one does at a proper British garden party. Don't you see, William? This reflects on you as well!"

"If my daughter becomes known for her mechanical genius, I will gladly bask in the light of her inspirations." He turned Constance around to face the metal dragon. "Now watch."

Madelaine opened a brass valve in the top of the box, then picked up a large jug of what looked like soapy water. She poured it all into the machine, then sealed the valve. Curious guests drifted closer.

"In honor of the Blue Dragon Festival," Madelaine said, "I have built this dragon. The Blue Dragon is one of the four guardians of Kyoto. Tradition tells us that the Blue Dragon is also one of the incarnations of Kannon, the Goddess of Mercy."

Constance glanced over at the Abbot. Mr. Fujita translated Madelaine's speech. The Abbot said something to one of the monks. Each monk took hold of one side of the chair and lifted it up, carrying it closer to Madelaine's dragon and setting it down in the shade where the Abbot would have a good view.

"Pious legend says the Goddess of Mercy gathers up the sorrows of the world and feeds them to the Water Dragon." Madelaine laid one hand on the metal dragon's shining neck. "My dragon will show you what I like to think the Water Dragon does with the sorrows of the world."

Madelaine bowed to the Abbot. He smiled and gave her a nod. Madelaine pulled a lever on the back of the dragon. The whirring of a large fan started up inside the wooden box. From the metal dragon's mouth there poured a shining cloud of soap bubbles, bright with the glimmer of rainbows.

The spring breeze blew the clouds of bubbles across the garden. Constance watched, waiting for the first outcry as a soap bubble burst against expensive satin or taffeta. The cries of wonder turned to laughter as people caught the soap bubbles and poked them or blew them toward each other. The breeze sent more bubbles swirling around the Abbot. One settled on his outstretched hand. He studied the bubble for a long moment. It popped. The Abbot nodded, as if witnessing something profound.

"Look, Constance," William murmured. "Look at what our little girl has created. Look at how happy she's made all these people."

Constance looked around her, at the British people in suits and gowns, at the Abbot and his monks in their robes. Eating and drinking and laughing and playing. Some of the men gathered around Madelaine's dragon, pointing to parts of it and asking questions. Madelaine raised one side of the wooden box to reveal the dragon's inner workings. Much nodding and pointing, more questions and answers.

All of Constance's anxiety over the details of the party disappeared in a sudden surge of relief. The men who were interested in Madelaine's work were too old for her, but some of them must have sons. The cat trap had removed a dangerous pest, and now this dragon added quite a unique feature to the garden party. Perhaps what Madelaine might miss during the Season in London, she could find here during the Spring in Japan.

Straight Flush

By Dover Whitecliff

Bloody amazing how easy it is to get yourself locked away for thirty days when your brother runs the largest syndicate on three continents. At least Briar saw to it that I was in with the *too dangerous for general riffraff* lot. Got room service, of a sort. Wasn't the posh experience I'd hoped for, coming here to the city of glitter and glamour, let alone missing out on stuffing myself silly at the buffet without having Kyree nagging about keeping in fighting trim.

Took maybe five minutes from the bars slamming shut behind me to find Inarion Blue on the first day in. Still couldn't think of him as Pascal Lovelace, boffin supreme. Not with those muscles. A quick brawl in the mud allowed for a conversation and the passing of the wild card. And then it was down to the waiting. No free rides inside the walls; everybody earned their keep. At least it helped pass the time.

I'd been maintaining my exo-suit, LUPA, since I was big enough to grab the hand grips, so it made sense that the warden would assign me to the machine shop. What didn't make sense was the fact that instead of a combine to plow and harvest the rice paddies, they used a couple of clockwork yaks, which, since spring planting was done, I found myself overhauling.

I was draped half upside down over the yak and hip deep in gears when Blue finally clicked all the number combinations into place.

GONNNNNGGG!!!

My skull vibrated in the melodic and unholy clang that echoed round the cavity when Blue thwacked a spanner on the brass yak housing to get my attention. I lost my balance and my vision split into stars when I wrenched upward and slammed the back of my head into a piston. I fell off the yak in a manner unbefitting the three-time Terceran bantam weight exo-suit champion and landed hard on my ass.

I'll say one thing for the eyepatch. It certainly cranks up the scare factor on the angry glare. Blue backed off, hands raised.

"Whoa. Sorry, Wolfy. Pax." He offered me a hand, and pulled me to my feet, then prodded the back of my head with his fingers. "No blood. No foul. You'll live."

"Thanks, Doctor Blue." I grabbed a rag from my back pocket and made a show of wiping the grease from my hands while I looked around. The shop guards had their eyes glued to the Dreadfulle Show. We had a few minutes at least. "So what's their takedown?"

"The Opening Ceremony. We need to get to Su Chan So Lake. Sooner the better."

"Wait. I saw the Grand Pavilion going up near the mooring yards when I came in. Lake's miles away. Why there?"

"The wild card threw me off. Jacquard combinations are at least twenty years out of date. There's only one Mechanical in a hundred miles that can read that card and it's at the lake. They're gonna use it to blow the dam. Tonight. Flood the opening ceremony with all those dignitaries around to blame each other for who did what."

I whistled, playing it out in my head. Bold move. Just about every nation leaderless and all their juniors jumping at shadows. Great way to start a war. But what if—no, Blue wouldn't pull something this crazy out of the air, and Fa would be representing Istavara at the ceremony, with Duncan Sarn bedridden. No way in the Void was I going to let Fa drown on my watch.

"Damn all. This isn't the arena, Blue. No suits, no backup. Just you, me, and the best two brains on three continents."

He smirked. "Best one and a half maybe. I got your back, Wolfy. Question is, can you get us out of here?"

"Leave it to me. I know somebody."

ೞಂಛ

Two brawls, a prison break that would dominate the aithercasts for a week, and a dreadful-worthy monocycle chase later, Blue and I lay flat on our bellies in stolen souvenir shirts peering over a low hummock of grass at Sparky's Boardwalk.

"You're serious. One of *those* can take out the Dai Sun Dam?" I stared incredulously at the Sea Serpents of Su Chan So. Never mind that they couldn't be *sea* serpents in a land-locked lake. The submersibles were shudder-worthy. Ear fins, silly grins, serpentine necks that waggled, and chartreuse steam curling out of their nostrils, each sea serpent a more eye-popping color than the one before, and named by mothers with no taste. Their bodies were riddled with crys-glass viewports distorting the faces of riders waving at friends waiting on the dock.

Blue shrugged. "I can see why they'd want to blow them up."

"You and me both, Blue. You and me both."

"Looks like two crew each."

"Pilot and attendant."

"Pilot must be for more than hitting the start button. Lake's too deep for tracks and they're going too far out for the ticket booth to run the cycle remotely."

"So. Two baddies switch out with the paid help. Right then. I'll take the pilot, you take the attendant and find the whatsit and make it stop. Unless you think bashing the thing would work."

"I'd have thought one bomb in the face was enough for you."

"Point taken."

"I count six rides. You?"

"A half dozen uglies it is," I said, watching for the pattern. They left the first dock and sank down until only the wiggling ear fins stuck up above the surface. They paralleled the shore at a mediocre clip to a swirling spillway, sucking excess water from the lake to spit it out into the channel below the dam, surfaced, turned, skirted half the length of the dam above water, and then submerged again to give riders the fish-eye view. The rest of the circuit took them to the opposite shore maybe a mile away, rounded the lake, surfacing at three or four points in the circle, until they stopped at a second dock to spit out the riders before gliding forward to do it all again. And again. And again. Maybe a quarter turn of the glass round-trip. "So which one is it?"

"No idea. You got enough for six rides?"

"Opening ceremony is set for about an hour after sundown. We don't have enough *time* for six rides." Thoughts chased round my head as the sun slid lower behind the hills, painting the sky blue and purple and the clouds orange limned in gold. The lamps in the submersibles' eyes began flickering on. Twilight. Nothing for it. Mr. Black Heart Pin was our only chance. "Be my eye for me." I pushed up into a crouch.

"Say again?" Blue and I scrambled down to the path leading to the boardwalk. I closed my right eye and pulled off the patch to stuff it in my pocket.

"Don't know if this will work. May split my head open. I'll try not to mess up your shirt if it comes to sick."

Blue looked down at the shirt adorning his chest, at the smiling sea serpent in a black and white bathing costume, straw boater, and goggles, and shrugged again. "I dunno. Might improve the look."

We passed the families queued up waiting to see the lake bed from the fishes' point of view and lounged between the fairy floss vendor and the ticket booth.

"Wait a tick, Wolfy." Blue turned to face me, grabbed my left hand and put it on his waist.

"Oy!" I protested, and smacked his hand. He snorted.

"Use me for balance. And if I can see what your peeper is doing, I may be able to help you through." He knew I knew he was right and he grinned. "Looks more natural, and if somebody gets nosy, I can plant one on ya."

"Yeah, yeah." I put my other hand on Blue's shoulder. "Public displays of affection blah blah people nervous blah blah." I turned toward the line of people clambering out of the hatch of a periwinkle and puce sea serpent with a brass name collar proclaiming it *Sparklypuff.* I hoped like the Void Blue didn't notice my hands shaking.

Focus, Girl.

Took a deep breath. Opened my eye.

Like that short second when I strapped into LUPA and dove through the drop doors into open air, there was a moment of nothing. No fear, no jitters, nothing but *me* in the silence twixt heartbeats. And then the world exploded.

Images clashed like me and Blue in the arena, slashing at each other, each shouting for notice and giving anything and everything to dominate. Real sight. Symbols scrolling. Colors flickering. Light pulsing until real sight turned bright, then red with blobs of different color sauntering through bold as you please. Parts of a map overlaid with directions and *Sparklypuff* grinning at me through it all. "Too much. Too. Bloody. Much." Everything threatened to upend. I felt wind and wet on my face. Blood pounded in my ears.

Then a voice whispered into the maelstrom. A familiar voice. "Talk to me, Wolfy. Talk to me."

I grabbed onto it and pulled. Opened my mouth and something unintelligible fell out.

"Need more than that."

Concentrate, Girl. He can't sift through what he can't see.

"Numbers, Wolfy. Do you see any numbers on anything?"

Real sight sparkled and hammers pounded on my head. Boom bada BOOM bada BOOM. "Can't do this, Blue. Can't."

"You the She-Wolf or ain't you? Don't you dare close your eye on me, Wolfy. Don't you *dare*. Focus. Numbers. Look for numbers. I need something to work with."

My eyes burned staring at *Sparklypuff's* goofy grin mocking me. I glared it down. "You. Will. Not. Beat. Me."

"There's the Lupa I know. You control it, not the other way round. Take it down. Find me some numbers."

I stood toe to toe with the monster under the bed. Looked it right in the eye. There, under the colors, past the colors, *through* the colors. A frame. Cradling them. A frame of *numbers*. "Gaaah. Numbers all over. Bunches of 'em."

"Bunches. How many in a bunch?"

I tried to focus, but the frame disappeared, washed away in a flood of opal and onyx shimmer. "Where'd they go? They're gone."

"I see the problem. You got two pupils in your right eye, Wolfy. Probably something to do with range or depth. You try too hard and they jam. Cross your eyes so they unfocus and try again."

Boom bada BOOM.

Ignore the pain, Girl. Do the job.

I crossed my eyes, or tried to, and everything went blurry.

"Better. Think dark arena. Look just to the side so you can lock onto your target."

That made sense. I remembered bouts in the Blackout Games. Audience could watch us through view-shields, but for us it might have been midnight as we stalked each other through the inky maze. You could see after a fashion, like the purse-lipped oraculars that made the caverns their home, by looking away to see head on. I tried the same trick.

"Different. Water isn't bunched. People bunches are colors."

"Are the submersibles different?" I shifted back to *Sparklypuff.* The ghostly frame of numbers clicked into place just as it slid away toward the loading dock.

"Yeah. Sixteen. Four by four. Damn all. Almost have—" I felt Blue's hand grab my chin.

"Don't turn your head. Movement will make it worse. Next one's almost there. Just hold on and do the same thing when it comes into view."

The colors and symbols spiraled until the violent green and magenta *Snuffleberry* lurched to a stop and disgorged its riders.

Look away to see head on. That's it, Girl.

"Do they repeat? Is there a pattern?"

"Tiles. They look like tiles. One two three four five. Every sixth set is all zeroes. And those ones go slantwise down and to the right."

"Zeroes. End of coding. Six sets. Six sets." Blue went off into boffin-speak. "Jacquard calculations are in the Diagonal Dodec. Every six is zeroes. Zeroes. End of coding. Four by four. Twelve plus four. That's it." I could feel his heart beating faster.

"That's what? Don't leave me hanging, Blue. What am I looking at?"

"Fourth row from the top. Two sets to the right of the zeroes. Read the numbers off top to bottom right to left."

"Eight. One. Six. Two. Four. Three. Zero. One—"

"Not the one."

"Bugger." The sun was gone now, and the bright lights above the boardwalk made it harder and harder to keep my eye open and not heave in the wash of color swirling through the sea serpent's exit. I gripped Blue's shoulder just to stay standing. "We're running out of time."

"Stay with me, Wolfy. Don't give up. The numbers are range and temperature. Next one."

I could almost hear each grain of sand slipping through the glass as another sea serpent came and went unchallenged. Both eyes were on fire from not blinking. A scream of desperation slithered up my throat, but I swallowed it back down.

Pull yourself together, Girl. Fa's life depends on you finding the right bloody sea serpent and stopping it doing whatever they've set it to do before it does it. Panic is not helpful.

The next in line was *Dimpledarling*, a blinding maroon and mustard job with a toothy grin. The frame of numbers blurred in and out. "Three. One. Six. No, no. Not six. Five. Two. Seven Seven Three Four Four Zero—"

"Heat. That's gotta be the one." I felt his hand in my pocket, and the eyepatch slipped over my eye. Two endless seconds of vertigo followed by blessed relief. "Catch it before they load."

We pounded down the pier as the sea serpent slid up to the loading dock; quite the sight for the tourists. The attendant reached for the hook to undo the rope and let the riders on board, but we pushed through to the front of the line amidst shouts of indignation. Blue elbowed the attendant off the dock, hurdled the rope and dove through the entry. I followed, turned to grab the hatch from the inside, and it slammed shut, wheel lock turning, and batten shoving home. I blinked, adjusting to the twilight.

"Did I do that?"

"What?"

"Secure the door."

"Probably set to seal when you close it so the ankle biters can't open it mid ride. We've got bigger fish to fry. Go. Cockpit's that way."

I shimmied down the narrow aisle between the seats to disable the controls, expecting the pilot to pop out any second. Heard Blue's steps ring on the steel flooring in the opposite direction. Hair stood on the back of my neck.

Think. You're missing something, Girl.

Wait. What had Blue said? *Set to seal when you close it.* Had I pulled on the hatch? I looked back, then looked ahead. The cockpit door. Ajar. *No. No. NO.* I had enough scars to know blood when I smelled it. No use feeling for a pulse with arterial spurt all over the smashed dashboard. I unstrapped the pilot, pulled her back into the cabin and propped her body out of the way in one of the passenger bays, then scrambled back to the cockpit to rewire the controls.

The thrum of the engine quickened. I looked up to see us gliding away from the pier.

How?!

A stillness on the dock caught my eye. An eye to the storm of chaos we'd left in our wake. An elegant eggshell linen suit and a stylish fedora with a burnt-orange ribbon and pink flamingo feather cockade. His smile was less idiot and more predator now. Garrick Bloody Winslow. He mouthed the word "BOOM," tipped his hat, and vanished into the crowd just as *Dimpledarling's* viewport slid beneath the lake. The engines thrummed faster as we headed full speed toward the dam.

"Wolfy!! Take us into the middle of the lake! Far out as you can go!"

"Working on it!"

One look under the console told me that rewiring would be a lost cause without an hour or two to trace the skein of mangled wires to the right connectors.

Think, Girl. You're moving already and the console is mince pie. Winslow's controlling it from shore. Has to be. So there must be something on board that he's controlling. Something connected to the rudder or the engine.

My footsteps echoed in *Dimpledarling*'s belly. Along with an unintentional 'oof' as I caught my hip on a seat back.

Why are these aisles so damn narrow?!

"Talk to me, Wolfy! Are we far enough out?! We have to ditch."

"Not an option!" I ran past toward the engine and hit the deck, scrambling across the plates and looking for something, anything that might be the whatsit Winslow was using to steer us toward the dam.

"I can't stop this thing. Not in time." Blue's voice was muffled behind the boiler. He poked his head out. Saw me. Made the connection. "What the—Who's driving?"

"That would be Winslow."

"Wait. Winslow? The flamingo?"

"Yes. The bloody flamingo. He's out there. We're in here. And if the damn dam doesn't blow, you can bet he'll be there at the ceremony with poison in the punch." I was running out of places to check for a control box. "Where *is* it? Nothing on the engine looks like it doesn't belong. No access to the bloody rudder from in here. If the receiver is—No. Wait. You said it *couldn't* be remote."

"Right. Dam's too far. He'd lose contact."

I banged my forehead on the engine housing, trying to knock an intelligent thought loose.

"How then?"

"We're missing some—" Blue shot to his feet and skidded down the deck toward the attendant's console in the back of the cabin. He yanked off the cover. There. The tail end of a card. This one undoubtedly punched, though I couldn't see the holey bits. I knew what Blue would say next, and my innards squirmed. "Need your eyeball, Wolfy." He pulled up his shirt and peeled off the wild card. Nice distraction.

Not the time, Girl.

"Abs ... solutely." Imminent doom made it a bit easier to ignore the excellent view. Just a bit. I closed my eye, pulled off the patch and faced the console. Breathe. Unfocus. Open.

"Give me the sequence on the card."

The numbers swam into view a bit easier in the dim light of the cabin. Overlaid themselves on the real sight. I counted off the holes in the card one by bloody one, expecting never to reach the next in the sequence. We had to be getting close to the dam.

"Got it. Move!"

I slapped the patch over my eye and opened the other in time to see Blue slip the wild card, now with crude holes in strategic coordinates, into the slot. *Dimpledarling* shuddered. Blue yanked out the first card and she listed sideways and upward, sending us sprawling. Blue grabbed my hand and we used each other as counterweights to stumble to the hatch. Suddenly, I could see the surface of the lake through the viewports and the spillway yawing to starboard like the Void. It looked as if we had been aiming to dive down its throat, but now we were following the true course. It took both of us with all our strength to pull the batten, turn the wheel, and yank open the hatch.

"On three!"

"On one!" Blue shoved me hard with his hip and we crashed into the surface of the lake, barely missing *Dimpledarling*'s tail as she pulled hard away from the dam and out into open water. I sputtered, gagging on a mouthful of spray. "Go Go GO!!!"

Only we weren't going in the way we were headed. I felt something hauling me backward. No way either of us had enough strength to fight it, but no way She-Wolf or Inarion Blue wouldn't go down swinging. Last thing I saw before the current dragged me down over the lip and into the spillway was night turning to day in the middle of the lake.

The Dai Sun spillway flushed us straight down and out into the channel below. We bobbed up like corks, gulping air. The walls of the channel had nothing to grab and the current didn't give us much of a chance to move to either side.

SPLOOSH! Whatever it was nearly hit us when it smashed into the water ahead of us, but whatever it was stayed afloat and we swam for it. Only when I grabbed hold and hauled Blue up next to me did I notice *Dimpledarling*'s goofy grin staring straight at me. Quite a few minutes passed before we could stop laughing. Blue gasped, reaching for a better grip on *Dimpledarling*'s ear fin.

"Uh, Wolfy ... You doing anything later?"

"You mean after ripping Winslow's heart out and security detail for the ceremony?"

"Yeah. Something like that."

"Want to join the detail? I. Er. We could use a guy like you if you're interested." My mouth sped on before my head caught up with it. "Or. Um. Got a room at the Tetra. We can clean up and hit the Kodo."

"You winking at me, Wolfy? Because, you know, it would be easier to tell without the eyepatch."

About the Authors

Sharon E. Cathcart

Award-winning author Sharon E. Cathcart's main focus is on writing fiction with atypical characters. She is a devout Francophile and is delighted to have been able to share a look at the June Rebellion with readers. She dedicates her stories in *Thirty Days Later* to the Occupy Movement, the modern-day Friends of the Abbaisé. Sharon also wishes to thank Prof. Peter McPhee, of the University of Melbourne, for his excellent course on the French Revolution.

Lillian Csernica

Ms. Csernica has published *Ship of Dreams*, a pirate romance novel, under her romance pen name Elaine LeClaire through Dorchester Publishing's Leisure Imprint. Ms. Csernica's short fiction has appeared in *Weird Tales*, *Fantastic Stories*, and *The Year's Best Horror XXI* and *XXII*. Her historical fiction has appeared in *Tales of Old* and *These Vampires Don't Sparkle*. She contributed two paired stories to the anthology *Twelve Hours Later*. Born in San Diego and a veteran of historical reenactment, Ms. Csernica is a genuine California native. She currently resides in the Santa Cruz Mountains with her husband, two sons, and three cats. Visit her at www.lillian888.wordpress.com.

Steve DeWinter

Steve DeWinter is a #1 bestselling Amazon action & adventure sci-fi author who has also co-authored two fantasy novels with Charles Dickens. Yes! That Charles Dickens. Steve's books have hit #1 on the Amazon children's action & adventure sci-fi bestseller list and his adult thrillers reached as high as lucky #13 on the Amazon action & adventure bestseller list. He also has the distinction of having nine books in the top twenty of the Amazon children's action & adventure sci-fi bestseller list all at the same time. Check out Steve's books on Amazon: http://bit.ly/SteveDeWinter-AZ

David L. Drake and Katherine L. Morse

David L. Drake and Katherine L. Morse are the award-winning, San Diego-based authors of *The Adventures of Drake and McTrowell—Perils in a Postulated Past*, a serialized steampunk tale detailing the adventures of Chief Inspector Erasmus Drake and Dr. "Sparky" McTrowell. The duo's many adventures are provided in weekly penny dreadful-style episodes at www.DrakeAndMcTrowell.com. They have produced four novellas since 2010: *London, Where it All Began; The Bavarian Airship Regatta; Her Majesty's Eyes and Ears;* and *The Hawaiian Triple Cross*. Drake and Morse won a Starburner Award for the radio show based on their first story which has run multiple times on Krypton Radio. When not cosplaying their alter egos at conventions all over the West, they are both research computer scientists specializing in distributed modeling and simulation. Mr. Drake is a nationally ranked foil fencer. Dr. Morse is an internationally respected expert on standards, but prefers to be recognized for her cookie-baking skills. They throw awesome parties, if they do say so themselves.

Anthony Francis

By day, Anthony Francis programs intelligent computers and emotional robots; by night, he writes science fiction and draws comic books. His stories here are prequels to his steampunk novel *Jeremiah Willstone and The Clockwork Time Machine*. Anthony is also the author of the urban fantasy novels *Frost Moon, Blood Rock,* and *Liquid Fire* starring magical tattoo artist Dakota Frost. Anthony lives in San Jose with his wife and cats, but his heart will always belong in Atlanta. You can follow Jeremiah Willstone at www.facebook.com/jeremiahwillstone, Dakota Frost at www.facebook.com/dakotafrost, or Anthony himself on his blog www.dresan.com/.

Justin Andrew Hoke

Justin Andrew Hoke is a short fiction writer, podcast personality, and Executive Producer at Dreadfully Punk. When he isn't writing, Justin is devoted to political activism and planet conservation. He aims to bridge the worlds of science fact and science fiction by promoting eco awareness, inspiring our youth, and fighting for a better future.

T.E. MacArthur

T. E. MacArthur is a San Francisco Bay Area author, artist, and historian. She is the artist and author behind *Shamanka: Oracle of the Shamaness* and *The Volcano Lady: Volumes I & II*, steampunk novels following the adventures of Victorian lady scientist, Lettie Gantry. Her novellas in *The Gaslight Adventures of Tom Turner* series continue with thrilling escapades following the time-honored cliffhangers of Victorian dime novels, penny dreadfuls, and weekly serials. She has written for several local and specialized publications and was even an accidental sports reporter for Reuters International News. Her blog can be found at www.volcanolady1.wordpress.com.

AJ Sikes

AJ Sikes writes noir urban fantasy and has published multiple short story stories and the alternate history novels, *Gods of Chicago* and *Gods of New Orleans*. He offers professional editing services to writers of speculative fiction, non-fiction, and academic material. He served in the U.S. Army, holds an MA in Teaching English to Speakers of Other Languages, and taught university level ESL writing and composition courses. He's a woodworker and toy builder in his spare time. AJ keeps a blog called Dovetails www.writingjoinery.wordpress.com where he talks about the similarities between woodworking and writing. Find out more about his editing services at www.ajsikes.com.

BJ Sikes

BJ Sikes is a 5'6" ape descendant who is inordinately fond of a good strong cup of tea, Doc Marten boots, and fancy dress. She lives with two large cats, two small children and one editor-author. Her stories in this anthology are prequels to her first novel *The Archimedean Heart*.

Emily Thompson

Emily Thompson is the author of the Clockwork Twist novel series. Although she adores steampunk and all things Victoriana, she also writes occasional sci-fi and fantasy. Originally from California, she takes every excuse to travel or live abroad, but now lives mostly in Washington because of the rain. Emily is a huge fan of Jules Verne, and loves to track down hard-to-find editions and translations. Her other hobbies include cooking, gaming, and watching bad sci-fi. www.clockworktwist.com.

Janice Thompson

JaniceT has been writing poetry for more than fifty years. She composes tightly woven, unforced verses that allow for as many levels of interpretation as are possible. Much of her poetry hearkens back to the English Lake District poets. JaniceT has been an avid fan of the steampunk genre since the early eighties, and its influence on her is apparent in some of her "steamier" poems, such as *Twist*, and *Train of Thought*. A few samples of her work can be seen on her blog at www.janice-t.weebly.com.

Michael Tierney

Michael Tierney writes steampunk-laced alternative historical fiction stories from his Victorian home in Silicon Valley. After writing technical and scientific publications for many years, he turned his sights to more imaginative genres. Trained as a chemist, he brings an appreciation of both science and history to his stories. His debut novel *To Rule the Skies* was published in 2014. Visit his blog at www.airshipflamel.com.

Harry Turtledove

Escaped Byzantine historian Harry Turtledove made his first sale in 1977, and has been telling lies for a living fulltime since 1991. He writes alternate history, other SF, historically based fantasy, and, when he can get away with it, historical fiction. He is perhaps best known for *The Guns of the South*; recent books include *Joe Steele*, *The Hot War: Bombs Away*, and *The House of Daniel.* He and his wife, writer Laura Frankos, have three daughters (one also a published author), one granddaughter, and two cats, Boris and Natasha. Watch out for Natasha. She beeps.

Kirsten Weiss

Kirsten Weiss worked overseas for nearly fourteen years, in the fringes of the former USSR and in Southeast Asia. Her experiences abroad sparked an interest in the effects of mysticism and mythology, and how both are woven into our daily lives. Now based in San Mateo, CA, she writes steampunk suspense and paranormal mysteries, blending her experiences and imagination to create a vivid world of magic and mayhem. Kirsten has never met a dessert she didn't like, and her guilty pleasures are watching *Ghost Whisperer* and drinking good wine. Get updates on her latest work at: www.kirstenweiss.com

Dover Whitecliff

Dover Whitecliff was born in the shadow of Fujiyama, raised in the shadow of Olomana, and lives where she can see the shadow of Mt. Shasta if she squints and it's a really clear day. She is a wild and woolly wordsmith, an analyst, and a jack-of-all-trades, but mostly a writer who has been telling stories since forever, and who won her first ten-speed as a fifth grader with a first place entry into *The Honolulu Advertiser*'s "*Why Hawaii Isn't Big Enough for Litter*" contest. Her stories in this anthology are prequels to her first solo novel *The Superspy with the Clockwork Eye*. She lives in Sacramento, California with her very patient husband and several hundred bears.